Divide and Rule

Divide and Rule

Elisabeth
Russell Taylor

HUTCHINSON
LONDON SYDNEY AUCKLAND JOHANNESBURG

© Elisabeth Russell Taylor 1989

This edition first published in Great Britain
by Hutchinson, an imprint of Century Hutchinson Ltd,
Brookmount House, 62–65 Chandos Place,
London WC2N 4NW

Century Hutchinson Australia Pty Ltd,
89–91 Albion Street, Surry Hills, NSW 2010

Century Hutchinson New Zealand Ltd,
PO Box 40–086, Glenfield, Auckland 10, New Zealand

Century Hutchinson South Africa (Pty) Ltd,
PO Box 337, Bergvlei, 2012 South Africa

Printed and bound in Great Britain

British Library Cataloguing in Publication Data
Taylor, Elisabeth Russell
  Divide and rule
  I. Title
  823'.914 [F]

  ISBN 0–09–174111–4

Dedicated to
Trevor Huddleston CR

If I am not for myself, who will be for me?
If I am for myself only, what am I?
If not now – when?
Talmudic saying.

I am sure there was no man born, marked of God above another, for none comes into the world with a saddle on his back; neither any booted and spurred to ride him.
Richard Rumbold. Executed June 1685 at the gallows in Edinburgh at Market Cross after the Monmouth Rebellion.

A condition of society in which there should be neither rich nor poor, neither master nor master's men, nor idle nor over-worked, neither brain-sick brain workers, nor heart-sick hand workers, in a word, in which all men would be living in equality of condition, I would manage their affairs universally, and with the full consciousness that harm to one would mean harm to all – the realisation at last of the meaning of the word Commonwealth.
William Morris.

The greatest thing in the world is to know how to be self-sufficient.
Montaigne.

PART I

Sunday

'It's on!' Professor Massimo Vardi had picked up the receiver before the telephone bell had rung. He was seated in his shirt-sleeves at his desk, the instrument at his side, and had heard the barely discernible click that precedes the bell. He had immediately clasped the receiver close to his ear and kept it there while staring ahead, expressionless, and then had replaced the receiver without uttering further words. As soon as the dialling tone started up again, he dialled.

'It's on!' he said, and put down the receiver at once.

Professor Vardi was in his study. The book-lined sanctum led off his bedroom to one side and the salon to the other, and both doors were ajar. His mother, the ageing countess, had been passing slowly to and from the salon and the bedroom where a servant, newly plucked from the medieval conditions that survived on the Vardi estate in Apulia, was packing the professor's suitcase to the evident dissatisfaction of her employer.

'Now, watch me!' the countess ordered breathlessly, with the impatience of one for whom the heat of a city summer was an annual calvary. 'Not like that. Like this!' The servant refolded the professor's shirts, all the while remaining mute, not knowing whether she was expected to react to the old lady's litany of concern for her son, a man in his fifties, which followed on her practical commandments. 'He's delicate . . . he pays scant attention to his diet . . . he lets people take advantage of him . . . All this travel, summer and winter . . .'

Aware that her son was no longer engaged on the telephone, the countess moved to the study door. 'One of your meetings?'

'One of my associates.' And Professor Vardi rose and moved slowly towards his mother.

'Come,' he said, gently placing his arm around her shoulder. 'Let's dine!'

The polished mahogany table occupied almost all the floor space in the dining-room. The countess had hardly enough room to pass between it and the highly polished sideboard. Every inch of wall was covered with darkly varnished, romantic oil paintings of Apulia – idealised out of recognition, to cater for those who wished their memories enhanced. The windows were draped in snuff-brown velour, in whose folds lurked reminders of past dinners and past cigars.

'Massimo, my dear, believe me, the English know nothing whatsoever about food. They eat their fish concealed in batter-coats, they overcook their meats to the consistency of shoe leather. And the only vegetables their climate permits them to grow are the sort we feed to our cattle. And you won't be offered the wines you like, just hop-water. It'll disagree with you. I really cannot understand why it always has to be you who attends these conferences. Couldn't your assistant make the journey on your behalf?'

'Mother dear, I go because I'm invited to give a paper. Only I can do that. It's an honour, you know, in recognition of my academic position.'

'An honour! An honour to be obliged to quit Rome for some English provincial city? An honour to sleep in strange hotels! Why, in pursuit of such honours you have also been expected to consume American food!'

Mother and son had lived together and alone for the greater part of Massimo's life. Their intimacy was total. The fact that the son did not confide his intellectual preoccupations and his political activities to his mother in no way lessened the couple's rapport. Indeed, the countess's happiness was the more complete for knowing that her son had a range of interests that, while they did not include her, did nothing to distance him from her emotionally.

It had been an unusually hot summer in Rome. Throughout the hours of daylight – even in the well-shuttered rooms of

4

the Vardi apartment – the air seemed paralysed. Mother and son waited to dine until late in the evening, when thoughts of food could be entertained with appetite. The countess had herself prepared the *panzarotti* and the various marinades for the chilled vegetables that Massimo's Vardi inheritance had schooled him to prefer. His mother never abandoned the Apulian diet of her son's childhood; she had acquired an affinity with it through her child – and it had come to suit her own constitution. While the countess carefully arranged food on a plate for her son, Massimo opened a well-chilled bottle of Sansavere del Tavoliere.

The windows had been thrown open. The lights of Rome twinkled below, the stars above. Inside, all was quiet. The servant had been dismissed to her room in the attic. Outside, the steady drone of traffic in the city would continue throughout the hours of darkness. Massimo and his mother talked quietly.

'You should be looking for a wife, my dear. Your old mother's not going to live forever!'

'Beloved mother! Not that subject, I implore you!' And reaching across the table, Massimo placed one of his hands over hers. 'I have my little encounters, you know that . . . But no one has ever meant anything to me. Apart from you,' he added quickly. 'You know I could never love another woman. I'm happy as I am.' Unseen, in the dim candlelight that shone on the gilt cutlery and crystal, the old countess smiled to herself.

Massimo drank strong black coffee and ate a pine-nut fondant. His mother fanned herself with a newspaper. How frail she looked, he thought, despite her weight, seated on the long damask-covered *chaise longue*, surrounded by burnished wood – gilt-edged. The heat was increasingly hard for her to bear; her feet, pressed into delicate Ferragamo slippers, were clearly troubling her. He could see how swollen her ankles were. And it worried him to see her continually wipe her neck and bosom with the gossamer-thin handkerchief, embroidered by the nuns, that she kept at her wrist. He too was intolerant of the heat – but not to anything like the same extent. Of course, in Apulia his mother had lived half in the open. In Rome that was not possible.

'I think I'll shower. I'm leaving early in the morning.' When Massimo removed his shirt he noticed, in addition to the smell of dust, the odour of stale sweat. It embarrassed him. The cold shower and a liberal application of Eau de Portugal left him refreshed. He threw off the towel round his loins and lay naked on his bed with only the bedside reading lamp lighted.

'Sleep well, my son. And may the Good Lord protect you!'

The countess turned off the lamp but did not leave the room. Instead, she drew up a chair and sat close to the side of her son's bed. She took his hand in hers and held it until his eyes closed. Only when she was satisfied that he was deeply asleep did she leave his room for her own.

Dr Julia Bruton and her husband, James, were seated at a narrow pine refectory table that ran the length of their kitchen–dining-room. It was a balmy evening; the french windows on to the garden were open, and the scent of tobacco plant wafted in on a faint breeze that was agitating bunches of long-stemmed buttercups suspended from a ceiling beam. A Sussex dresser along one wall was chock-full of salt-glaze, slipware and spongeware on the upper shelves, and below, on the pot board, huge dough-bowls were ranged in orderly, even military file, providing storage space for apples, potatoes, carrots and onions. On the walls Vuillard prints celebrated domestic contentment and culinary skill; alongside the prints hung brass ladles and medieval farm tools.

The couple were seated at the garden end of the table. At the other end stood a Masons jug – part of a Victorian toilet set – crammed with garden flowers: roses, phlox and delphiniums. Scattered around the jug were papers, books, keys, a torch, a billiard cue, a pair of shoes for the menders, a jacket for the cleaners. A cat lay sprawled on the papers, her nose fastened to the shoes, breathing in ecstatically.

'I remember it very well indeed,' James insisted. 'It was the day we just happened upon that stunning tapestry. And

6

then we hung about in Angers to eat, and had a bottle of this wine. My memory's not that bad. Anyhow, if *you* remember, I bought a whole case of the stuff when we got home; I'm not likely to have forgotten that.' James was opening his last bottle of Sancerre to go with the *salade Niçoise* Julia had prepared.

The two ate and drank without giving attention to either activity. Julia's thoughts were divided between the paper she was going to give the following week to the delegates at the conference on Peace Research and Conflict Studies at Oxford, and instructions to James, who was going to have to manage on his own for a week.

'Please, please don't forget the Tubby-Tabby. I know you're not crazy about her . . . And don't forget to lock the windows as well as the doors when you go out. And the garden shed. There's a ladder in it.'

'Julia! I'm forty-six . . .'

'I know, but I'm not sure memory improves with age.' And she rose from the table and threw open the door of the fridge. James's eyes followed her.

'My God! There's enough for the Berlin Phil! Our Boys' Club group amounts to less than half their brass section – on a good night. I don't understand why it is that you always over-provide.'

Julia closed the fridge door and returned to her chair. 'I suppose it's because I can't bear your accusation that I'm impenitently academic. I always have to prove to you that I'm just as interested in cooking and cleaning and all the other domestic things as you are in putting up bookshelves and unblocking drains. Anyhow, will you listen to this and try to give me an unbiased opinion?'

James gave Julia his divided attention. When she stopped reading and put down her papers, he paused before saying that, if past experience was anything to go by, he imagined she'd get some sympathy from some of the Scandinavians.

'I really don't think our lot will go along with you, though – even if they concentrate enough to follow you. You haven't modified your original proposition, have you? 'The Autistic

Society' called too much into question too quickly, and it's far too psycho-analytical. Most of us don't accept that for people to get damaged by society there doesn't have to be overt violence. We've lived with our present institutions for generations. Why is it suddenly now that they're supposed to be doing so much damage?'

'I've dealt with that: As people emerge from a certain type of serfdom, and multiply, they flex their muscles and discover resistance.' Julia delivered this homily in a sing-song tone – indicating her general dismissal of James's point of view and the fact that she had rehearsed this argument with him before. She went on impatiently, 'Why can't you see that by preventing people from developing their full potential *you are being violent?*'

'Look, I know part of this is getting at me. I know you think banking is repressive. Well, if banking's repressive, what is education? I believe that some are destined to lead and others to be led. One sees this clearly in the animal kingdom— ' Julia's impatience exploded. 'I can't bear your comparing human behaviour with animal behaviour! The whole thing about being human is that we're responsible for our actions; we take thought about them, we have a feeling response to individual circumstances. But I forgot. You don't like admitting to feeling responses.'

James walked over to the fridge, opened it, and started fiddling with the interior bulb which appeared to have burnt out. 'What I can't stand,' he said in a hard voice, 'are the discussions about feelings that go on among your friends in analysis – professional patients forever picking about in their navels and their friends' navels. They've given feelings a bad name – at least, with me they have.'

Julia ignored this. 'Can't you see? Violent behaviour is a response to repression.'

'Is it? I should have thought it was the result of lack of discipline.'

'Whose discipline?'

'Parents, teachers, the clergy . . .'

'And what gives parents, teachers and the clergy the moral

authority to impose discipline? If what you're after is civilised behaviour, it can only be *loved* into people. People need to be consulted and co-operated with. And, incidentally, the only discipline worth anything at all is *self*-discipline.'

But Julia knew it was no good arguing with James. Nor was he the only hurdle to acceptance. 'Anyway, you're certainly in august company!' she told him. 'No one in my department has a good word for Galtung, and if they've heard of Erich Fromm they've never given a clue that they've read him. I can't imagine Gladyse Baker and Gerald Smith getting together to discuss *The Art of Loving* or *To Have or To Be*.'

'I find both books unreadable,' James admitted coldly.

'*I* think Fromm is something of a saint.'

'He's certainly unworldly.'

Julia held out her glass for James to refill. As she drank she turned and looked out on to the garden. 'I really don't understand, sometimes, why it is I choose to put myself through these hoops,' she said abstractedly. 'Part of me longs to be a stay-at-home, walk the dog, get the garden the way I want it, do some leisurely cooking, keep nice tidy cupboards . . .' She felt despondent. Perhaps if James had been a more demonstrative and feeling man she wouldn't be so academic. She might even have been more creative.

'That would suit me very well indeed,' said James. 'There are a lot of people I ought to entertain, you know, but I don't burden you with it because you're always so busy preparing lectures and writing articles and so on.'

Julia seemed not even to hear this. She got up, went to the sink, and turned on the taps. 'I bet they're all going through my paper with a nit comb at this very moment,' she said. 'It's funny, circulating a paper in advance. One knows that students can only take in three facts in fifty minutes, but you'd expect these international high-octane academics to manage a bit better. I suppose they're all rushing to incorporate my findings into their own papers before they submit final drafts for publication.'

Dr Julia Bruton was a senior lecturer in the International Relations Department of Thomas Paine College, University of London. Over the gates of the purpose-built college (miraculously it had escaped destruction in the bombing of World War Two) were the words: 'My country is the world, and my religion is to do good.' Within the walls the aspirations were less exalted, and there was bigotry and prejudice. But Julia Bruton ploughed her own furrow and rejoiced in the fact that the principle of academic freedom protected her too; if her colleagues found her views anathema, they did not have the right to depose or dismiss her. Occasionally, when she and two other members of the department were interviewing students, she was able to influence the acceptance of a black or Asian candidate by making it clear to her colleagues that she saw through their objections. Only recently, she had witnessed the unseemly contortions of her professor, Gladyse Baker, as she struggled to explain how and why it would be more appropriate to appoint a candidate for a junior teaching position who had neither a doctorate nor a single publication to his name – Maclaren – rather than another who had the former, and a string of the latter, to his – Levy. In the event a compromise was struck: neither was appointed. The 'cuts' were blamed.

James Bruton had gone straight from Oxford into a merchant bank. A friend of his parents – his own godfather – had been keeping the job warm for him; James, he thought, would approximate to the old merchant banking type – loyal to King and country, honest as the day is long. James looked the part and maintained the gentle, unruffled air of a man for whom the future is secure. Life had indeed dealt him a good hand and, as a result, everything about him was consoling.

His appearance was boyish; he had blond hair and blue eyes that had retained the ability to look surprised. When he was not dressed in immaculate city stripes, Hawes and Curtis shirts, he wore tweeds, a Barbour, a corduroy peak cap and green wellies. He had a mellifluous speaking voice, and when he was interviewed for television on economic and financial matters he had the effect of making women sound shrill and men shifty.

Julia and James had met at Oxford and married as soon as

they graduated. James started at the bank immediately, so that Julia had been able to get on with her research at Thomas Paine. In the early years of their marriage they lived in Stepney in a rented flat, but when Julia got her doctorate and was taken on to teach at Thomas Paine, things looked up. James's parents owned a house in Hampstead; his father, a naturalist, had long wanted to move to Selborne but had failed to wean his wife from London. However, when he was commissioned to write a biography of Gilbert White he held all the cards he needed, and his wife agreed that she might even enjoy exchanging the town for the country. They generously offered their house in Hampstead to James and Julia.

It was a beautiful house, part of a small terrace built in 1760, and preserved in pristine condition. The fronts of the houses rose sheer from the pavement; the backs looked on to a flag-stoned terrace, shared by all the residents and uniformly embellished with earthenware pots and stone urns. Whereas most of their neighbours confined themselves to architectural plants – foliage specimens – James liked scent and colour and a more nineteenth-century approach to gardening, so that even in winter the terrace was bright with Christmas roses and pansies, and in summer, giving way to an exuberance that no one who knew him professionally would have suspected of him, he raised scarlet geraniums, white tobacco and all colours of sweet peas and phlox.

'I must iron your shirts now,' Julia said. 'Then I'll get my own things together. I'll be in a rush and a sweat in the morning. What d'you think I should take? No, on second thoughts, don't bother with suggestions. I'll think about it while I iron and you take Bates for a pee.'

James took the lead from the hook on the kitchen door and climbed the stairs to his study where Bates was sleeping. 'Come along, old chap!' Julia heard the front door close. She revelled in the quiet. The loudest sound was that of steam flushed from the holes in the iron as she slowly pushed it back and forth across James's shirt. She was conscious of a deep contentment – something produced by the union she forged with her surroundings. Overcoming what was to her an awesome experience of separateness – whether from persons, ideas or objects – was a preoccupation with Julia. At some profound level her attachment to the world seemed tenuous. She made conscious efforts to achieve a state of union and harmony, wondering, in her inability to prolong it for more than seconds, whether its continuity was acquired only in death.

Yet she had it within her to enjoy life. She had a companionable marriage; she took it for granted that she loved her husband although neither declared the matter – they had not done so since their courting days. She had fulfilling work. The fact that she spent her days in the company of demanding colleagues and students led her to crave distraction in the evenings, and at least twice a week she and James went to the theatre or to concerts and out to dine. Their house was comfortable and well-appointed, even luxurious. They had first-class stereo equipment because they were passionate music-lovers. Each had a word processor. There were tv sets in the kitchen, the bedroom and in James's study; they tended to listen, rather than watch, however. Having spent long hours in the carpentry workshop at school – and enjoyed it – James proved good at do-it-yourself, patient and exacting. Julia had a flair for finding old objects – early wireless sets and sewing-machines – the appearance of which contributed to their stylish environment.

James was relaxed about work. In the office he applied himself diligently, but in return he expected to take days off when he felt like it, and when Julia was not teaching. They drove into the country to rummage in junk shops and second-hand bookshops, visit the studios of artist-craftsmen, and wander in markets. The spring holidays that they always took somewhere in Britain meant that they knew their own backyard – important, Julia felt, if she was to speak with authority about Britain and the British. If James wanted to look for business abroad, he would do so when Julia was free to accompany him. And when Julia had to attend a conference James often asked if she would like him to come along. Although his company made going abroad easier for Julia, from time to time she insisted on travelling alone, if only to force herself to experience fully the intensity of a strange place. Both accepted that they could rely on one another. They were considerate of each other, and on the surface this emerged as an unusual courtesy, upon which friends remarked. Without their realising it the Brutons excited curiosity and envy. However, Julia did not altogether escape problems. There were her parents.

Julia's father had been a maths teacher in a grammar school in central Birmingham, and her mother secretary to a solicitor in Edgbaston. When the school went comprehensive, Jack Fowler went mad. He handed in his notice on the very day St Bartholomew's fate was announced in assembly, saying he wasn't going to teach 'a tribe of gollywogs'. His wife Jill, a meek woman, swelled with pride on hearing Jack's report of how he had told the Head what he could do with the maths department. She liked the way he had acted so dramatically, and stuck up for himself and for her. But if they both coincided in agreeing that what was best for Jack was best for Jill, it was not because they discussed anything much. Jill provided the roast on Sunday, cold meat on Monday and shepherds' pie on Tuesday, but it never occurred to her to ask her husband if that was what he wanted, and it never occurred to Jack to consider whether he might prefer some other dish. In a world of candlewick bedspreads, the *Telegraph* and holidays on the Norfolk Broads, there was deep discontent – but no contention. Mr and Mrs Fowler's relationship was cemented with the grout of conventional wisdom. They had complete faith in the rightness of things matching: curtains to covers, plates to dishes, gloves to shoes – and their opinions on everything. They enjoyed the heady air of the moral high ground, and a favourite expression employed by both, and often in unison, was 'We could not countenance that!' They took much for granted – religious people were good people and Conservative-voting Anglicans the best. The British were better than foreigners in every way, particularly in their cooking, and their ability to govern their inferiors.

These and similar generalisations provided the ballast that weighted them so firmly to the ground of suburbia.

'Julia's always been devoted to her father,' Jill would confide over the garden fence. 'She doesn't tell me much. She's fond of me, I know, but she's close, if you know what I mean.'

In fact Julia was neither 'close', nor fond of her mother. She had been fond of her father when she was very young, and because she had shown signs of being unusually clever, he was proud of her. But as time went on, Julia's studying was undertaken less and less in order to please her father, and more and more in order that she might one day escape her parents' world.

'Our Julia's bright! A bright kid! Mark my words, she'll go far!' Jack Fowler told the family at their annual Christmas get-together.

'Oh no, she'll not be going into the biscuit factory,' he added, to the deep embarrassment of Julia, and the fury of his brother whose child, Patricia, was.

Jack would take Julia to one side and tell her, over and over, that all he wanted was the best for her and that she must study hard and do all her homework and not waste time with sports . . . 'Nor acting and painting!' Jill added. 'Just you concentrate on getting good marks!' If she 'did well', they both explained, she would be 'respected'.

Julia did not question her parents at the time, and it was not until she had fulfilled their five-year plan for her and won a place at Oxford, that she vaguely began to recognise that it might have been built on false precepts.

In January of her first year at St Anne's Julia's parents emigrated to South Africa. Her father had no difficulty in getting a job teaching maths at a public school in Johannesburg, and her mother had no problem in accommodating to a routine which involved sitting by her new mini-pool in an unfashionable suburb and gossiping with her all-white neighbours. The sale of the Birmingham house, and the advantageous exchange rate, meant that Mr and Mrs Fowler achieved a standard of living they had never dreamed of back in England. It was so convenient, Jill wrote to her daughter, having the little concrete hut for the maid tucked away at the bottom of the garden behind the trees. The maid was able to do almost all the work before Jill was up in the morning, so she wasn't obliged to have her around the house during the day. They had a gardener, twice a week. It wasn't a large garden, Jill explained, but there was the pool to keep clean. Unfortunately they didn't have a tennis court, she added, but nice Mr and Mrs McFadyan next door ('they have a son doing medicine, a bit older than you') had invited them to use theirs whenever they liked ('People are so friendly out here!').

Julia had not been ignorant of the situation in South Africa when her parents announced their intention of emigrating. She had a vivid mental picture of the poverty of the great black majority, herded like cattle to work where it suited the white man, separated from husband, wife and children; but she had very little idea of how the whites lived, and how their remorseless contempt for blacks affected their whole outlook. It was only when she visited her parents at the end of her second year at Oxford that she saw the results of the disease of prejudice. She had read Trevor Huddleston's *Naught For Your Comfort* and Alan Paton's *Cry The Beloved Country*; she was prepared to be saddened and indignant. But in the event she was outraged. The fact that her own father and mother – whose genes were her genes – accepted the South African situation and were ready to benefit from it, appalled her.

Contacts at Oxford led her not only to the lush prospects of Houghton but also to Soweto. The gap between rich and poor that had long worried her in Britain seemed a mere oversight when compared with the complete disjunction between the lives of blacks and whites in South Africa. 'How can you live with yourselves?' she asked her parents. 'Why teach white children in segregated schools when you could teach black children and help bring about their emancipation?'

Jack spoke his piece. 'I've not come here to change society, Julia. I've come to enjoy it, as it is. Out here they respect the white man, know what he's worth. Look around you! See for yourself what the whites have made of this country, and see what the blacks do with it. They live like animals.' There was a pause. Julia's father savoured the expression of his profoundest beliefs. 'I'm looked up to here!' (*Ah, there it is.*) 'I can choose my company here. I don't have to rub shoulders with the blacks like I did in Birmingham. And if it doesn't suit you, my girl, you know what you can do!'

Julia knew, and did. She left earlier than she had intended, but not before expressing her feelings. In a ruthless row with her father, who became beetroot-red during the scene, Julia told him precisely what she thought of him. Jack put his hand to his heart, feigned angina, and hit Julia before slumping into an armchair. Jill, who had never seen Jack so roused, stood up, flapped her arms, and screamed, 'You're killing your father!', then rushed from the room and took to her bed. By turning on the fan over the bed she was able to drown the raised voices still bouncing off the walls of the lounge, but later she heard Julia telephone the airline office and change the date of her departure. She also heard her take her suitcase from the cupboard under the stairs.

Mrs Fowler kept her arrangement for a shopping expedition with her neighbour next day, hoping Julia might see the error of her ways and make it up with her father. But as soon as her mother had left, Julia confronted the only wall in the house not occupied by a print of Clovelly or one of great-aunt Agnes's watercolours, drew a six-foot square outline in indelible felt pen, and inside wrote facts and figures that she hoped would etch themselves on her parents' minds.

	Black	White
Population of South Africa	85	15
Distribution of land (%)	13	87
Average monthly earnings (Rand)	320	1350
Educational expenditure per child/per year	238	1654
Health. Population per doctor	40,000	400
Life Expectancy	53 years	70 years
Infant Mortality	200 in 1000	15 in 1000

And she rounded off her statistics with a quotation from the Reverend Allan Boesak: 'Whites are afraid we will do to them what they have been doing to us.'

When Julia was back in England Jill tried to make peace, and in response to her attempts Julia now regularly sent her mother a token card at Christmas and on her birthday. But she never wrote to her father or sent him a message. It was her father who had taken pride in guiding her morally and intellectually when she was a child; seeing him in his true colours had been an unerasable shock. She did not dare expose herself to him again. It was not that she feared acquiring his views; she feared her views would kill him.

Julia's apparent orphan status was a matter of concern to her parents-in-law who sought, tactfully, to encourage Julia to re-establish proper contact with her parents. 'After all, they live thousands of miles away and it's not as if you're going to have to see them.' But Julia demurred. In a discussion with James, after a dinner at his parents' when the matter had been the subject of conversation on and off all evening, Julia explained that she saw no reason to make allowances for relatives that she would not make for acquaintances.

'If they want my affection then they're going to have to earn my approval. They've got to meet minimum standards of decency. Choosing to live in South Africa is incompatible with decency itself!'

'What d'you have to say about those people who live in South Africa and *do* something about the situation?'

'Well, in the case of Huddleston and one or two other churchmen I say, wonderful! But I'm less convinced by "liberal" politicians, academics and intellectuals. They're too compromised; their morality is ambiguous; they benefit too lavishly from the black man's inferior status. Not only would they not have the *renommé* in Europe that they've achieved out there, but they would never enjoy the material comforts. And everything they put back into society goes to the whites!' Julia paused before adding, 'I'd like to live long enough to see the day when black families can choose to have white servants. After all, unlike me, the whites have no moral objections to having others do their chores for them. So let them try it!'

James winced.

Monday

It was 8.30 a.m. when Jeremiah Jenkins, a seventy-five-year-old scout at Marlowe College, felt he might decently enter the rooms of Edmund Marshall, a normally late-rising post-graduate. With some difficulty – for his back was stooped and his hands arthritic – he pulled back the curtains on a brilliantly sunny morning, and with every evidence of habit having attained ritual status he recited an elaborate weather report. He observed the situation as it was: sunny; he forecast the likely situation in the afternoon: hot; and he continued by observing the seasonableness. He had addressed his obser-vations in the direction of the garden, but now he turned to Mr Marshall to remind him that his peace was due to be disturbed within a matter of hours by the conference on war and peace that was opening that day at Marlowe.

'Without meaning any disrespect, I foresee that it will be our peace their conflict upsets,' he volunteered darkly. 'There'll be upwards of fifty foreigners on our staircases and in our bathrooms and eating in hall!' He shuddered. 'Not to mention scattered about our lawns.'

Mr Jenkins had retained a conservatism that many of his 'gentlemen', he noticed with distaste, had renounced. He did not hold with international anything, and sorely regretted the parlous financial situation that had overtaken Marlowe and led to the Master touting for conferences. 'If you'd known it in the old days, Mr Marshall . . .' Mr Jenkins was generous with his reminiscences, and in the fifty-five years he had been a scout had acquired the manner and vocabulary with which to impart them. He now confided in Edmund his view that

19

international relations could have little future in a world in which *national* differences were proliferating, and proving recalcitrant.

'If I might suggest, Mr Marshall . . . You go up to Scotland for the fishing!'

Edmund, roused at last, jumped out of bed, hauled on his dressing-gown and joined Jeremiah at the window. He was very much looking forward to today, but his anticipation had little to do with the conference and even less to do with fishing. The local refrigeration plant was on strike, and this was providing him with first-hand evidence of the true relationship between pickets and police – a golden opportunity to compare what actually happened with what was reported to have happened. Edmund's thesis on post-war industrial relations could do with first-hand experience – leaven for a study he admitted to friends was proving stodgy.

The two men watched in silence for a few minutes as three gardeners carefully swept the lawns. Shortly they would tidy the already immaculate flower-beds and take feed to the deer. While Edmund braced himself for a bath that was never really hot (the antiquated heating system was inadequate for the increased demands made upon it), and Mr Jenkins savoured a sight that had not changed in all the years of his service, activity outside quickened. Other college servants, struggling under the weight of sheets and towels, crossed to and fro along the little paths that linked the eighteenth-century building where Edmund roomed with the earlier, medieval buildings that housed the domestic offices. On the newly swept lawn, men in suits laid out a vast canvas banner on which were painted in red letters CONFLICT STUDIES AND PEACE RESEARCH, and at each end they threaded stout rope through punched holes. The job completed, they gathered up the banner and between them carried it away towards Marlowe Tower.

At roughly the time that Edmund got into the bath, Professor Massimo Vardi checked in at Rome airport. He carried his crocodile-skin briefcase, but entrusted the matching holdall and wardrobe-case to an airport porter who wheeled them on a trolley. The professor indicated to the porter, with a single finger, that he should wait in the queue at the check-in desk while he went to buy newspapers. When he returned he was carrying French, German and Italian papers under his arm, and Havana cigars in his hand.

By 5 p.m. the crush of delegates in the porter's lodge round the single typed sheet of room allocations was so great that when Dr Julia Bruton and her student, Margaret, arrived together from London they only just managed to squeeze through into the main quad. They sat on the rim of the cloister fountain for a while, enjoying the sun, before setting off to wander round the staircases, and see if they couldn't find their rooms for themselves. An hour later the lodge was almost deserted, and by 6.30 p.m. all delegates had been safely housed and were sipping sherry in the Master's drawing-room.

Sir Augustus Eddington, Master of Marlowe College, was perhaps less than one hundred per cent comfortable in the twentieth century. Knowing this of himself, he had encouraged the Dean to take care of those matters for which he was demonstrably unfit, in particular Marlowe's disastrous financial situation. However, he did have one important contribution to make to the Dean's efforts – and the Dean was not unmindful of it, and made great play with it: Sir Augustus was second to none as a figurehead.

As the most distinguished Anglo-Saxon scholar in the country, Sir Augustus had occasionally been invited to make brief, scholarly appearances on television, but it didn't take producers long to realise that Sir Augustus's eccentric delivery and peculiar behaviour made him that rare and blessed thing, a television personality, and the appearances soon became less and less scholarly and more and more frequent – with the happy result that it was the name Marlowe, and not Baliol or Magdalen or Christchurch, which tended to spring first to the minds of those whose job it was to hire conference accommodation. In all sorts of other publicity arenas Sir Augustus's eccentricities also paid excellent dividends. Americans particularly warmed to the untidiness of the man, and the fact that he was more likely to display his toothbrush in his top pocket than a silk handkerchief. Other, more rarefied nationals found it engaging that Sir Augustus should assume their knowledge of fifth-century invasions of his country to be as wide and as deep as his own. And wealthy businessmen revelled in the esoteric pleasure of raising a blue Roman glass to their lips while taking sherry with Sir Augustus, and being informed in minute detail as to its provenance. 'Faversham! Kent!' he would exclaim excitedly. 'But not *made* there. Dear me, no! *Made* in Somerset!' And without pausing for his visitor to put a rather puzzled question, Sir Augustus would urge them to visit both Faversham and Glastonbury, and hurtle on to provide them with a passionate description of the greatest of Anglo-Saxon treasures, loyalty. 'Ah yes, we're very proud of the artifacts of the period, aren't we, but less mindful of its moral lessons. Pity! Great pity! Yes, British law, my friends, British parliament, British language and literature all owe their origins to the Anglo-Saxons, yet we British have jettisoned their ideals. We have done so at our peril!'

'And are you "conflict" or are you "peace?",' the Master enquired now of a dumbfounded delegate. He was revelling yet again in the sight of a troop of paying-guests in his drawing-room. His vision being somewhat impaired, he had not noticed the banner defacing the tower, and his hearing, being of the variety that is liable to fail when the subject under discussion is of no interest, was not violated by the Babel of voices. But a sudden cessation of conversation did attract his attention.

'Something untoward?' he asked, several times, over the heads of his guests.

The Dean, spotting the Master's unease, came quickly to his side and explained that it had been announced on the seven o'clock news that three railway stations in Italy had been devastated, simultaneously, by bombs, and that it was estimated that at least eighty men, women and children had died at Rome station alone. When Turin and Milan supplied their figures the total was expected to be in the hundreds.

'Good heavens!' exclaimed the Master. 'And is this the act of barbarians, or a response to barbarism? That's what I should like to know.'

A German delegate who found himself standing at the Master's side offered his view that in Germany and Italy the legacy of fascism was such that it was as difficult to neutralise as atomic waste. At which point a Swede broke in to hope it would not be a matter of *millions* of years before every vestige of fascism had been erased from the soil of Europe.

'Today it's the same organisation that finances and operates the destruction of both Left and Right in Italy. It's anathema to these hooligans to see a coalition trying to maintain even a semblance of national harmony.'

'National harmony is only possible under a dictatorship,' Professor Vardi chipped in.

'Or under socialism,' the Swede moved.

'Perhaps we'd do better to aim at peaceful discord,' Dr Bruton suggested. 'At least that's within the bounds of possibility.' And then someone challenged the German, maintaining that the chaos in Italy was the responsibility of the Left, and the German became heated and said that was certainly not the case. 'Italian communists are far from being a bunch of thugs! They're educated idealists! I know it's fashionable to be cynical about idealists, but I myself am not. Nor do I mind being labelled unfashionable.'

'Nor I, my dear fellow!' the Master exclaimed delightedly. At last, someone who would understand the value of his thoughts on Anglo-Saxon vendetta! 'Do tell me, is this dreadful act in your opinion one of total lawlessness? Or does it have its rules and regulations? You see, I've been writing a little monograph . . .'

By 8 p.m. the Master's drawing-room had become intolerably hot and stuffy, despite the windows and doors being flung wide open. The Master had hijacked out on to the lawns first the German delegate, whose escape was only achieved by an ostentatious departure for the lavatory, and secondly two stunningly beautiful Ugandan delegates, whose magnificent *tenues*, in the dim presence of a good deal of academic crimplene, positively blinded the male delegates with their stylishness. The more sober delegates were clearly irritated by the Master, who now sat with his arms extended along the back of a garden seat, one Ugandan beauty on his right and the other on his left, interminably discussing the differences between vendetta in Uganda and vendetta in Anglo-Saxon Britain.

Julia observed the Master's tactics with amusement. She had noticed, over the years, how it is often the least attractive men who succeed with the most attractive women. Was it, she wondered, a case of the women being patronising, thinking to themselves: poor dear, he can't possibly imagine . . . ? Or was it that women did not like the competition that elegant and confident men pose? She couldn't imagine herself competing for attention with a man – but then she couldn't get involved in any sort of fight or competition. She had been born without the ingredient that makes some people wish to succeed at all costs.

She would certainly never fight over a man . . . Or would she? It was something she had never had to do. She and James had got together so early in their adult lives. And since then they had found enough in one another to keep them interested and content without making sorties from the straight and narrow on to the shadier by-ways. It was not, she imagined, that they had made a religion of sexual fidelity, or believed it was proof of anything much, just that they had recognised the dangers inherent in having affairs. Anyhow, neither of them had the time.

These and other tangential thoughts were in Julia's mind as she moved from one group of delegates to another, recognising some, and being introduced to others she had not met. All the time, she was peculiarly aware of the presence of a large man, not strikingly good-looking but strikingly evident. He was following on her heels as she passed from group to group. She was struck by the way he paid equal attention to male and female delegates, and seemed unaware of the difference between the extraordinarily dowdy women from – she regretted to have to admit – English universities, and the ravishing foreign visitors. He seemed to behave as graciously to the exquisite doll-like women from Asia, wearing traditional silks, whose presence revived memories of exotic paintings and embroideries, as to the Austrian valkyries whose dress had its roots in the Tyrol and, when it did not conjure up images from *The Sound of Music* reminded Julia of the heresy of Aryan 'purity'. Julia was disturbed by the man's dominance: she noticed that while he appeared to bestow himself generously, he actually gave nothing of himself away.

She would have known he was Italian even if she had not heard him introduced. His name was Vardi and he was a professor from the University of Rome. By comparison with other delegates Professor Vardi, immaculately attired in a cream linen suit, appeared cool, and Julia had been somewhat surprised to see him take a sage-green silk handkerchief from his breast pocket to mop his brow. His skin looked matt. It had been just after he had heard the Dean inform the Master about the railway station bombs in Italy. Julia had been drawn to observe him as the Italian listened intently to the German delegate's declaration that fascism was a continuing problem in Europe, but apart from the single comment – that national harmony could only be achieved under authoritarian rule – Professor Vardi had not contributed to the conversation. Julia wondered if the professor was advocating dictatorship or merely observing how difficult, even impossible, it is to obtain national harmony?

The Master's party was a success; delegates stayed on until the light faded. A French delegate realised with horror that it was after 9 p.m. and therefore almost impossible to get a meal in Oxford, and left. Having sorted themselves into their appropriate slots, Peace Research, Conflict Studies, other delegates followed. Half an hour later Julia saw Professor Vardi stride into The Randolph with a group of Conflict delegates. She herself, together with an American Peace delegate, continued up St Giles. They had been invited to a late supper with an American historian in Oxford on sabbatical leave.

Tuesday

Breakfast was laid in Hall. It was a magnificent prospect; the medieval oak-panelled room was bathed in soft sunlight as if smiling with satisfaction at the sight of abundant food and abundant company to enjoy it. Along the length of one wall a refectory table groaned under the weight of kidneys in a huge chafing-dish, platters of freshly grilled bacon, tomatoes and sausages, and fried eggs kept warm on hot-plates, a York ham on the bone and every variety of bread known to Scottish, Welsh and English bakers. It seemed that the staff were determined to model the presentation of the breakfast feast along medieval lines.

Although a number of delegates were breakfasting in hall, it was quiet. More sound was created by the turning of confer-ence papers and newsprint than by conversation. Julia found a window seat. Just as she sat down, she saw Margaret enter and make her way towards her.

'I'm in a rush. I've got fourteen Greenham women coming to the seminar that the Danish delegate is giving,' she said. 'I've got to be at the bus station to meet them in ten minutes.'

'It's a pity you have to rush,' Julia said. 'It's a real treat having this huge choice of food that one hasn't had to prepare oneself. I'm seriously considering starting at the top with prunes and working my way through the whole cooked bit down to the toast and marmalade.'

'What? At this hour? You must be mad!'

'No! Hungry. That American historian had a very casual approach to Sunday supper . . .' Julia watched Margaret gulp her coffee. Over her head she saw the German delegate enter hall with a couple from the University of Geneva. Behind them she saw Professor Vardi.

'May we join you?' the German asked. Julia smiled and nodded. She did not welcome the prospect of conversation over breakfast, but since most delegates had by now left Hall she was surrounded by unoccupied seats; there was nothing she could do to protect her privacy without appearing rude.

'It's always said that the English breakfast is their best meal of the day!' the German observed with a touch of malicious satisfaction as he stared down at his brimming plate. He turned to Professor Vardi who had taken the seat at his right hand and was clearly not enjoying his black coffee. 'You're not eating, my friend!'

'I'm rather fussy. I've a rather delicate constitution.'

Oh, he's rather fussy and he's rather delicate, is he? Too bloody bad! In her thoughts Julia became uncharacteristically xenophobic.

'I really do recommend the full breakfast,' she tried, a touch over-politely. 'The ingredients are first-class, and the whole thing has been well prepared.' Professor Vardi did not reply. Julia thought that she detected a vague smile hovering round his lips – but there was nothing of it in his eyes.

'I'm going to take advantage of this glorious weather and work in the garden this morning. I've got some last-minute additions to make to my paper. And then I propose to reward myself with luncheon at The Mitre. Can I persuade you to join me?' the German asked, looking amiably around him but without singling out anyone in particular.

'What is The Mitre? And where is The Mitre?' one of the Swiss delegates enquired. It was a question, indeed two questions, that Professor Shein had longingly anticipated. He was a man of enthusiasms, and his delight in expatiating on them was unleashed by the merest hint of interest from another. He explained that his passion was for old travel books. The reason he attended, slavishly, all the conferences in his field was largely because they provided him with the opportunity (funded) to follow in the footsteps of travellers of long ago, and observe what remained unchanged since those redoubtable explorers had chronicled the far reaches of the world.

'I have with me *Travels in England* by the eighteenth-century Karl Moritz. He was such an acute observer . . . and he himself was travelling in the footsteps of Milton. So I propose to put my feet down where Moritz and Milton trod. It's extraordinarily romantic.'

'And they visited The Mitre?'

'Precisely! Indeed, they stayed there.' Julia decided not to tell the professor that The Mitre was now a Berni Inn – poor man, he would find out soon enough. Indeed, the Swiss couple delightedly agreed to accompany Professor Shein, and there was much enthusiastic anticipation. The professor was so delighted at having corralled the two delegates that he did not notice that neither Julia nor Professor Vardi committed themselves to his plan.

Julia propped the conference programme against her coffee pot. I must learn how to clamour, she thought to herself, and wondered why the thought had swum into her mind. On what tide had it drifted unbidden? It was so difficult to account for these things. She must attend Pastor Svenholm's lecture. His book *Freedom and the Church* raised a number of questions in her mind. I shall have to tell him, she thought, that far from the Church setting anyone free, it was man tasting the fruit of the tree of good and evil that did that; man acted against God's orders and became autonomous. It might sound rude saying this to the Pastor, but she had found that bottling up strongly-held opinions only made her depressed. She had once heard her own professor, Gladyse Baker, say to a student outside her office, 'I think we should tell them that if they shoot the American hostages we shall line up their diplomats and pick them off, one by one!' And she had found no way to challenge Gladyse. First, she could not do so in front of the student; secondly, she could not see a way of bringing up the subject later when Gladyse would almost certainly have forgotten the occasion. And, of course, Gladyse had a perfect right to her point of view – even though the student would feel pressured to confirm it if he or she wanted to do well in the department . . . Giving the stick back to the dog, it was called.

Julia had not known what to say to the student. Her student. In the event she had organised a seminar, the subject of which was 'Intolerance of Intolerance. For and Against'. She held the seminar at a time when first-, second- and third-year students would be available to attend, and she had had a very full house. She was gratified to discover that the majority held the view that intolerance of intolerance was a necessary component of a free society. On this occasion she was, therefore, spared depression.

At five minutes to eleven Julia pressed her knee against the unyielding weight of the door marked 'Extra-Parliamentary Protest'. As she did so she caught sight of Professor Vardi walking into the adjacent room where the North/South Divide was under discussion. For some reason, she found herself very much hoping that he had not seen her, and did not know that she had seen him. She felt oddly attracted – and repelled – by him. Clamour, she thought. A lot of stuff was banging about her mind in an unco-ordinated way.

The Danish delegate, Dr Sussi Sorensen, was sitting on the edge of the huge mahogany table, chatting to a group of women dressed in the Oxfam uniform of protest. Dr Sorensen looked so wholesome, as if she had been peeled from a packet of Danish butter. The women were describing their life on Greenham Common. Dr Sorensen asked them about the effect that their mode of life was having on their children, and how they coped with cooking meals on a primus stove, and how they kept clean and warm.

'Are the local residents hostile to you? Or do some invite you in for baths and food?' There was laughter, and it was good-natured. 'Yes, they're all hostile,' one of the women insisted, adding, 'But I really don't see how they could be anything else. The sort of people with property, brought up the way they've been brought up, are far more concerned about litter in their gardens than the possibility of the destruction of the world. And war has a nobility for them that financial ruin, in the shape of diminishing property values, has not.'

Julia felt warmly disposed to the Greenham women. They were friendly, reasonable, enthusiastic and optimistic. By ten past eleven three men had joined the seminar, and by a quarter past the hour all the chairs round the table were taken and the occupants fell silent for Dr Sorensen's lecture.

As she delivered her paper, Dr Sorensen developed her argument in response to interruptions from the delegates. Her subject was one that put Julia's peace of mind under threat; she likened the effect Dr Sorensen was having on her conscience to the effect that *Pears Medical Encyclopedia* had on her nerves: when she opened its pages she found that she had every disease from Abdominal Cancer to Wryneck, whereas in fact all she suffered from was over-indulgence, fatigue – and suggestibility.

'We must – here and now – take a stand. We must – here and now – stop colluding with the system by plagiarising its forms and practices. We have to find an appropriate anarchism, and adhere to it.' Dr Sorensen concluded her paper.

A lecturer from an English provincial university complained that his presence at Greenham Common had been rejected by the women. 'How can we hope to co-exist between nations if we can't co-exist between the sexes?' he whined.

'Can't you see,' a Greenham Common woman piped up, as if talking to an imbecile, 'we women are obliged to confront the most serious issues of life and death *alone*. After thousands of years of men's failure, we're setting an example of how it should be done – and we have to do it by ourselves. It's a transitional period. Once our abilities have been properly tested, and once they're duly recognised, we shall welcome you in to help consolidate the peace we shall have won.'

'How can you argue with a swarm of bees?' The seminar over, the four men grouped at the far end of the room. They would not take issue with the Greenham women, who outnumbered them, but simply consoled each other with their well-rehearsed prejudices; all women were irrational – and these women were not even feminine. Laughter exploded from them like wind – bar-room laughter that lacked gaiety. Julia looked over towards the men and found them distasteful and pathetic. She reflected that James was not like them. One of the Greenham women, who had been observing Julia and seemed to have been following her unspoken thoughts, turned to her and quoted: ' "O, if we but knew what we do/When we delve or hew." ' Julia smiled as she gathered her papers together, and with Hopkins ringing in her ears asked whether anyone would like to have a bite to eat at Binsey. Dr Sorensen knew nothing of Gerard Manley Hopkins, nor of Binsey, but liked what she had seen and heard of Julia and said, 'Why not?'

As they left the seminar room, the group broke up into small clusters – those who would lunch in town, those who did not want lunch at all, and those who would join Julia at The Perch, on the river. Julia was idly speculating on whether people were making their choices according to the views they held on Extra-Parliamentary Protest, when she bumped into Professor Vardi in the corridor.

'Are you busy for lunch, Dr Bruton?'

'Have you capitulated to Dr Shein and The Mitre?' Julia enquired, laughing. But she felt embarrassed. Was he inviting her to lunch with him alone?

'I most certainly have not!' Vardi replied.

'Well, as a matter of fact I've just arranged for a party of delegates to have lunch with me at a pub on the river. Perhaps you'd like to join us?'

In the space of time it takes for a clap of thunder to sound, Julia realised that she felt equally glad and sorry, that Vardi accepted the invitation.

In the event eight delegates made for The Perch, three in Julia's car and five, including Professor Vardi, in the unsympathetic Englishman's. It was not until Julia was out of the city that she remembered Margaret, but since no Greenham women were among her party she could not discover why Margaret had failed to attend the seminar.

Coldston had been planned, as some had put it, a 'decent'

distance from the centre of the university city. Had a man from the moon dropped into Oxford and passed a day wandering through the medieval colleges and their gardens, the nineteenth-century residential streets and the Botanical Gardens, and then leapt, on the following day, into Coldston, he would have formed the view that different species inhabited the two adjacent sites. On the one hand, Oxford – organically progressing, aesthetically pleasing, financially secure – on the other, Coldston – a slice of frozen 1920s time, ugly, poor, neglected, a place in which neither man nor vegetation was expected to burgeon. The spiritual needs of the people of Coldston were catered for by a half-boarded-up Victorian church at the edge of the estate. Their aesthetic needs were overlooked. Their education was confined to schools that were architectural infelicities with concrete playgrounds, door-less lavatories, and classes of up to forty children. Indeed, the only needs considered when Coldston emerged from the drawing-board had been those of the factory bosses, whose houses were sited just outside a seventeenth-century village five miles away.

The estate had been organised round a series of figures-of-eight, with two open spaces at the centre of each group of eighty houses. The designing architect may have had in mind open fields of long grass scattered with buttercups and daisies, or circles of municipal planting serving as a meeting place for adults and a playground for children. However, when it came to the point the council proved to have no plans for the spaces, and had spent no money on maintaining them. The local canine population seized the opportunity and used the dereliction for its lavatories. A few blades of grass pushed heroically through the undernourished clay soil, and in the gutters where the rain collected and the drains overflowed, children's boots mashed longer grasses into a series of little bogs. During the hopeful 1960s some attempt had been made to encourage the grass to grow, and access to the open spaces had been curtailed by barbed wire, to give the grass seed a chance – but the wire had been cut, and the wind had hurled fragments of black plastic bin-liners and other bits of refuse onto the spikes.

Now, in the mid-1980s, Coldston's appearance revealed to all who cared to look both the lot of its residents – undermined and living at subsistence level – and the attitude of the local authority – unpardonable indifference.

The self-image of the people of Coldston was no more dignified than the reflection they received from the mirror held up to them by their local authority. They were at a peculiar disadvantage; congested with despair, they felt themselves continuously despised. They lived with the example of Oxford only four miles distant – yet, in the sixty years of Coldston's existence, not one of its sons or daughters had gained a place at any one of the Oxford colleges – except in the capacity of servant.

In recent times, with the virus of unemployment rampant, the male population of Coldston rarely ventured into the city but hung around the few shops still trading on the estate. On The Parade, at the intersection of one of the figures-of-eight, there was a cinema, a newsagent's, a chemist and a supermarket – of sorts – that sold cans of beer and cider. The men met outside the supermarket and, taking their cans with them, they would wander down to the edge of the estate, to the banks of the river, and sit on municipal concrete benches to drink and exchange desultory conversation. They preferred to meet at 'the bottom' rather than 'the top' because 'the top' was the site of the surgery, where the women gathered with their bronchial children and their 'women's complaints'. There too was the vet, to whom their distempered dogs, their mangy cats and their enteric canaries were taken – and put down. The men could not abide uninterrupted chatter about ill-health. It was bad enough to have no job, no money and no prospects; they did not want to be reminded of illnesses, dying and death. Added to which, the betting shop had its premises at 'the bottom'. It was the women who, in more confident days, had found the strength to see to it that this temptation was not sited on The Parade. They had their bingo in the cinema in the afternoons; that was quite enough. It was no use their trying to oppose the betting shop altogether, they knew this, but out of sight was out of their minds at least, they said.

The women did get into the city; both the colleges and the Oxford residents employed them as cleaners. Some academic wives rehearsed arguments moth-balled since the 1930s: 'It's our *duty* to employ as many of these unfortunate people as we can afford.' But few of the Coldston women working as domestic servants earned a proper wage. None was regarded as a 'treasure', few were accorded a 'Miss' or a 'Mrs'. And over luncheon quiche and Sancerre their employers gathered to lament their clumsiness in handling Royal Worcester, their ignorance in the use of Antiquax and the ironing of raw silk – and their musical preferences. Women who prided themselves on being liberal-with-a-small-'l' expressed some sympathy for the plight of their domestic skivvies, but it was a phoney sympathy; none would have relinquished any of her own privileges to achieve a better quality of life for her employee. As liberals they regretted the gap between the classes, and between rich and poor; as members of an upwardly mobile class, every one of their actions endorsed what they deplored. And the strike at the refrigeration plant at Coldston was universally condemned. 'You'd think in times like these those men would be pleased to have a job at all – whatever the job and whatever the pay!' chorused women who lived off their husbands, and whose only occupation was the preparation of the occasional dinner party and an afternoon a week spent handing out books at the local hospital.

Coldston expressed the very sorrow of existence. At Coldston the real and actual was the sole option. The inner life of the individual had been so neglected as to have been destroyed. Once, Coldston men had worked for a wage packet, created a few children – partly from habit, partly to insure themselves against destitution in old age and partly from ignorance. They had taken their wives to the pub or the cinema on Saturday nights and, possibly, spent five days at Butlin's in the rains of summer. Today, unemployment led the men to stay in bed until eleven or later, and hang around the house with the transistor and the television blaring, reading the *Sun*. Following a solitary 'dinner', consisting of beans on toast, they would gather by the river with others who had also been made redundant. They did not discuss the roots of their dissatisfaction, that would have been too painful. They considered why – and how – their wives had less allure than Page Three girls, and what they would do if they won the Pools. Their lungs became increasingly damaged by smoking, their livers increasingly rotted with beer. Their children got on their nerves, asking for things the men could not afford to buy. The men were getting violent at home; two from one estate were up for manslaughter in September, and no one even kept count of the cases of GBH any more.

The National Front had moved in, attracted by the contagion of instability. Like birds of prey, the thugs knew when a collective animal was done for; what they lacked in intelligence they made up for in instinct. Few of the Coldston men could be bothered to go into Oxford to set light to the cars of rich Asian and Jewish students, but more were willing to gather in the laundrette and outside the betting shop and enlist in the so-called 'armies' of the Right. Unseen leaders drafted phoney words of sympathy and phoney solutions, and waited patiently for the crucial moment to order their minions to pour them into the decibel-damaged ears of their victims.

The Coldston men had earned a reputation in the North for being unreliable. These workers did not have the *esprit de corps* of the miners, who knew that the wretched are open to flattery, and that the sort of flatterers that wait and watch for prey are deceivers, robbers and murderers of the wretched themselves. It was this knowledge that had brought the miners' flying pickets to Oxford bus station and diverted Margaret from her purpose. Instead of returning with the Greenham women to Marlowe, she simply put them on the right path to the college and then trudged the five miles to Coldston with the men.

'Jesus Christ! Just look at this place!'

The phalanx of North Country trades unionists had emerged from the lane that ran along fields of ripening grain, protected by ancient hedgerows and magnificent old elms whose crowns were studded with crows' nests. The contrast was striking as they rounded a corner and came face to face with blocks of tear-stained concrete – the factories of Coldston. Most of the buildings were shut, their windows shuttered. Notices warned intruders to KEEP OUT, and alerted them to the presence of guard dogs. One factory was still operating; black smoke poured from its chimney and litter from sacks and bins lay scattered in its yard. At the opposite side of the lane, overlooking the factories, the windows of the houses of Coldston stared expressionless over their unkempt gardens. To the stench of some unidentifiable effluent was added that of faulty drains.

'Once working men and their families are seen to put up with this sort of squalor, management knows it's demoralised them, and the men'll be ready to accept anything shovelled their way. It's a danger to the whole working class when things get this bad!'

Margaret nodded, stunned.

There were no more than fifty Coldston men standing at the gate, but there were at least forty police observing them from the opposite side of the lane. As the men from the North rounded the corner and moved towards the factory gates, the police strung themselves across the lane and blocked their way.

'Keep back, you lot!' an officer shouted through a megaphone. 'I don't want any trouble from any one of you. If I get none from you, you'll get none from me. But I'm warning you, you'll do as I say. You'll keep to the verge, this side of the lane.' And then he spotted Margaret and walked over to her.

'And you, my girl, what brings you to Coldston on this nice sunny day?'

'I'm a student!'

'A student, are you? Well! Well!' And he looked her up and down. 'My advice to you, young lady, is to get back to your studies!'

'These are my studies!'

'Is that so? Well, I don't know what the world's coming

to. So these are your studies, are they? My work your study? This strike is potential civil disobedience, Miss Student!' And turning to a fellow officer, he confided well within Margaret's hearing that this was proof – if proof were needed – that women did not deserve education. 'If you're going to "study" Coldston's troubles, I'd be obliged to you if you'd do so from this grass verge,' he said. 'I don't want to have to speak to you again. You've been warned.'

It was just after Margaret had received the police officer's admonition that she noticed a young man, notebook in hand, taking down the exchange. It was Edmund Marshall from Marlowe College. They fell into conversation.

Julia found that the crush and hubbub in the pub were not only uncongenial but also a further embarrassment; she had chosen The Perch, she was responsible. She would like her environment to appear at its best. Professor Vardi looked peculiarly out of place. Was it that he contrived to look out of place in order to establish that he was special? His straw-coloured linen suit (or was it raw silk?) had the effect of making everyone else's clothes look cheap and the pub look fusty. Yet, in the past, Julia had liked the way the English have of not caring about the vintage of their dress, and she had been pleased that The Perch's landlord had done nothing to hide the kippered ceiling of the bar or replace the faded cretonnes. She was irritated that things she had been satisfied with were being put to shame by the presence of the Italian.

While her group ate moist crab sandwiches stuffed with cress, and drank ice-cold lager, Julia orchestrated the conversation, bringing to notice a timid member and discouraging those who hogged the attention. Unlike the others, Professor Vardi seemed not to be affected by heat or noise; Julia felt that this indifference could be laid at the door of his pride. Nor did he contribute much to the conversation. The rest of the group did not appear to notice his silence. He had a way of nodding assent from time to time so that he drew attention to himself – without proving contentious. And no one could have failed to notice that he was not only physically striking

37

but also unusually well-kempt. Unlike the English, who studiously contrive a style thrown together by an east wind, the Italian showed every sign of having carefully chiselled his face and modelled his body, and then chosen after-shave and clothing that could be relied upon to bring out their finer points. There was something a bit show-biz about this man! His fingernails were too clean; he might even have drawn a white pencil under their tips.

'I could do with some air.' Julia rose from her seat. The group looked up and smiled and carried on talking. Professor Vardi pushed back his chair and stood up. He did not explain himself. He joined Julia on the tow-path.

'I'm going to walk,' she said, pointing upstream.

'I'll join you!'

They walked without talking for a few hundred yards. With each step she took Julia was conscious of the silence between them, and was made uncomfortable by it. There was something frightening about his power to fascinate her. The hairs rose at the back of her neck. It crossed her mind that this man might throw her into the river. The idea itself was terrifying enough; that she should be suddenly entertaining it was dreadful. I'm being hysterical, she thought.

'D'you know the poetry of Gerard Manley Hopkins?'

Professor Vardi did not, he had never heard of Gerard Manley Hopkins. Julia was grateful; she told him at once that Hopkins had been a religious, a nature-poet, a Victorian. 'He read classics at Baliol.' What a relief it was to know a great deal about Hopkins, to have an uncontroversial and impersonal topic of conversation. And, nearing Binsey, she recited for him 'Binsey Poplars'.

'Hopkins wouldn't be a jot surprised by that ghastly industrial scene,' she said, looking out from the place of the felled poplars, over the meadow towards Oxford.

Vardi followed her gaze. 'You're terribly sentimental! Where would your country be without its industries?'

It would be useless, Julia thought, to take issue. It would be useless to try to make him see that that was not the point.

Julia led Vardi into Binsey churchyard. She would explain

how it was that Binsey Well had earned its reputation for being magical. 'In the Middle Ages people believed that these waters restored the fertility of barren women.' Vardi was clearly uninterested.

'D'you have children?' he asked.

'No. I never wanted children.'

'And your husband?'

'I think he regrets not having them. Now. But in the early days of our marriage he wanted me to pursue my career. I feel rather guilty about it, today. But,' she added after a pause, 'I did join him in the Society of Friends.' Realising, perhaps for the first time, that this concession probably did not altogether compensate James for the loss of parenthood, she laughed in embarrassment. And anxious to change the subject she asked, 'Did you ever read *Alice in Wonderland*?'

'I did.'

'Well, this is the treacle well!'

It was cool in the churchyard; the yews kept out the light and warmth of the sun, and the untended grass and ivies kept in the damp. Julia wandered among the headstones noting the Oxfordshire names. And then she heard voices; other delegates had found the place and were invading it in an effort to escape the intense heat. Some had plonked themselves down on low tombs, others – with a respect for the dead often denied the living – stood around awkwardly like uninvited guests.

Conversation was desultory. At last they all found something upon which they could agree; they would return to college, to its thick, damp stone walls, for a siesta . . .

Julia peeled off her cotton dress and filled the wash-basin with icy water. She plunged her head into the basin, soaking her hair, her face and her neck. And then she dipped her arms into the water and wet them up to her shoulders. She eased her feet from her sandals and cooled them in the basin. She threw back the bed covers and, still damp, lay on the bottom sheet. She felt utterly exhausted.

A knock on her door did not surprise her. But her heart thumped against her ribs. 'Who is it?' she said disingenuously.

Professor Vardi entered so quietly, it was as if he were melting into the room. He did so in a cloud of Eau de Portugal. How, Julia wondered, could he have a change of trousers and shirt that looked as if they had just left Valentino? She felt a little frightened and drew a sheet over her naked body. 'What on earth . . . ?'

'My dear,' he said, closing the door without making a sound, and locking it, 'this is surely what we both want?'

She was cross; he was deplorably presumptuous. But what he said was true. Other such thoughts came to Julia as she watched the Italian placing his trousers and shirt meticulously over the back of a chair. She wondered whether she should try to stop his advances. But how? Did it look odd to him that she was putting up no opposition? She pinched her thigh. This was happening, and it was happening to her, and shortly there would be no way back.

No one need ever know, she thought. If I am going to be unfaithful it's better that it's with a stranger, no one known to the clan. And in the space between two split seconds she thought of Amanda, whose affairs were picked over by all her friends and acquaintances, commented upon, assessed, judged . . .

He is bound to make love as elegantly as he does everything else . . . or am I about to discover that Latins are lousy lovers?

It was forty minutes before Julia's questions would be answered in full. Professor Vardi proved an accomplished lover; he satisfied his partner because not to do so would lay him open to the charge that he was careless. He would not have objected to the accusation of being uncaring, but to be careless was inimical to his style.

'How innocent you are for a woman of your age!' he murmured as he slid out of her bed. 'But English women so often are!'

Post coitum . . . Julia felt confused. She was as disappointed as she was surprised that, once satisfied and rested, Vardi replaced his clothes and prepared to leave. He had become fidgety; he was bored. It was humiliating. He was treating her like a whore. She was clearly not to become an insolent encroachment on his time. As he was unlocking the door he turned towards her and smiled – but he said nothing. Julia was unable to decide whether the smile was one of friendship, conquest or conspiracy. Had they established any sort of contact? She wondered. She knew his name and he knew hers, but neither had uttered the other's. 'Massimo' she whispered to herself as the door closed.

'Make love not war!' Julia's thoughts slipped back to the banners her students at Paine had hung around doors, windows and light-fixtures when their ire was raised in protest against some banana republic's dictator or in support of the victims of injustice. 'Make love not war!' Surely that silent sexual encounter could not be dignified by the word love.

Her uncharacteristic behaviour had left her bemused, although her earlier exhaustion had dissolved, replaced by an unfamiliar feeling of physical repletion. Her mind was filled with Massimo to the exclusion of all else. She plus Massimo equalled adultery. She had committed adultery! She tried to work out how she felt. Above all, she must not express her feelings and risk being hurt.

Julia had trained herself to think consistently over extended periods of time. It had been a long haul; she had started as a student, thinking three minutes at a time on some concrete subject and going back to the beginning if her mind wandered. Years later she had developed the capacity to consider an abstraction for as long as she needed. The term 'adultery' was not one she had dwelt on before. Now she lay brooding on the word – and not in the abstract. Ordinarily, she was not given to analysing herself. She accepted that her behaviour, like her heartbeat, was something that could take care of itself, needing no interference from her. But her adultery raised the issue of betrayal. This was the first time that she had betrayed James – even in her thoughts. How did she feel about him? How would he feel about it? Would she need to tell him? And how far could she compromise herself without losing her integrity? Her life at home and her work were of a piece. The implications were starting to seem overwhelming.

On the fringes of her friendships were ranged acquaintances

who relieved the boredom of lives spent shopping, playing golf and organising charity balls with soft drugs and wife-swapping. And there were orgies at the Red House that abutted Hampstead Heath where she and James walked Bates. However little Julia would have wished to swap places with Maralyn, whose husband was in armaments and bored for Britain, or with Miranda Blunda, whose husband was a leading member of the jetsam set, those women had not 'betrayed' their husbands – they had conspired with them. Husband and wife had taken a joint decision to play the field in the company of any number of partners. And sex in that context was far removed from the sacrament of love.

Julia dressed and made up with particular care. She chose a faded pink Jean Muir dress – a timeless garment, beautifully detailed. She hung a beaten-silver and coral necklace round her neck. She fastened her shoulder-length ash-blonde hair in a matching clasp at the nape of her neck. She felt desirable. She hoped Vardi would be in Hall for dinner; she hoped he would dine with her – and sleep the night with her.

Julia watched the delegates leaning forward over bowls of iced vichyssoise and picking inquisitively at prawn cocktails. From where she stood it seemed that all the seats in Hall were taken. She spotted a vacant seat – between two Africans clearly not on speaking terms – and as she moved towards it she saw Massimo Vardi out of the corner of her eye. He was engaged in animated conversation with three Conflict Studies friends. One of the Africans rose from his seat as Julia drew out the empty chair, and waited until she was settled comfortably before returning to his seat. He introduced himself as Dr Jo Machito, and for the duration of dinner discussed the problem of Africanisation facing his country, Zimbabwe. From time to time Julia surreptitiously snatched a glimpse of Vardi, but he was never looking in her direction. She found it impossible to give her undivided attention to Dr Machito's plan for the decolonialisation of thought in Zimbabwe, and she barely noticed what she was eating. It seemed astonishing – and wrong – to have been making love with a stranger some three hours ago, and equally astonishing for him to have returned, immediately, to the status of stranger.

Vardi had changed into yet another set of clothes. His deep tan and glossy black hair, his caramel-and-white-striped shirt and duck-egg-blue tie, distinguished him from those around him. He could never pass unnoticed in a crowd, Julia thought; he sticks out like a sore thumb – no, rather, a jewelled finger. When eventually Dr Machito led her into the smoking-room where coffee was being served, she noticed Vardi leaving by a side door with one of the Indian women delegates.

Julia felt sick. She was no longer able to keep up the pretence that the problems of Zimbabwe were her most urgent concern. She excused herself on the grounds that she had some preparations to complete for tomorrow. Dr Machito rose from his chair and bowed formally until Julia was out of his sight.

What was it that had made her stray into such unfamiliar territory? What was so intriguing about being disregarded? What was she re-enacting? What dissatisfaction was she redressing?

Wednesday

'I'm sorry! You must have wondered what on earth had become of me!' Margaret was waiting for Julia just inside the Dish of Tea, and as Julia pushed open the door Margaret spotted a vacant table for two and drew Julia towards it. 'It's much nicer here than in all that magnificence, isn't it?' she said.

It was ten-thirty. Elderly country women, whose dress made no concession to fashion, had done their shopping and come to spoil themselves at the cake trolley.

'I met a post-grad from Marlowe on the picket line. He's also doing something on industrial war and peace.' Margaret chatted on – she had a lot to tell Julia – and did not notice that Julia had refused hot buttered toast. 'The pickets were convinced that Edmund – that's his name – and I were management "plants". They couldn't so much as entertain the idea that we might be sympathetic to their cause. It was only the way the police behaved towards us that convinced them we were on their side. The police! Talk about "a little power". . . ! You might be forgiven for thinking civil war was raging throughout the country. What's so odd is that the police and the strikers come from the same class and the same part of the country, and probably worship the same God. I do wish you'd come down and see for yourself.'

'There's a midday seminar I particularly want to attend,' Julia told her student, adding that she would try to get along to Coldston in the afternoon. She thought how young Margaret looked. She wondered whether Margaret could detect

44

something changed in her. It was Margaret who should be having an affair . . .

Since yesterday, Julia had felt a wholly unfamiliar disturbance within her. Although in her mind she fostered some interest in the subject of the approaching seminar, in less easily identifiable parts of her being she was consumed with interest only for Vardi. She wondered where he was, what he was doing – and with whom. Was this not how the young feel? Insecure; jealous; obsessed.

The seminar paper was entitled 'Negative Creativity' and was being given by an American psychoanalyst, Fred Traisom, whose book *Frustration* had recently been received in Britain with a fanfare of approbation from sociologists on the Left, and boos of hostility from psychiatrists on the Right. Dr Traisom was an accomplished intellectual acrobat; he walked a tightrope between heady idealisms. But when he landed, he did so upright, with his feet firmly on the ground. His arguments were accompanied by practical solutions: if the British were willing to pay for *all* the nation's children to be given the kind of education provided for the mere eight per cent who buy it in the so-called public schools, the nation would actually save money.

'The men you imprison for crimes against person and property cost you more to incarcerate than they would to educate properly. You can't call most of the schooling you provide "education". And you have only to look at the truancy figures to see how unsatisfying pupils find their *training*. Boys, particularly, emerge unrealised and dangerously frustrated. They go on feeling this way in adulthood because there's precious little to interest them and make them feel valued in the world of work – if they get any. The more gifted are resentful that they haven't been prepared for more demanding careers. The result: the nation pays out in a vast range of illnesses created by the palliatives of smoking, drinking and pill-popping; in absenteeism, and in vandalism. It's vandalism that I refer to as "negative creativity".

Julia's attention was caught, but she wondered whether Traisom's figures had been checked and agreed. Would it really be cheaper to send everyone to Eton? She wondered about his assumptions. *Would* the outcome of universal public school education result in a less frustrated society? Of course, universal intake would modify public school *mores* . . . And if it could be proved that a less frustrated society would emerge, why was it inconceivable that such an experiment would ever be attempted? Was it that Britain could only operate on the layer-cake principle - a thin coating of icing for the most fulfilling jobs, some jam for the money-makers, and for the remaining eighty per cent, crumbs?

The bus drew into a lay-by and deposited Julia and a dozen local lads a mile from the centre of Coldston. The youngsters went on ahead, bashing their fists into one another's arms, shrieking with sounds that had to make do for laughter. Julia noticed that fluorescent socks in the colours of wine-gums were a favourite with them all.

The hedges separating the fields from the road had given way to barbed wire. Evidently, the most popular entertainment hereabouts was attaching pieces of black bin liner to the spikes. Or was it the wind? One of the walls of the first factory Julia approached had been painted white – why make it stand out? – but not recently; green lichen-stain clustered round the down-pipes, of which there were many. The air was hot, but dull; no sunshine penetrated the thick cloud that hung menacingly over the houses, their roofs compressed by impenetrable gloom. The vile smell invading her nostrils made Julia wonder whether the effluent from the factory always excluded sunlight from Coldston. What about the wind? she wondered. And then she heard shouting.

'What do we want? Work! What do we get? Birks! What do we want? Jobs! What do we get? Yobs!'

Julia watched, horrified, as police pushed youngsters past the factory gates, shouting at them to 'Move along, there!' She spotted Margaret with a young man (too easily identifiable as an Oxford student, she thought), and she walked swiftly towards them.

'You'd better introduce yourselves,' Margaret said, her nose in her notebook. 'We've just been booked; I hope you don't meet the same fate.' Julia rather hoped not, too; Gladyse Baker would be tartly critical if one of her staff was featured in the tabloid press.

Edmund and Julia shook hands quickly, and then stepped back as they heard the sound of approaching lorries. The lorries, as yet still out of sight, were obviously accelerating hard – clearly, they were hoping to sweep into the factory through the gates, just twenty-five yards from where Edmund and Julia were standing. The lorries rolled into view. A great roar rose and exploded as pickets thundered '*Scab!*' and rushed the police barrier. They hurled themselves to the ground in front of the approaching lorries. In the mêlée Julia found herself knocked down. Before Margaret and Edmund could get to her, two policemen had taken an arm each and had dragged her on to the grass verge on the other side of the road.

'Teach the likes of you to come meddling. Now, will you all kindly clear off – right away – back where you came from.'

Julia was shaking. She did not know whether she was shaking from fear or from anger. Her muslin-thin skirt was torn and her shirt had lost a button. An obstinate smell filled her nostrils, a combination of gas and iron, of dust and sweat. A huge man had knocked her down with the force of his shoulder. He had not done so on purpose; he himself had been hurled forward by the pushing, shoving crowd. She held her right arm with her left hand.

'It's nothing, really,' she assured Margaret. 'I expect I'll have a bruise, that's all. Nothing broken!'

The crowd was raging. Like a stormy sea, it had developed an uncontrollable momentum of its own, and no one, certainly no single, reasonable human being, would be able to control it or contain it. She did not know who most she feared and hated, the police, or the strikers and their minions. One violence confronted the other, kept smouldering by the taunts of the pickets.

Julia's reason had been a casualty of her experience. In all the time that she had spent considering conflict in the abstract, it had never occurred to her that being thrown to the ground herself, and manhandled, she would emerge so fearful and so disgusted.

Margaret and Edmund had succeeded in interviewing strikers, flying pickets and police. Indeed, the police had been anxious to put their point of view, once they had seen that the other side, so to speak, had expressed theirs. A picture was beginning to emerge, of unyielding conflict in which the interests of the factory bosses and their shareholders were seen as being unfairly protected, while those of the men who actually created the wealth were ignored.

'They don't give a witch's tit for any of us,' the men complained, 'yet it's us as makes them so bloody rich.'

Margaret and Edmund had managed to keep their cool, but Julia was devastated. All she could think of was getting out of Coldston – quickly. When a woman who had been watching the violence from the safe side of her garden wall called to Julia and invited her to come into her house to 'clean up', it was the last thing she wanted to do, but somehow she found herself accepting.

The woman was grubby; she had damp patches under her arms, and to the strong odour of her body was added that of cat and boiled whiting. Her complexion was grey and her eyes were sunk deep in their sockets. She pointed Julia to the bathroom. The lavatory pan was stained and discoloured; the bath and basin seemed never to have been cleaned. Meanwhile, Margaret and Edmund, who had followed Julia into the house, waited self-consciously in the front room, their eyes hypnotised by two black bananas festering in a pyrex bowl, and flies grazing on a saucer of cat food. Underfoot the lino was whiskered and pock-marked, and on the walls the paper was peeling.

'Me 'usband used to work there but there was an accident and 'e died.' Margaret longed to ask questions. She contented herself by looking around. The meagre dwelling spoke volumes.

'Thank you so much! It was most kind of you!' Julia

emerged from the bathroom and stretched out her hand to say goodbye, but her hostess had not done.

'Me 'usband said they was all bastards, the lot of 'em. They said the accident was 'is fault, 'e shouldn't 'ave tried switching off the machine; that was the foreman's job, see. But me 'usband saw danger ahead and acted quick, like. Got 'isself badly burned for 'is pains. Sixty per cent, they said. 'E died within the month. I'd not put my lad there if it were the last place on earth!'

Back in the carefully maintained gardens of Marlowe College, it was the very absence of sweet-wrappers on the lawns, of groundsel in the herbaceous borders and dog dirt on the paths, that struck Julia. How finely tuned were the sensibilities of 'gown'! But how was it that sensibilities so finely tuned to the appearances of things were deaf to the clamour of social inequality? It could be no coincidence that Coldston had been built at a dead end, for example. Access to it from Oxford was by a single lane from a part of the city unfrequented by 'gown'. 'Gown' never had to pass through Coldston to reach any of the exquisite villages appropriated by retired academics, or visited by undergraduates in search of spiritual and/or corporeal refreshment.

Margaret was unable to contain her indignation and was venting it upon Edmund. 'How can you *bear* being here?'

'I couldn't bear being anywhere else! I love it; it's so beautiful, I get excellent supervision, the libraries are well stocked, I have my friends around me . . .' Edmund paused. He knew what was Margaret's drift and he anticipated her next accusation. 'It's perfectly democratic. Anyone who takes the Oxbridge entrance and passes can get in.'

'That old chestnut! You don't expect me to fall for that! It's only the public schools that know how to prepare pupils for Oxbridge!'

'Not only,' Edmund replied softly.

'At least eighty per cent of the undergraduates here come from the private sector,' Margaret insisted.

'Well, whatever the case, it's a good thing I got in. If I'd refused a place on the grounds that Oxford's elitist, I'd have lost the opportunity to expose things as they really are. As it is, I can do an inside job.'

'And I hope you will! But Oxbridge perpetuates Oxbridge. You'll probably send your children to your old school and they'll automatically come on here just like other public school products.'

Margaret had chosen Essex for her undergraduate studies. She had stayed on an extra year to be president of the student union. She was a thoroughly entrenched political being, the product of card-carrying Communist parents. She was eminently practical; she could whistle up a fleet of charabancs to bus pickets wherever they wanted to go; she had a tame printer who did her cheap leaflets at a moment's notice. And because, together with her committed authority, she had natural good manners, she could charm a hall or a meeting for money for a cause from the most hardened, irascible bureaucrat.

But there was another side to Margaret that made her unusual. Impatient though she was with the prevailing system, when she came into contact with dyed-in-the-wool Tory ladies and blue-blooded landowners and farmers, she was always able to find in them some redeeming characteristic. She liked people.

She admired Julia as a teacher and valued her friendship. However, it had not escaped her notice that, very close friends notwithstanding, Julia was someone who probably loved humanity more than the individual. And Julia had once admitted to Margaret that rather than tip the girl who washed her hair, she lectured the hairdresser on paying realistic wages.

Julia looked down into the stream that ran though Marlowe's rear quad and decided not to take up cudgels. Yellow flags lined the shallow edge of the water near one of the arches of the bridge. At Coldston the river was filled with rubbish; she had noticed how an old pram had been ditched and somehow moved to the centre and stuck there, and how a ring of scum and plastic bottles attended its slow disintegration. The waters of Marlowe's stream were clear; a few trout were basking in the sunlight, Julia could smell the scent of watermint. While she was making her comparison she became conscious of someone leaning over the bridge, looking her way. She looked up into the sun and although she could not make out his features, she knew from his outline that the man was Massimo Vardi. She watched him as he slowly came down the steps by the side of the bridge and walked towards her along the tow-path. She wished she were alone. She felt her heart thumping. She felt physically excited. She couldn't wait to be with him.

The moment Edmund and Margaret suggested that they all go to Mrs Flemming's Tea Shop, Julia knew it was a mistake. However, for Margaret and Edmund not to include Massimo Vardi in their suggestion would have been impossibly rude. Julia realised that matters were not in her control and a feeling of torpor overcame her – not so much a physical torpor as a mental lassitude. She avoided meeting Massimo's eye. As he stretched, pushing his legs down hard against the floor of her car, he asked, 'Is it far?', as if a long drive in a smallish car was not something that he would contemplate with relish.

The four of them sat round a slatted pine table in the garden on which Mrs Flemming had lavished her creative talents for more years than anyone could remember. Undergraduates, graduates, come and go; Mrs Flemming would go on for ever. Huge, blowsy Nellie Mosers pushed their way up one side of the cottage door, over the lintel and down the other side. Bees glided among a blaze of annuals, piercing deep into each bloom for nectar and retiring backwards, pollen-laden. Julia was grateful to the flora and fauna; they provided a badly needed distraction. She allowed the conversation to proceed without her while she concentrated on Mrs Flemming's gardener tut-tutting in the vegetable patch, waging war on the insect population. Blackfly clung to the nasturtiums, planted beside the broad beans for their protection; greenfly clung to the hedge of sweet-peas grown for the table. Julia watched as the gardener leant over the veronica, severing the tiny cobwebs that spiders had strung between their spikes.

'Did you by any chance hear the news? Did they give the latest mortality figures for the station bombings? I overheard someone at Coldston saying there had been English holiday-makers among the estimated two hundred dead . . .'

Massimo was fastidiously loading tiny, bite-size pieces of scone with clotted cream and did not look up. 'Yes, I did hear the estimate of two hundred. Of course it sounds a great many because they all died at once. But it's not many, really, if you compare the figure with those who die on the roads, or of cancer of the lungs.'

'It's one hell of a lot if someone you happen to know is one of them . . .' Edmund remonstrated. 'I've friends in Florence . . .'

'Yes, I suppose so.'

In an effort to move the conversation from a topic which, for a reason she did not understand, she felt was becoming contentious, Julia asked Massimo if he liked English tea-time fare.

'Yes,' he replied, but his voice rose, as if he had intended, 'Yes, but . . .'

'How was your seminar? What is meant by negative creativity?'

'Traisom's coined the phrase for violent and/or destructive acts which he sees as the individual's expression of frustration. He says these acts arise from situations that thwart the individual's natural impulse towards growth. According to him, if you accept that everyone has the impulse to fulfil himself, you have to allow that if he is prevented from fulfilling himself – for social or psychological reasons – then his frustration will build up and either implode in depression and suicide, or explode in violence and murder. Traisom sees this syndrome as being the reverse of the artist's experience. Hence, *negative* creativity.'

'It occurs to me,' murmured Massimo, 'that the Anglo-Saxon is always far too concerned with the problems of the

52

individual. His rights can only be the first concern of nations whose communal good has already been secured.'

'And what is the "communal good" if the individual's freedom has not been secured?'

'You play with words, my dear friend. Take the behaviour of the workers at Coldston. They are on strike to preserve an industry for themselves and their progeny that cannot sell the products it manufactures!'

'But it's not their fault! There's been insufficient investment. If the management had modernised and put in new machinery . . .'

'The management knew that the Italians would produce cheaper, better-designed and longer-lasting refrigerators. Just take the example of our people. Our Calabrians willingly moved to the north, to the smog, got used to margarine in lieu of olive oil, and they have prospered – and our nation has prospered. Your workers are unambitious, unrealistic, and expect to be maintained by the state from cradle to grave.'

'That's unjust! And it's a calumny! Take my forebears, Highland Scots. Britain was so utterly indifferent to their needs that thousands of Scots upped and left and were obliged to settle in Canada and Australia. The Highlands were virtually depopulated. In the long run it was Scotland that lost out.' Margaret was showing rage.

'But your precious individual benefited! He prospered!' Vardi was triumphant.

'If you mean that in the short term he acquired material benefit in his new environment, that's perfectly true. But that's not my definition of prosperity, and judging from the way in which expatriate Scots defend their heritage, it's not theirs. They would far rather have lived and worked for modest financial rewards where their ancestors had lived and worked – in the glorious Highlands and Lowlands.'

'It's really extraordinary,' Edmund agreed, 'that to this day men are still required to uproot themselves and their families to follow work. It was understandable during the mining booms, and when communications were in their infancy, but today there's absolutely no reason whatsoever for not building factories in unemployment areas – prefabs – and setting men to work on renewing the infrastructure. All over the country our roads are in an appalling condition and our sewers are collapsing. It's the will that's lacking – and the imagination . . . Anyhow,' Edmund continued, 'the principle of preserving the differences between peoples is a good one, and it should jolly well extend to respecting the English, who don't like moving from their place of birth, school and marriage. There are plenty of nomads in the world to do the shifting about. Why can't we do the settling down?'

Julia did not join in the conversation. It was obvious that both Margaret and Edmund felt deep hostility towards Vardi. Julia was in an embarrassing position. She did not want to find herself defending Vardi to her student – he was indefensible. On the other hand, she did not want to spoil her chances with him. Throughout the conversation, as he held forth with hardened right-wing views alien to her own, Julia found him fascinating her with his eyes in a manner which seemed to confirm that some intimacy existed between them. It was an ironic situation; her hostility to his views seemed only to heighten his interest in her. And it was compromising that she enjoyed his signal. But it was not this sexual undercurrent that Julia feared Margaret might observe. It was the patronising tone Vardi applied to his criticism of Traisom's theory that she did not want her student to pick up.

The conversation turned to the problem of guest workers in Germany.

'If the Germans had to have Turks to run their factories, it would surely have made much more sense to have built the factories in Turkey and given the Turks the means to survive in their own country, with their extended families and their existing social institutions.'

'You preach a counsel of perfection, young man!'

'No, not perfection – this is the real and actual world and I only expect the decent. As it is, the Germans have created a miserable environment for their guest workers and given their own nationals an outlet for their endemic racism.'

'Have you noticed,' said Margaret, 'that the Germans have

the Turks to do their dirty work, the Israelis have the Arabs, and the White South Africans have the Black South Africans. And everywhere the rich have the poor. *Ugh!*'

So saying, Margaret rose from her chair and Edmund with her. They took their leave of Julia and nodded in the direction of Vardi. 'We'll walk back,' Edmund explained.

'You've kept very quiet!' Vardi said accusingly to Julia as soon as they were alone.

'I simply hadn't anything much to contribute.'

'And do you share the views of these young people?'

'On the whole, yes.'

'I'm surprised. They are immature views. Ones you should have grown out of.'

Julia gave no sign of having felt the barb and said she felt strongly that a country that did not respect its nationals at home was unlikely to respect foreigners abroad. 'Indeed, in my view, English class prejudice – for it is always the poor who are misprized – and our traditional contempt for foreigners, probably have their roots in the same ground.'

And then, fervently wishing to restore harmony, Julia suggested that they explore Mrs Flemming's garden. 'You should see it. It's a real English cottage garden, quite different from anything you have in Italy . . .'

On the journey back to Marlowe – a journey that was much longer by car than by foot along the river and across Christchurch Meadow – Vardi described to Julia his estate in Apulia. He was at pains to emphasise his preference for Italian olive groves over English apple orchards. Julia would rather have heard about his emotional background. Was he married, she wondered? He was utterly incurious about her, and asked her nothing about herself. When she suggested he might like to wander in the Botanical Gardens which they were just passing, he ignored her, evidently still preoccupied by thoughts of Apulia. Julia wondered why it was that his imperiousness tantalised her; it was not a characteristic she normally found attractive. She noticed too, how economical he was with his likes and how lavish with his dislikes – although he never appeared to be expressing excesses. Indeed, he had the effect of making her seem over-enthusiastic about everything. Julia realised that she had an almost desperate desire to please this man. It was humiliating; she wanted to go straight back to her room and sleep with him. At the same time she was infuriated by him. He's like the cock in the farmyard, she reflected, he thinks his crowing makes the sun rise . . . She did not like the man, she thought, but she was hypnotised by him; she was desperate for him to think well of her. While she considered these matters in the seconds it took to cross the road from her parked car to the college, she blushed inwardly. She had not felt this way since she had been a mite at school, anxious to do well in class and please teacher.

'Some other time,' Vardi said, waving his hand non-chalantly backwards in the direction of the Botanical Gardens.

So there was to be another time? Julia's mood changed. Something lifted; clouds of confusion gave way to a ray of optimism.

The public telephone was sited at the far end of the entrance hall, at the doors to the cloisters. If she was to ring James, as she had arranged, Vardi would be sure to overhear her conversation. Would his interest in her dissolve if he knew that she was contentedly married?

'I'll see you at dinner, perhaps,' she tried. 'I've got to make a call,' and she pointed to the telephone.

'I'll wait for you.' Julia could not make out from Vardi's expression whether he was being deliberately indiscreet or whether he felt that because he had slept with her once, he had claims on her all the time. He was evoking in her all the confusions that go with desire, but she knew in her heart that he was unlikely to provide any of the compensations that go with emotional involvement.

'James? It's me. How are you managing? Good! Good! Yes, very much. Very stimulating company!' And then after a long pause, 'I've gone through it yet again. I think it's all right but I'm not looking forward to presenting it. Yes, all right, I'll ring tomorrow. 'Bye!' When she replaced the receiver, she found that she was alone. She had not noticed precisely when, during her short conversation, Vardi had slipped away . . .

She was lying on her bed in bra and pants, reading, when Massimo knocked on the door. He did not wait for an answer, and Julia had left the door unlocked. His love-making – if, Julia asked herself later, that was an appropriate description of what ensued – was assertive; he penetrated her as if he were waging a private war against his own frustration. And while he rammed her, he cursed her, reproaching her for her innocence. He turned her face-down, mounted her like a dog and in a soft voice sneered, 'Loathsome bitch!' in her ear. His lust satisfied, he appeared to be overcome with that peculiar feeling of indifference – even to his own desires – that so often accompanies conquest; it was as if the air at the summit had been too thin to nourish further enthusiasm.

Julia had experienced an awesome excitement but no satisfaction. Her feeling of unsatisfied desire was intolerable, and she was furious as well as hurt that Massimo had not considered her pleasure – merely used her ruthlessly for his own. Yet there was something gratifying about being the object of a man's lust, about being so immediately necessary for another's satisfaction. Massimo lay like a beached whale by her side. He was bathed in sweat. His black hair was plastered to his forehead, and rising above the odour of after-shave was that of sweat. She wanted him again – and again; but she had no intention of risking an approach and letting him know that he had left her unsatisfied. She wondered whether the sexual static that accompanied him attracted all women. She thought of James. James's attraction was his decency, his dependability, his evident interest in other people. She compared the love-making she shared with James with the sexual drama she had just experienced: two quite different activities. But that, she gauged, was fine, for she would not wish to replicate the tender expression of devotion between her husband and herself.

She longed to know what Massimo was thinking but was determined not to enquire. She felt an overwhelming tenderness infuse her. She wanted to caress this man, take him to her breast. But something prevented her and she settled her head on his shoulder with her cheek against his chest.

'You English women are so prudish. Sexual abandon is unknown to you. You offer yourselves rather as some optional extra in an all-in social package – like early morning tea.'

'I'm sure you'd know!' Had Massimo listened to her, he would have heard Julia's note of bitterness.

'I've come to the conclusion that sexual performance reflects political attitudes. In people who are suspicious of violence, sexual passion is more often than not lacking. You must set your face against the sentimental, my dear, if you are to enjoy yourself and have others enjoy you. You must abandon the league of possibilitarians who live in a permanent conditional tense, fastening on to some unattainable perfection in the hope of acquiring some of it for themselves.' If this is pillow-talk, Julia thought, I would rather something else. But Massimo had not exhausted his reflections.

'Idealists! I have no doubt that you regard me as cynical – even perverse – in believing that idealists are absurd. What are needed, both in bed and out of bed, are realists!'

No, a thousand times no! Man must live in the service of great ideals, and if he cannot ascend to the summit of his aspirations that is no reason for resting in the foothills.

Massimo made as if to get out of bed. Julia was stunned. She put her arms around his neck and kissed his cheek. On no account must Massimo leave her. He could insult her as long as he wished, but he must make love to her again. But he untied her arms. She sat up and watched as he poured himself a glass of mineral water and walked to the open window. He had his back to her; she wondered what he was looking at. Then he drank, turned towards her, threw back his head and laughed. He lay down beside her again.

'You've lain down for the police and you'll lie down for me!'

This time Julia came.

'Ah! So we've made it.'

She had had to. It was a question of Massimo's pride.

'Don't go! Not yet! Please!'

'Don't be foolish!'

She felt pathetic; she knew that she appeared pathetic.

'For heaven's sake don't start confusing your heart and your glands!' He was staring at her unblinkingly. Aggressive. Hostile. If he had wanted to buy her he might have looked her up and down. He didn't even want to buy her. He simply wanted her to know that he rejected what he saw. Oh, the tyranny of sex! Her feelings of desire for this man were so urgent and so strong. Someone, she could not remember who, wrote that it was pious fraud to believe yourself in love when merely sexually aroused. It was not, however, that she 'believed' herself in love. She 'felt' herself in love. The feelings she was experiencing bore no relation to any others she had ever entertained. A sudden stab of loneliness struck her chill.

'I'm not going to become embedded in your fantasy,' Massimo informed Julia as he drew on his trousers. And she knew that he would never satisfy the appetite that he had created in her. She knew too that she would continue to desire, and to repudiate, her lover – and that he in turn, for quite different reasons, would desire and repudiate her. It was almost a case of precognition; she had fallen for the wrong man, yet she had fallen, and there was no way that she could reason herself out of the situation.

She was reminded of the morning the Tubby-Tabby raced in from the garden with a blue-tit between her teeth, and how distraught she had been. The furry animal whose usual position was on her lap and in her bed had become another thing altogether. She growled deep in her throat, she did all she could to evade Julia. Because Julia was unable to prise the terrified bird from the cat's jaws, she cornered the cat, picked it up and threw it back out into the garden, with the only feelings of loathing for her pet that she had ever experienced. Throughout that day she had felt shaken. She thought she had reacted over-vehemently; it was the cat's nature to hunt and to present her with her prey. Julia imagined that the sight of the powerless little bird in the jaws

59

of the powerful animal had sparked off a complex of feelings which had never, previously, revealed itself.

If there had been a vacant place beside Massimo, Julia wondered, would she have joined him at dinner? She was still smarting from the sting of their pillow-talk. In the event, Massimo was seated at the middle of one of the long refectory tables, surrounded by all the Strategist delegates, whose views on conflict were attracting a disproportionate amount of attention – and approval.

The devil has all the best tunes, Julia thought. One of the Unilateralists had said that in an age which placed so much confidence in certainty, it was hardly surprising that an argument which seemed to convey the promise of delivering was becoming increasingly popular. But Julia wondered if it was not perhaps the delegates themselves who won recruits – they had more drive than her lot. Massimo was in excellent form, fluent and confident, bowling names and theories to his admiring acolytes. Julia ate disconsolately, within earshot. It was, perhaps, *post coitum* depression that was colouring her view of her Unilateralist companions. She could imagine the sort of contempt for their idealistic attitudes that Massimo and his group must feel. Mercifully, Professor Shein intervened to take the conversation into the English countryside, the herbaceous border and the English public house. He had read extensively on all three subjects.

At this point, as his allies bent their attention to what he obviously regarded as trivialities, Massimo turned to a psychologist and asked him if he had ever wondered why it was that women but not men had a propensity to confuse the heart with the glands. With the confidence of a man who has just received the tablets on Sinai, and had no need to hear the view of a mere psychologist, Massimo offered his own explanation.

'Women cannot abide the biological. It's understandable, in a way; they have so much of it in their lives. That must be why they choose to interpret what is biologically determined in their emotional lives as a function of feeling. I think, too, that they imagine they flatter us in this way.' Massimo's utterance had the fine edge of a well-maintained cut-throat razor, and one or two women delegates received it in stony silence. However, Julia noticed two male delegates surreptitiously smiling into their burgundy.

'In my view, the trouble with Western men in general,' the psychologist parried, nodding deferentially in the direction of an Indian delegate, 'is that most are so alienated from their feelings that the only way they can justify their sexual drive is to say that it's a function of their biology, over which their feelings – let alone their morality – have no control. For example, when a man seduces a woman he doesn't consider whether this is something the woman actually wants. He believes it flatters her to show desire for her, and he takes it for granted that his glands and hers have some preordained appointment. If he presses his attentions upon her against her will, he interprets her resistance as "playing hard to get"; if he shows her hostility, even violence, he counts this as "natural" and shores up his confidence about his behaviour with examples from the animal kingdom. In fact he's on very uncertain ground here. It's not the glands that are responsible, but the feelings of guilt and a need for supremacy. Men who don't experience the joy of love find solace in hate. I always feel that once one understands the part that guilt has to play in individual human behaviour, it should make us take great care not to arouse it in our enemies.'

'Oh come, come! The case for guilt has surely been vastly overstated. Mr Freud muddied the waters. Anyhow, psychology is not an exact science.' And looking around for support, Massimo added, 'What we need are hard facts – not speculation.'

'I would have said that just the reverse was required – a feeling response.' The psychologist was demonstrably irritated.

'Being in possession of the facts has never modified a prejudice,' someone muttered darkly.

'Anyhow, facts do not always add up to the truth,' the

Indian remarked, 'and what's more, the precise truth is invariably not the whole truth.'

'Be that as it may,' a delegate with a dog-collar intervened, ' "It is the truth that shall make you free." St John rings deafeningly in my ears whenever I hear a politician doling out lies to the public for his own and his party's benefit.'

Vardi's nostrils flared. 'Politicians know very well indeed that the last thing the mass wants is freedom. They couldn't handle it, it would be altogether too threatening for them. The mass prefers to submit. Man chose wrongly in the Garden of Eden, when he was offered the choice, and ever since he hasn't dared to risk making another irreversible mistake. The one freedom left to him is to obey.'

The cleric was silenced. A woman seated next to Julia sighed. Julia turned to her.

'But what's so ironic is that I heard one of the men out on strike at Coldston saying just what the professor said, from a different angle, of course. He maintained that, "The only freedom we have is the freedom to obey orders." Not that this was a recommendation – it was an observation. He went on to advise the strikers not to hold the bosses exclusively responsible for the threatened closure of the factory and the loss of their livelihood. "It's the older generation that brought these troubles on us," he declared. And he stressed that this was as much the fault of *their* forebears, who put up with the conditions that laid the foundation for the present situation, as it was the fault of the bosses who took advantage of them. "The men should have refused to work altogether," he said, "as soon as they saw they were being palmed off with out-of-date equipment. They should have known their product wouldn't be up to competing in world markets!" And he talked about the casuistry of the Church of England whose role was not to relieve the suffering of the poor, but to convince them that their place in the scheme of things was to do their duty and to accept their lot. "Our forebears obeyed orders. They were positively addicted to orders!" And he rounded off by stressing that the present strike wasn't called to uphold the right to work, but to proclaim the right to live decently.'

Julia's companion was quick to observe that she was glad her field was the causes of hostilities between *nations*. 'Even if we discount the view that the causes are always rooted in economics, they're still easier to determine than the causes of *industrial* unrest. The national interest has to be made to appear homogeneous or the support needed can't be mobilised. Industrial unrest has more to do with the expression of discontent, and that can have its roots in any number of areas of man's experience. And then, the individual has to decide for himself whether he's willing to risk his livelihood over matters of principle.'

'What you say links with Fred Traisom's theory of negative creativity – always an individual response. That's why the causes of political violence come under quite a different heading. It's not the result of individuals' decisions, it's the response to the demands of one outside authority by another.'

Julia saw Vardi rise from his seat. She followed him with her eyes. She wanted him. She wanted the feel of that heavy body lying on top of her, dragging an orgasm from her. He did not exit in the direction of the smoking-room, where coffee was being served. She wondered where he was going. She would have been relieved if she had seen him making for the telephone and known that he was speaking to his mother. She would have been less consoled if she had heard him speak.

'Dearest, how are you? Yes, I'm well. No, not very interesting, these things rarely are. I heard about it. Absolutely ghastly. Of course, I knew you wouldn't be anywhere in the vicinity . . . Has the press suggested who might be behind it? Oh, really!' And then there was a pause before Massimo Vardi laughed conspiratorially. 'You know me, mother. I don't allow the grass to grow under my feet. I don't ignore the opportunities that drop into my lap. Yes! But nothing serious, of course. Sunday evening without fail. May God be with you!'

When Julia did at last see Vardi in the smoking-room, he was in deep conversation with a Swedish woman. Julia knew who the woman was, Professor Lunquist from Stockholm. She was not only singularly beautiful, but universally known to be brilliant; she was careful not to associate herself exclusively with either 'peace' or 'conflict' and she was, therefore, wooed intensively by both sides. Julia's well-known admiration for the theories of Galtung did not endear her to Professor Lunquist, and Professor Lunquist's proximity to Massimo did not endear her to Julia.

But these thoughts gave way to more uncomfortable feelings. The very sight of Massimo talking to the beautiful Swede was making Julia feel physically sick. Perhaps he found Professor Lunquist more attractive than he found her. Professor Lunquist was so beautiful! Perhaps he would not want to make love to her again, and would take up with the Swede . . . Was this what falling in love felt like? She couldn't think of anything but Massimo Vardi and what Massimo Vardi thought and felt about her. She drank down her coffee and shakily placed the cup on the table next to her chair. She was going to get out of the smoking-room and she was going to do so without looking in the direction of the two professors. But why hadn't he spoken to her? Why hadn't he taken coffee with *her*?

Thursday

It was impossible to enjoy breakfast. The press, indifferent to the needs of the delphiniums, the dahlias and the annuals, had swarmed across the wide border beneath the window of Hall and with their noses pressed against the ancient glass were watching the delegates feast. Everyone was united in contempt for the press. The scouts serving tea and coffee despised them for their evident lack of manners – 'They're not gentlemen . . .', and the delegates had no wish to be made to sum up their theories in palatable phrases of three words, to be regurgitated to an uninterested public. In fact the press was gathered in Oxford in considerable numbers, drawn not by the conference but by the strike. But 'killing two birds' is devoutly to be desired by those who administer expense accounts. The press had been ordered to Marlowe.

A straw poll was taken. Delegates agreed that Massimo and Julia, representing respectively the Freedmanite and the Kentite views on disarmament, should first deliver short statements and then answer questions. Jeremiah Jenkins, whose dislike and distrust of the press amounted to paranoia, went out on to the lawn and told the journalists and their photographers that if they would kindly step out of the flower-beds and on to the paths, spokesmen would come out in a quarter of an hour to answer their questions. He directed them to a gazebo in the adjoining field.

The attitude of the press was not only cynical but, at first, hostile. They wanted to know what the usefulness of these expensive get-togethers could be. Although it would have been evident to a child that Professor Vardi was using the

65

conference for personal ends, he dealt with the press in such a skilful way that they felt flattered by him, and pulled their punches. Julia, on the other hand, expressed simple enthusiasm for the opportunity to exchange views with people from all over the world and to come up against adherents to theories other than those held by Europeans. For her pains, the press noted the length of her legs and estimated the size of her breasts.

'Why is there no Soviet delegate?' the *Guardian* reporter enquired. Julia was not altogether sure, she was not one of those who had organised the conference. She suggested that the invitation to the Soviets might have been extended late. 'I know that the Soviets tend to need a rather longer time to consider these invitations than we do in the West.' And she looked towards Vardi for some confirmation.

'It would be quite pointless for the Soviets to attend. If they had agreed to participate it would only have made difficulties. They would have been disruptive. It was with this in mind that I and my colleagues who sent out the invitation couched ours to the Soviets in language which gave them an excuse to turn it down, and at the same time feel a warm glow of one-upmanship for so doing.'

Members of the press drew two chairs into the gazebo and suggested that Vardi and Julia would be more comfortable sitting down to give their statements.

'Would you – in a couple of nutshells – outline the current multilateralist and unilateralist points of view?' Vardi motioned to Julia to make her statement first. She refused. 'Very well. If that's what you want!' Vardi turned away from Julia and looked towards the press.

'There have always been wars. It is logical and reasonable to believe that there will continue to be wars. That being the case, it is desirable that we in the West should be able to defend ourselves. My prime concern is with the best type of weapons for the job. I want to know their nature and their number. Of course, it would be eminently satisfactory if everyone agreed to disarm. But they won't. Indeed, as we speak there is evidence that a number of small nations –

Libya, Israel, Pakistan – have the know-how and the materials with which to produce their own nuclear weapons, and are doing just that. What we have to do is to get agreement between the two great powers to balance not only their own nuclear arms but those of their allies. It is balance we are after. If one of the great powers disarms more thoroughly than the other, the whole basis of super-power relations – which depends on mutual deterrents – is undermined. If we don't have arms the Soviets have no reason to disarm.'

'Nothing new there!' someone muttered loud enough for Vardi to hear. 'And I'm not interested in *moral* arguments,' Vardi continued, unruffled, 'unless the argument rests on the assumption that our first priority is survival. My thinking on this subject has its foundations in the concept of the "just war". The state *must* protect its citizens from threats from the outside, whether they are physical threats or cultural threats or spiritual threats.'

The emphasis gave his delivery theatricality. The crowd that had gathered was listening quietly.

'The "just war" has as its objective the promotion of good and the elimination of evil; each of us can choose where we live, it is up to us to live in the country whose ethics we approve – and then strive to uphold them. And it is not enough to pay lip-service, we must be ready to defend our country in whatever way is available to us. Long-range nuclear missiles are the best deterrents we have against the threat of Godless socialism.' A number of people raised a 'Hear, hear!'

Professor Vardi answered supplementary questions with equal expertise – and charm. It was evident that he relished the sympathetic atmosphere that he had established with the press.

'Will you give us your statement, Dr Bruton?'

It was unusual for Julia to wonder how she looked before she spoke. She had dressed in a white sharkskin suit but as Vardi turned towards her she felt naked.

'Since Professor Vardi has raised the question of the so-called "just war" I think I'd better deal with my position regarding that right away. I have very mixed feelings about

67

the concept. Of course, there *is* an irrefutable obligation on the state to protect its citizens from any enemy. However, the citizens themselves must feel that this protection answers their need for them to become personally involved. Currently the state is not protecting its citizens from the internal enemies of poverty and injustice.'

Julia looked about her and paused to see whether she had driven home her point before continuing. 'The intention of the "just war" is to promote good and eliminate evil, but if peace at home hasn't resulted in that, what is the likelihood of war producing it? The fact of a nation going to war to protect its territory from being overrun won't necessarily result in the promotion of good, even if the enemy is defeated. It seems to me that there's no question but that the Second World War had to be fought. However, had the world upheld the values that Hitler tried to overthrow in the years preceding the march into Poland, war would not have resulted. It is because the democratic world wasn't vigilant that tolerance, justice and compassion died in Germany. I have to agree that the good of humanity was undoubtedly served by the overthrow of Nazi Germany. But one has to face the fact that the war did nothing to save human life; the Russians lost twenty million men, the Jews lost a third of their race, not to mention the losses on the part of the British, the Americans and others.

'And I would like to question whether it was right to destroy German cities in the way we did. If we agree today that it was not right, how much more reprehensible would it be to use the weapons of mass destruction today when we have had time to consider the implications? It is double-think that appals me. Many people believe that it's wrong to destroy a society which we don't approve – and to risk being destroyed ourselves – but at the same time maintain that the manufacture of the weapons of destruction is acceptable. It seems to me that it's impossible to defend the slaughter of innocent men, women and children in an effort to ensure our own justice, peace and order; we can't hope to achieve our own objectives, ones we can honestly claim are moral, by using the methods of those we regard as immoral. Nor can we use these weapons purely as a threat in the belief that the threat will be the deterrent that results in peace. All threats of violence lead to fear. Fear can lead to flight but often leads to fight. I wouldn't press the button to bring civilisation to an end, so I can't support a system that advocates deterrence. I propose to think more and more about the dynamics of conflict until I come up with something better than arms stocking. I know that it's conventional to have an army to "defend" us but, to my mind, nothing that I hold dear can be defended by aggression. And while we have weapons, they will be used.

'I believe in non-aggression. If some country wished to invade us, let them. They will find a population unwilling to co-operate with them and they will gain a Pyrrhic victory, for what natural resources do we have greater than our population? It would refuse to obey orders; we would all go on strike. We'd be fined and jailed and curfewed and, eventually, the whole operation would fail and the invader would either be obliged to make peace with us or withdraw. If the invader wants us, for his own logistical reasons, to set up bases, he would have to import staff and build roads and his own communications. We just wouldn't help. What would be happening would be a political struggle rather than a military one. And supposing we failed. Supposing they shot us – all of us. Would it be any worse than shooting the men who would otherwise have been conscripted to battle *on our behalf*?'

Massimo Vardi, unable to restrain himself, interrupted. 'I really must interject,' he insisted. 'Your naïveté knows no bounds. A much likelier scenario is as follows. The enemy (who would not have heard of non-violence), finding that your men would not co-operate, would shoot them. The women would be lost without them and would fear for their children, and so do whatever the invader expected of them. Thus, the invading army would have all the women they needed to create their own future . . .' And as he looked around for approval it seemed as if there were plenty in the crowd to give it. Confident of the effect he was making, Vardi ostentatiously indicated to Julia that she might continue.

'Let me deal with your first question: whether I believe that a third world war is inevitable. I don't. I don't see why we must assume that because there always have been wars there always must be wars. In the past, particular conditions and antagonisms have led to hostilities. If we could find out what those conditions and antagonisms were, we might be able to avoid the outcome in which they resulted. We might, equally, find better ways of solving our differences.

'At present a large part of our economy depends upon making weapons of destruction. Imagine how much happier, healthier and better educated we might be if the money involved in defence – as it's called – were spent on hospitals and schools. As for the balancing act favoured by Professor Vardi and his "macho" multilateralist friends,' Julia turned to face Massimo in an attitude of confident hostility, 'I can only confess that I find this strategy indecent. Dealing in the type and number of weapons capable of destroying the world, in an attempt to get parity between nations, is no answer at all. Someone has to find the courage to say that because the Soviets have ten thousand rockets, that's no reason why we should have to have ten thousand too. And I must stress the point: once you *have* arms, you *use* arms.

'The possession of nuclear weapons is immoral in itself. Not only could the money be better spent relieving suffering – one must not forget that three-quarters of the world is destitute, sick and hungry – but we, in the so-called developed world, might actually cure ourselves of the state of anxiety in which we live. Anxiety's a condition caused by a fear of annihilation, you know.' She paused to see whether she had driven the point home. She repeated it. 'Professor Vardi says that he's not interested in a *moral* argument that does not see survival as our first priority. It's because I want survival that I believe we should be rushing to be the first to disarm. But I have a rider to add: the real threat to peace may not be the amount of arms we stockpile but the racist, socially inequitable society that we have created.'

The crowd rumbled. There was movement, people were coming and going.

Vardi and Julia avoided one another's eyes. Their positions regarding nuclear armaments placed them at opposite ends of the political spectrum. So too did their social attitudes. Vardi was unconcerned; Julia, while feeling that her stance was the right one, admitted to herself that it would have been cosy to have been able to stroke her lover politically.

'No, I don't think war is inevitable,' Julia continued, 'but I have to admit that to prepare the ground to make it *unthinkable* is not only going to be an arduous task but one which is bound to meet with suspicion. First, we must go back in history and try to work out what have been the conditions that led to war. We must analyse the structure, the patterning in international social behaviour. For by observing the systems, we can actually change them. Secondly, unless we see to it that every individual is offered the opportunity to fulfil himself and absolve himself from fear, we shall continue to prepare the ground for war. I myself don't cleave to the view that man is naturally aggressive. That is to say, he isn't naturally any more hostile than he is co-operative. I do believe, however, that, being by nature programmed for survival, the energy that man generates to survive can easily be channelled into actions of hostility if he's thwarted from realising himself. Under present conditions the majority of men only feel secure with what they call "their own kind" – co-religionists, blood relations, members of their political party and so on. Such human beings are not truly "individual"; they have no real sense of, or confidence in, their separate identities, they are very easy to conscript for a hostility which makes them feel part of a larger community. Although I'm not suggesting it's done consciously, I do believe that by keeping the mass unfulfilled, we continuously preserve a fund of cannon fodder.'

'Thank you, Dr Bruton.' Someone was wanting to staunch her flow, she was sure of that. 'Now, Professor Vardi, will *you* tell us whether you believe a third world war is inevitable?'

'Yes. I think it is. During the twentieth century, in addition

71

to two world wars, there have been at least one hundred and fifty small wars. This proves – at any rate to me – that man *needs* war. Whether there is some natural balance-correcting going on, I don't want to say. Certainly, the world is over-populated and, as medicine advances and fewer men die from diseases, some correction of numbers is needed or food and fuel and so on will be exhausted. War is about ascendancy. Victory is evidence of superiority – economic, physical, moral – and maybe even spiritual. We live in a world divided into two ideologies. The Soviets believe in their system, they believe in it blindly, despite the overwhelming evidence that it has done nothing for the people so devoted to it. On the other hand, we know that capitalism and Christianity are morally and spiritually superior to Marxism: they have pro-duced superior physical and economic strength. Senti-mentalists hold that under the skin all men are equal and similar, needing and wanting the same things. This is demon-strably untrue. From time to time, in an effort to sort out the good from the bad, the strong from the weak, man engages in conflict. He has to; he has a natural urge to do so. It's an animal instinct. Yes, I think we shall have another world war.'

Vardi sat back in his seat, pleased by his performance, feeling that he had regained territory momentarily lost to Dr Bruton. Another journalist asked him his opinion of the strike at Coldston. He replied that he had none, but went on to say that no strike ever settled a dispute. This statement produced a rumble in the large crowd that had by now gathered round the gazebo. Julia saw that Edmund and Margaret, the Green-ham women and various members of the press whom she had seen at Coldston, were there. From the crowd a man from the *New Statesman* asked Julia whether she detected any con-nection between industrial unrest and international conflict.

'I think industrial conflict may be compared with small wars of liberation. Indeed, I think they do stem from similar causes. I regard both outbursts with optimism; I find it aston-ishing and heartening that men and women who have been denied property and power for generations, on the grounds of their class or colour or religious affiliation, can actually muster the energy to get up and insist on their rights.' In her mind's eye she thought of the woman who had lent her bathroom. 'I don't feel this way about wars between nations, of course. I agree with Clausewitz: "War is nothing else than the continuation of State Policy by other means." '

In the space of half an hour, the press had succeeded in personalising the differences between Professor Vardi and Dr Bruton. Julia had no difficulty in imagining the lurid headlines they would employ to highlight the warfare going on in the tranquil surroundings of Marlowe College. (While their differences had remained confined to academic theory – acknowledged but not advertised – Julia had succeeded in putting them to one side while she and Massimo consummated their one accord.) The Conference on Peace Studies and Conflict Research had been set up in order that adherents of both sides could meet in agreeable surroundings and make some attempt to bridge the gap between them. In the event, delegates had been inclined to keep to their own camps, but there had been little overt hostility. The press had changed all that. Julia found herself surrounded by Greenham women and by their two allies in the press, who were prodding her to expose Vardi's political attitudes. How could she now be seen to be socialising with him? And it was not only that: the man she so passionately desired was a man to be feared. Everything he said was destructive. He was a man out to punish, and had not Goethe written that one should especially distrust those in whom the urge to punish is strong? Julia remembered having told her students as much. Massimo was well-integrated – too well. His authoritarianism, his punitive and restrictive attitudes were reflected in his behaviour in bed. But it was not only at a personal level that Julia felt vulnerable. Tomorrow, when she read her paper 'The Autistic Society', she would be vulnerable as an academic. It was not that she felt her arguments could not withstand his. It was that she knew that what she felt for him in terms of desire would come between her thoughts and their delivery.

Surrounded by the Greenham women, Julia let them represent her to the reporter from *City Limits* while she considered her dilemma. She agreed to meet the crowd at The Perch for lunch. She wanted to get back to her room, to be alone for a while before she attended a seminar on 'Non-violent Action'. But Vardi must have noticed her detach herself from the crowd and he caught up with her at the door to her room.

'Julia!' It was the first time he had used her name.

'I don't want to discuss it with you,' she said, turning to face him.

'Discuss what?'

Julia could not believe it! Was he ignoring their political differences? Had he not understood the extent to which she had been alienated? 'Our differences!'

'Oh! That!' He was dismissive. 'No, I don't want to waste time on that, either. I just wanted to ask you whether you would agree to accompany me to Lord Stanton's for dinner, tonight.'

Massimo held open the driver's door and watched as Julia swung her legs into the car. His expression was uncharacteristically appreciative. She at once leant over and unlocked the passenger door and pushed it open, and Massimo actually thanked her. And when they were both settled comfortably and Julia was about to put the key in the ignition, Massimo kissed her cheek.

'Why didn't you join Professor Lunquist and me last evening for coffee?'

'You didn't invite me!'

'My dear child, this is a conference, not a social gathering!'

As they drove out of the city into open country, the light was fading. The river caught the last of the sun's rays, gleaming like a silver ribbon cast across the soft green fields. Soon night would crawl into the valley and rob the countryside of its colour.

'Isn't Oxfordshire glorious!'

'It is!'

Julia was inordinately grateful that Massimo was being positive, affectionate even, and certainly charming. He was uncritical of her and of the countryside. She was careful to avoid asking him what it was that was responsible for this sea-change.

She knew the way to Stanton. She knew Stanton Place – but not from the inside. She and James had made a pilgrimage to the little church on the estate, to view a medieval wall-painting that had been discovered and exposed a year before. It had lain under layers of whitewash for centuries until a child – intent on mischief – had got into the church armed with a penknife and had unwittingly uncovered a fragment. A restorer had been sent in - someone James knew – and the Brutons had driven down to see him at work. They had seen Stanton Place from the meadow that separated it from the church, and had regretted that it was not open to the public. It had seemed a most romantic building – moated, with a keep. The man restoring the wall-painting told them that the foundations had been laid in the thirteenth century, but it was obvious that most of the residential quarters in use today dated from the seventeenth century.

'Is Lord Stanton a particular friend of yours?'

'I always see him when I'm in Britain. I know a number of his associates and we get together from time to time in Europe. Stanton was close to the Duke of Windsor. I met him originally in Paris with the Windsors and some of their political allies.'

Drinks were being served in the north corridor. Most of the other guests were formally dressed, but although Massimo was in a lounge-suit and Julia in a calf-length dress, she did not feel self-conscious because nearly all the women present were old enough to be her grandmother. Massimo introduced her to Lord and Lady Stanton; the latter took her hand, limply, and smiled wanly but did not address her. Julia stood by Massimo's side while he and Lord Stanton exchanged news about a certain Carlo Lambrossi who, it appeared, was 'lying low' in London. 'The extradition requests failed, the court wasn't satisfied that a *prima facie* case had been established.' Massimo thanked his host for sending on the papers and said he would be in touch next week. From their conversation Julia gathered that Lord Stanton and Massimo knew one another quite well.

'We've interests in common,' Massimo told Julia as they stepped back into the crowd to allow their host to talk to another guest. It was clear to her that Massimo had said all he was going to say about his relationship with Stanton.

Julia and Massimo had been among the last to arrive, and it was not long before they were ushered into the huge dining-hall where a liveried Phillipino waiter conducted them to their seats. Julia observed, as she passed down the table, that almost all the names on the place-cards had prefixes and suffixes. This was not a milieu with which she was familiar, but she recognised its nature at once: these were the people who regarded their privilege as a right. This was 'the leprous upper-crust of society'. These were the folk who formed a scab over the wounds they themselves inflicted. Looking around her, before the asparagus had made its way to her plate, Julia was reminded of an advertisement for a zoo that was currently being shown on television. It depicted a dinner party much like this one, but through the eyes of an innocent young girl. Each time the girl's attention fastened on a member of the company he or she turned into an animal, as if such haughtiness as the women displayed could only be truly represented by the sniff of a giraffe, and such crude table manners as the men deployed, by a pig.

But above all it was the women's dress that fascinated Julia. It proclaimed, we are rich, rich enough to ignore fashion. And clearly, rich enough to fly in the face of sumptuary laws. No gift of the garb here! Every throat was choked in diamonds, emeralds and rubies, every wrist clasped and weighed down with gold, every bosom encrusted with beads. As for the men, their dinner jackets had obviously done a lifetime's service; many were green with age, and stained – no doubt with foie gras, caviare and quail's eggs. Julia had previously only seen advertisements for 'Marcel Waves'; here, she saw the waxen quiffs themselves. These women were in some sort of 1930s time warp. The men had been transfixed in the 1940s; many of them sported military moustaches on their congested faces, and they stuttered. Six silent Philippino waiters, wearing Lord Stanton's livery, moved gracefully round the table serving the food.

Julia had been seated on the right of Massimo. On her right was a man in his seventies who introduced himself as Sir Bogum Forsyth and then immediately – before Julia could give her name – switched off his deaf-aid. His wife, seeing what he had done, explained to Julia from the opposite side of the table, 'It whistles so. And he does like peace to enjoy his food.' Julia organised an understanding smile. Meanwhile, Lady Bogum turned to the man by her side and continued her conversation. 'He wanted to keep on his signalman's uniform but I was adamant. Since he's been retired and has so much time for his trains, he hardly ever takes it off. He still feels a great sense of injustice that his father insisted on him going into the army when he was intent on becoming a station master.'

'My wife, wonderful woman, knows everything and everyone. 'S'why I married her, by God!' Sir Bogum did not need his deaf-aid to follow what his wife was saying. Julia wondered whether he lip-read or whether it was simply that his wife always conducted the same conversation at dinner parties. Sir Bogum did not appear to object to his wife sharing these intimacies. But he was such a mess, it was almost as if he were falling apart in front of her; his hair had come out, his stomach was coming out over the waistband of his trousers, and his teeth were mostly out – his gums, presently dealing with a bread roll, resembled a machine for mashing farmyard bilge . . .

Julia looked around her. There was no one she found less offensive; they all belonged, as it were, to the same club. They had all come to flatter one another, they were practised in the exercise of the art and appeared to enjoy it more than the food – and almost as much as the wine. As they ate, and between snatches of conversation to their neighbours, they kept an eye on Lord Stanton. They must not miss one of his jokes, they must not fail to support his edicts. He surveyed his company from the head of the table, which was wide enough to seat four but which he habitually reserved to himself. From his lonely position he assumed a pose of Olympian hauteur:

'A capital way of making the masses happy is to put it abroad that their Christmas bonus is to be discontinued. Let the report fester in the press and on the television for a week or more, and then have the Minister of Whatever come on the news and say of course this caring government wouldn't countenance such a thing, that the bonus is actually going to be increased by forty pence!' His guffaws, produced by his taking in air and puffing it out, echoed round the dining-hall.

A man with that look of total concentration that does nothing to conceal utter boredom, caught Julia's eye. She could not, however, talk to him – he was a little too far down table. He was younger than most of the men present but their sort nonetheless: Eton, Brigade of Guards, sexually nebulous; no wayward sucker that had left the main stem on a route of fantasy or intellect. His wife, Julia was sure, smelled of chypre, even if her eyes had a faraway look. She sat facing Julia.

'I simply *have* to visit Venice once a year. If I don't I get withdrawal symptoms, I feel aesthetically deprived, don't you?'

Straight out of Proust. Mme Verdurin! Julia so hoped that no one would come between the woman and her self-expression; it was such a treat to watch someone 'expressing her uniqueness', as Julia was sure she would put it.

'I see life as an artistic experience, don't you? I must live in a world that looks lovely, smells fragrant and tastes succulent!' She'd better avoid the inner cities, Julia thought, dazzled by the woman's lack of self-consciousness.

'But I've spoken too much about myself,' she whined on. 'Do tell me a little about yourself!' It was the word 'little' that Julia savoured.

'I entirely agree with you. I love Venice.'

'Do you? Do you? And do you always stay at the Cipriani?'

'No, actually, I don't.'

'But you *must!* There's really nowhere else!' And calling down the table to her husband she begged him to confirm the fact.

'Absolutely! Nowhere!'

Elsewhere the conversation was being conducted with all the imaginative fervour of a board meeting – but that was understandable, for everyone present had one ear open for Lord Stanton.

'Are you enjoying yourself?' Massimo asked, his right hand on Julia's left thigh. She had not been enjoying herself at all, but with his touch came her delight.

'Very much,' she was able to reply enthusiastically.

Even before the salmon had been served, Julia had begun to dread the moment when she would be obliged to 'join the ladies'. She had had about seventy-five minutes to consider what she knew would be an ordeal. By sitting silently and absorbing the conversation around her, she had managed to gather that she was a guest of the founder of a group called The British Band, a name that had surely been chosen for its ambiguity, since by masquerading as a music group it could not be accused of being a party within a party – the Conservative Party. The Band had been inaugurated in 1964 when Harold Wilson came to power and brought with him the threat of socialism in Britain.

'We couldn't stand for that,' someone said in Julia's direction. 'Dear me, no! What would've happened to the likes of us? We'd 'ave been shot before dawn unless we took steps.' The ensuing discussion on the dangers of socialism was predictable. Men who had inherited their titles and their lands, and women encrusted in inherited jewels, agreed with one another that 'giving' the masses equal opportunities could lead only to their moral deterioration. 'People don't value things unless they earn them!' they noted.

'The church's gone soggy. We've got bishops that deny the virgin birth and the resurrection. I can't imagine what our dear Queen must think . . .'

'Oh, the clergy! Seems to me they spend the best part of their time on their backsides on committees upholding the rights of Jews and Blacks and other scum this country could well do without. Don't see them standing up, preaching against homosexuality, adultery, self-abuse. Or telling the masses to pull their weight. Well, if they won't, we must. And I'll tell you what I've just been organising . . .'

Julia suddenly realised that she was privy to a discussion involving a private army – terrifying enough in itself – but she also learnt that members of Conservative Head Office were *au fait* with the arrangement – knowledge that was even more alarming. And the adversary to be confronted by this private band was 'the enemy within': all those who dissent from the view of the rightness of 'the rich man in his mansion, the poor man at his gate'.

'There's just one problem I'm having to face,' Lord Stanton admitted regretfully. 'The young men I'm recruiting out at Coldston cut no figure! No education! No background! They feel as we do about repatriation: they won't work for the Jews, either. They're patriots to a man – but it's not enough that they get out their bicycle chains and their knuckledusters . . . They should be showing that they come from somewhere, don't you see? And where have they come from? Nowhere much, you understand. We've got to recruit some of the young lads from the universities – both of them – to lead our game-wardens and our farm labourers. See what I mean? But it must be done carefully, very carefully. I heard that old Colonel Welsh was recruiting in Northamptonshire, and so as the men would find their way to his house without advertising its name, he put a notice on his front gate – "End Immigration, Start Repatriation". Some busybody got lost up the lane on holiday and reported the matter, and do you know? Welsh was forced to take down the notice! It's a free country, mind, but you can't put a notice up on your own gate. See what the country's coming to? Well, I suggest you just put up "The British Band" and draw a bugle by the side.'

Julia leant over and whispered in Massimo's ear, 'Did you know Stanton Place was a fascists' nest?'

'Just labels, my dear,' he answered nonchalantly. 'I enjoy

seeing the old guard maintaining its position, its standards,'
he whispered. 'Your egalitarian ideas produce nothing more
coruscating than the old peoples' homes of East Berlin. You
wouldn't get asparagus and caviare and salmon there . . .'
And he laughed. 'I've been entertained in People's Palaces all
over Eastern Europe, I know what I'm talking about.'

Of course, fascism in Italy was something that the whole
nation had experienced, something Massimo had lived
through. These derelicts, fantasising over their imagined paradise, over the sort of kingdom-of-hell-on-earth they hoped to
create with their skinhead foot-soldiers and a handful of wealthy industrialists to fund them, were nothing to worry about
– especially since the Conservative Party had marginalised the
raving-Right by absorbing into the party the more dangerous
far-to-the-Rightists who would promise their votes in return
for respectability.

A log fire was burning in the grate in Lady Stanton's
dressing-room. Incapable of commanding either herself or her
guests, the old lady was accompanied everywhere by her maid.
Julia had noticed the maid sitting beside Lady Stanton at
table, slightly behind her chair, to assist the old woman with
her food. It was the same maid who led the women upstairs
to powder their noses after dinner. An elderly, bejewelled
woman remarked to Julia with an air of finality, 'Simplicity
is always the best solution; when one's young one has no need
of bijoux.' And it was only when Julia heard the maid address
the woman as Lady Muir that Julia learnt her name. Like
many in her class Lady Muir had been raised to talk thus to
her inferiors, but as she aged she had come to assume that
anyone she did not know must be an inferior, for did she not
know the whole of society? Julia registered the woman as
dotty, but then quickly reconsidered. Such a label absolved
her of all responsibility for her views and her behaviour. Her
conversation and that of the other women showed an obsession
with the trivial, and assumptions of rightness that were terrifying. Nevertheless, these women, although old, were in full
possession of their faculties.

A woman in her fifties was addressing another about the

cruelty of keeping hens in batteries. How easy to have battery hens as your most pressing concern! To condemn the frightful conditions in which these poor creatures were born, laid their eggs and died, had clearly become this woman's cause. But her presence at Stanton Place was proof that she was not exercised by man's inhumanity to *man*. It was a modern phenomenon; men and women eager to protect the whale and the seal – and send Black people to the bottom of the sea.

The appalling consequence of belonging perfectly to a particular class, Julia pondered, is that it tends to produce people who do not consider what they do or become, just so long as they remain firmly in their niche. These people lack all conscience, she thought.

Back in the drawing-room, the men were gathered in small groups round three huge fireplaces where logs and pine cones spat and roared. It was high summer, but the old walls of Stanton Place were damp, and every day of the year fires were lit to keep the house from crumbling. The windows, however, were open and night sounds filtered in. Julia heard an owl hoot and waited expectantly, hoping to hear its mate reply. But her attention was caught by the word 'Coldston'. A group of men were discussing the strike.

'Marxist trouble-makers, as usual. We shall have to deal with these men, eventually. Can't understand why the government hasn't . . . They don't understand that we the shareholders can't go on investing in these factories if what is being made isn't good enough for world markets. I told the chairman, I said, Geoffrey, you've got to get rid of the lot – or we'll have to do it for you.'

'Of course, you're quite right. The workers are utterly selfish, never prepared to make any sacrifices for their country.'

Julia was so angry that even if she had wanted to speak up – and she had decided not to for fear of arousing Massimo's ire – she would not have been coherent. She moved away, and joined Lady Muir and her husband – because Massimo was seated nearby.

'Of course, we should have had the Anglo-German Pact!

We were very near to it. We just didn't get that little extra support we needed, Churchill and Vansittart are hung in effigy by our youngsters at their get-togethers, you know . . .' Julia heard. 'It's the French we should never have backed. We've had trouble with the French throughout history.' Colonel Reid, aged about eighty, was confiding his prejudices with relish to Brigadier Jones of the same generation. Massimo had drawn up a chair beside the two old warriors, and, seeing him, Jones turned and said, 'As an Italian, you would have been spared the desecration of your country if we'd urged the case for Germany.'

'Indeed. And I'm not sure we'd any of us be the worse for it today,' Massimo replied. 'Mussolini was rather misunderstood.'

Sir Bogum must have switched on his hearing-aid, for he was in a state of some agitation. 'Did I hear someone say Mussolini? Did I? A genius with the trains, y'know. Our lot are hopeless,' he added sadly. 'Can't get them to work, to run on time . . . So what do they do? Abolish them! That's what. Abolished them altogether hereabouts. Abandoned us to the motor car, and a very poor substitute it is too. Trains! Trains! There now, that was something we were really good at in the old days!' But Sir Bogum's reminiscences passed without comment and the old warriors continued with their own. 'You know what the trouble was, of course? Hitler wasn't a gentleman. You can say what you like about his ideas, they may well have coincided with our own – but he wasn't one of us! And he'd never have become one of us! We couldn't have taken him to dine at the club, now, could we?'

'You're right, Buffy. But if we'd gone in with the Germans and backed Hitler just for a while, Windsor and the rest of us would have known how and when to ease him out. We could've replaced him with a good front man, one of the Prussian aristocrats. Prince von Arlstein, for example. We couldn't have gone on doing business with a house-painter. Von Arlstein would've gone down a treat with our Royals, don't you think?'

'It's too late regretting all that now, dear boy. But I think we may be seeing some of the old ideas coming to life again quite soon. I've found myself quite cheered by those brave boys behind the station bombings in Italy. They seem to me to be a damn clever lot. They bomb to the right of them and they bomb to the left of them and it's very unlikely they'll ever be rumbled. There're enough people in Italy wanting to destabilise society and get back to *proper* authoritarian rule . . .'

Lady Muir, who had been listening attentively, was not convinced that bombing, in whatever cause, was aesthetically pleasing, and she asked tentatively why it had been necessary to destroy some very architecturally interesting buildings in order to show up the deficiencies of democracy.

'Don't you worry your pretty head over a few *palazzi*, my dear. Our architects will fill in the gaps – you won't be able to tell the difference.' And Lady Muir was given no time to demur. Someone else had something to say about democracy – a funny thing that had earned a respectable name, but signified damn all. 'Giving a man one vote every three or five years is a sop to the masses, but it doesn't completely convince even them. What we need is strong leadership. We like that; the masses expect it. They respect our sort, always have, always will.'

And all, with the exception of Julia, murmured their accord. Julia tugged on Massimo's arm, but he shook her off. He moved away with two men who were discussing calling a meeting sometime in the autumn. 'I think we should have completed plans for the whole military set-up by then.'

'How many British MPs have you behind you?'

'So far? Ten!'

'Breed like rabbits! It's the same old story, the pure races must be on their guard against the inferior races. All that breeding they do is a threat to us; it's as if they hope to make up in quantity what they lack in quality. The scientists of today, don't ye know, *could* produce genetic perfection!' And he nodded, his underlip thrust upward by his chin, confirming his knowledge, and the advisability of its being put into practice. 'We want *efficient* people. That's what the state needs –

efficiency. Can't afford these long-haired louts, intellectuals and poets, they don't make the nation rich . . . You'll always get your clever men rising to the top of the vat to lead; the rubbish – the lees of society – will always sink to the bottom. What we've got to ensure is that they stay there, and rot. Intermarriage will destroy them. The physically and mentally ill-equipped should be made to mate together . . .'

'One thing's sure: we've still got to be on our guard against the Jews. It's the same old story with the Jews. They're a virus. They get into the bloodstream of our cultural life, our scientific life *and* our political life. And you know, old man, there's no antidote to a virus. It seems to me that what we have to do is learn their methods – beat them at their own game.'

'I don't see quite what you mean here . . .'

'Racially-based world domination's what I mean.'

'You mean, forbid a Christian fornicating with a Jew?'

'I mean just that!'

'I think that'd be difficult to legislate . . .'

Julia did not hear the end of this exchange. She moved away, wondering what the two old men thought about the holocaust. They probably believed either that it had never happened or that it was a tale put about by the Jews to attract attention to themselves – or that it was a wonderful idea that had fallen short of completion. She had once heard two men talking over the catalogues at the British Library, saying that the Jews had deserved all they got but that they hadn't got enough – there were too many about still. She had tried for months to get the men's names as if somehow that would give her domination over them and their fate. But she had failed. Each time she went into the Reading Room she looked to see whether one of them was there, but it seemed they were not regular readers. No doubt both would have been perfectly at home at Lord Stanton's.

Remembering this episode, Julia caught fragments of a conversation about 'Band Band'. At first she heard 'bang bang' and imagined the speakers had strayed back into child-hood. But no; The British Band had a radio station in the

Midlands. Despite objections pouring in to the Commission for Racial Equality and various MPs, it seemed that the station had managed to elude the police for three years. The Band had friends in the Midlands constabulary and got tip-offs from them when a raid was imminent. The blueprint for Band Band was being sent to other parts of the country and local cells were being encouraged to establish radio stations in their areas.

'Band Band is a most valuable asset. I'd say our recruitment success in the Midlands was fifty per cent due to it. The trouble with the post is that it can be intercepted. That's not to say we don't have our friends among the sorters, but they're not the brightest of our members . . .'

Julia was a practised listener. She was one of a small coterie of academics who were as interested in the processes of teaching as in their own research and she knew from her years at Paine that by listening closely to a student she could discover how to generate in him the confidence he lacked; were she to interrupt and fill him with ideas of her own, she was as likely as not to arrest the student's intellectual growth. The time to disseminate her own ideas was in the lectures she gave, and these she photo-copied for distribution after she delivered them. In the three hours she had been at Stanton Place Julia had listened avidly. Although some of the guests must have remarked that Julia was not a member of their community, the very fact of her presence among them conferred upon her membership of 'The Band'.

Julia amused herself in a ghoulish way wandering between the groups of guests, picking up the threads of their conversation and hearing them weave nightmarish fantasies. Every view expressed was one she deplored and despised. Her first appraisal had been correct; these people did indeed regard their privileges as some God-given right which they had a God-given obligation to protect by any means they thought fit. And not content with ninety per cent of the wealth of the country, they were out for one hundred per cent of the power as well. Their conversation kept returning to the heyday of their power in the 1930s. They felt it had begun to be seriously eroded at the end of World War II, and that the cause lay somewhere in the working of the House of Commons. They were laying plans to buy off more MPs.

'Every man's got his price. If you pay a Papist enough he'll back abortion.'

And there was a recruitment drive on. Although clearly considered somewhat undesirable, it seemed that it was gauged necessary to gather members of the under-class into the fold. Numbers were needed: unemployed men and women from the inner cities who blamed immigrants for the lack of jobs; small shopkeepers whose businesses had gone to the wall with the arrival of supermarkets headed by Jews; disaffected schoolteachers unable to adapt to the comprehensives; all who felt their status threatened. The plan was for each founder member of The British Band to take control of one particular area, each area group to be armed and commanded as a self-contained unit.

The overall aim of The Band was to restore power to the eight per cent who owned the wealth of Britain. All Blacks would be repatriated and all Jews given a single ticket to Israel. Homosexuals would be forced to have aversion therapy, and if any homosexual was found to be practising his perversion he would be sent to prison and solitary confinement, – that is, until capital punishment was reintroduced. Gypsies would be offered tickets to Ireland or France unless they agreed to live in sub-standard housing in the inner cities and become the garbage collectors. The universities would be most carefully supervised; the State – that is, The Band – would contract the universities to do the research it required, which would thus be patented in the name of the State so that publication of 'unsuitable' findings could be prevented. That way, dissension would be controlled out of existence. The press would also be in the hands of the State. According to their intelligence, tested by the State's social scientists, children would be allocated to the various schools – training for all but the top five per cent needed to run the country.

The Band's organisation, by means of a system of self-contained cells, had been instigated by Reginald Waterstone,

Julia discovered. Trained in intelligence, Waterstone had learnt a great deal from the example of the Soviets. However, he had been careful not to reveal to members of The Band the model for his organisation – they would have been deeply suspicious . . . It was Reginald Waterstone who now took Julia into a corner and attempted to elicit from her exactly how she came to be at Stanton Place. He had not seen her before. As it happened, he had never met Massimo Vardi either. Julia explained that Massimo was 'an Italian contact' of Lord Stanton's; this cleared her with Waterstone. And when she told him that she lectured at Paine College, his suspicions about her political outlook were completely dispelled. Julia knew why: Gladyse Baker was renowned for her Rightist stance. She very often took up her pen to complain to the press that all incoming students had been indoctrinated at school, through peace studies, and to a man (and woman) arrived at Paine hardened Marxists – giving the impression that she saw it as her bounden duty to remedy the matter. However, Gladyse was rarely successful in her efforts to carry the students so far to the Right of the political map that they hung off the edge of it with her. In earlier days, when Julia first joined Paine, Gladyse's determined efforts had been something of a problem in the department, but since administrative work had become an almost full-time occupation, Gladyse spent more and more hours in front of her computer and fewer and fewer lecturing, and she had recently given up taking tutorials altogether.

'D'you know Professor Gladyse Baker?'

'I work in her department.'

'Oh! I see!' And Reginald Waterstone was confirmed in his ignorance.

A man approached. 'D'you mind?' And with a hand on Waterstone's arm he started to draw him away.

'Will you excuse me?' Waterstone asked Julia, who nodded. The two men moved a couple of feet to her side.

'Don't worry about extradition,' Waterstone told his companion, 'our courts are very fussy. If they're not satisfied that a *prima facie* case has been established in the case of Lambrossi in Italy – and I've reason to believe that the crime for which he was convicted in his absence is not one which corresponds to anything in our law – he can sit it out here for as long as he likes. D'you want him moved to a safe house round here?'

'It would help. But how long is this legal state of affairs likely to last?'

'I imagine, for as long as we need. You know how slow grind the wheels . . . The government says its intention is to tidy things up so that anyone accused or convicted of serious crimes abroad can't escape the consequences by coming over here. But I don't see them moving against Italy unless there's something in it for them – and what's Italy got to offer us?

'And deportation? Could Lambrossi be deported?'

'Not with the new EEC law. Anyhow, old man, we've got impeccable contacts in the Home Office. Don't you worry on that score. There's a gentleman's agreement: Italians of the Right convicted in Italy can stay here just so long as they keep their noses clean. That means giving no offence to the neighbours – not frightening the horses, that sort of thing. If they keep their noses clean they're said to "constitute no present threat". And bear in mind, Italians are White . . .'

'Safe as houses!'

'Safe as safe-houses!'

Twice Julia had tried to distract Massimo and suggest that they leave, and twice he had ostentatiously ignored her. Finally, just after midnight, he indicated that he was ready to take his leave of Lord and Lady Stanton.

'Did you enjoy yourself?'

'What? You must be joking! I've never been in the company of such ghastly people before, and I hope never to be again. Everything about them is either dangerous or pretentious, or both. They're the sort who preach charity on Sunday between ten and eleven, shoot and fish and consume in the afternoon, and for the rest of the week make every attempt to get as much power for themselves as they have land and money.'

'They're the backbone of your country. They're the men who've done their duty.'

'Oh, yes, I know all about men who do their duty. They

start by doing what they're told to do and end by insisting we all follow suit. They're addicts to duty. And like all addicts, they're never content unless everyone around them is as hooked as they are.'

Julia had downed an exceedingly large brandy shortly before Massimo signalled his willingness to leave Stanton. As she drove carefully down the quiet, dark country lanes she remembered, 'The path which leads to the fascist terror has a most attractive entrance.'

Massimo remained silent. He was clearly not in the least embarrassed that Julia had seen what went on at Stanton Place. Julia wondered whether the whole thing could have been a joke, some sort of theatrical performance? It was a full quarter of an hour before Massimo took her left hand from the steering wheel, kissed it, and then placed it between his thighs at his open fly.

'Shall we stop here?'

As Julia slowed to round a corner, Massimo gently pulled on the hand brake. He took Julia in his arms and kissed her and caressed her, and with his hand and probing fingers he deftly made her come. She felt delicious; her whole being was filled with desire for Massimo. He drew her out of the car, into a field that had recently been harvested. Shocks of corn lay evenly scattered on the ground; the stubble between the shocks was an inch high.

'Kneel! Go on! Kneel low! Let your forehead touch the ground! Now, lift your skirt!'

The stubble was digging into her knees and her forehead. Massimo placed both his hands on Julia's haunches; he was shrieking with pleasure. 'Bitch! Loathsome bitch!' And as he ejaculated he pushed her from him, brusquely. She fell over on to her back. What on earth was she doing? She felt that she was colluding in her own rape.

The moon was full; around Julia the field was bled of colour. The night air was balmy, she could smell earth and stubble; it was delicious. Massimo lay down beside her on his jacket.

'You are very lovely. Very desirable,' and he leant over her and sucked her lips into his mouth and bit them. She was again consumed with desire. The slightly ferrous taste of blood in her mouth was appetising. Massimo was pulling open her dress and exposing her breasts; he caressed them with his hands, he kissed them with his lips, he drew the nipples into his mouth and sucked. Julia stiffened. She knew with every fibre of her being that he was going to sink his teeth into her nipples, and as he did so she shrieked with rage, with pain. With a strength she did not know she had, she pushed Massimo off and struggled to her feet. She stood over him and within her rose the urge to shit over him. Horrified by this impulse, she yelled down at the prostrate figure, 'You brute. You disgusting animal!'

Massimo was enchanted, he laughed loudly. 'Yes, my innocent child. I am an animal and so too are you, and that is what is so absolutely delightful!' And then he rolled on to one side, rose to his feet, and winding his arms about her thighs he held Julia aloft. Somehow he managed to divest her of her dress; he threw it out into the field where it landed on a corn shock. Holding her in his arms he walked between the shocks as if dedicating Julia to the moon. He was enraptured by her and he told her so. 'You are beautiful, you are intelligent, you can't do without me!' and he laid her on the ground, stood up with one leg either side of her body, and while he talked of her beauty, her desirability, her brilliance, he sent a hot stream of foul-smelling liquid over her breasts and her belly. And then he lay down on top of her, penetrated her, aroused himself to orgasm, withdrew and poured his sperm over her body. Julia took his head in her hands and drew it to her own. She kissed him with tender passion.

'And so you have enjoyed me?'

'I have. But I don't enjoy being hurt.'

'You say you didn't enjoy the pain, but I know you enjoyed the passion. Women like to be treated with a firm hand. They're like the peasants on our estate. To function, women need to know their place.'

Oh God! She had colluded with the man!

The word 'collude' that formed in her mind suddenly took

her away from the immediate experience. She had colluded all her life in one way or another – with her father's expectations for her, with James's way of life. She had played into their hands, so that when the break with her parents came they were quite uncomprehending. Throughout her early life they had believed – and she had allowed them to believe – that she was like them and espoused their thinking.

There had been very little expression of feeling in the home of Jack and Jill, very little space left for anything but the programmed round of duties. And James believed that passion was the reserve of women's magazines . . .

Massimo was caressing her from her cheeks, her neck, down, down to her feet. He had removed the final vestiges of her clothing and with his fingers he sought to arouse her again. Just seconds before she would have arrived at orgasm, he withdrew his hand. 'Get up! Walk over there to that tree.' As she did so, she wondered what it was that was making her walk naked over the stubble in the moonlight. As she reached the tree and turned, a light shone in her face. Massimo had a torch with him, and with its beam he scanned her body.

'Masturbate!' he ordered. 'Go on! Let me see you!'

Friday

It was four in the morning before Julia and Massimo walked through the gates of Marlowe College. Dawn was rising. They stood together by the fountain at the centre of the cloister garden, and looked up at the sky. Patches of blood-red showed between dark clouds.

'There may be rain.'

In the wake of his peculiar display of violence and degradation, Massimo behaved with tenderness towards Julia. 'There, you see how good it is when you submit to me.' Julia wondered whether he was not ashamed of the ordeal he had put her through. Did he not know that his sexual appetite was aberrant? Did he admire her only for her tortured obedience? From her point of view, it was hardly less perfidious to have endured sexual humiliation than it was to have provoked it. She remembered that one of the Coldston men had argued that it was as wrong for their forebears to have accepted humiliating terms of employment as it was for the factory bosses to have imposed such terms on them. She had to face the fact that she had wanted the sexual attention of Massimo and had been prepared to pay any price for it. The forebears of the Coldston men had accepted their lot in return for a subsistence wage. There was not a lot of difference between her and them in terms of individual humiliation, but they were less compromised than she at a moral level: they had to live, they had to support their families. She had a husband she loved, with whom she shared an intimate sexual life. What did she want with this man? A man she had allowed to pee over her! Did other men do this? Did other women let them?

She was fascinated by him. Massimo was devastatingly attractive. The fact that every view he held was the opposite to her own, and actually frightened and disgusted her, was a challenge; she would not submit intellectually, and perhaps she would even convince him, eventually, of the rightness of her views, and in exchange for his sexual authority would impose her moral authority. And if she could get him to share even a few of her ideas, would it not change his behaviour? But she doubted she would.

The intellectual arguments on the multilateral and non-pacifist side were politically attractive, and easier for the majority to grasp; they could be made to seem reasonable – and there was nothing the majority liked better than to be called 'reasonable' and 'rational'. The unilateral and pacifist stance was always referred to as 'idealistic', a word now deprived of its positive connotations through the clever but coarse propaganda of the Right. And the argument for strong leadership was particularly persuasive in the present climate – one that was hostile to individual rights, and therefore failed to encourage individual responsibilities. But Julia was convinced that among the pacifists who believed in equal rights, who had no need to jostle for power and position, the moral argument was won. In due course it would become clear to all that there is no argument stronger than the moral one.

It was these and other such thoughts that preoccupied Julia as she lay sleepless in bed until it was time to rise, bathe and dress. When Jeremiah Jenkins knocked on her door at seven-thirty she was already at her desk, working on her paper.

'Despite the red in the sky, I believe it will keep fine,' the old scout informed her. He was standing awkwardly at the window, not knowing quite what to do since the ritual of drawing back the curtains and opening the windows had been wrested from him. 'It's a pity to stay in reading and writing on a day like this,' he observed, adding regretfully that he supposed it was what people like Julia preferred. 'Had you thought to take out a punt, yet, Miss?'

'No, I hadn't. But what an excellent idea!'

When he discovered that Dr Bruton would like to follow up his suggestion, Jeremiah Jenkins became quite animated. He would, indeed he would, prepare a picnic for two. That is to say, he would supervise the kitchen's preparation of whatever lavish spread Dr Bruton would care to order.

'This looks astonishingly prodigal, my dear.' Massimo was gazing down at a foie gras mould surrounded by packed ice. He had tied the punt to a tree. Julia had already discovered that Jeremiah Jenkins had forgotten nothing: the rug, the wine in its cooler, napkins, cutlery . . . And the food was a triumph. As a coda to the delicious cold collation, a small olive-green melon had been scooped out, and the hollow filled with berries macerated in brandy. The lid of the melon had been so carefully cut that neither Massimo nor Julia had suspected its contents.

'Little wonder that your young friend, Margaret, had reservations about Oxbridge. I can't imagine that this sort of luxury would fit her idea of what constitutes university education.'

'At the risk of your regarding me as inconsistent, I do see this as part of education. I like to think that students emerge with a desire to reach high standards in whatever they're doing. I don't see anything elitist in good food well prepared, good clothes and good housing . . .'

Massimo looked at Julia, looked at her 'good clothes' and was demonstrably unimpressed. Julia remembered: no matter what an English woman wears she can never – or, only rarely – approach the chic of a French or Italian woman. Why? Oh why?

'Come here!'

'I've fallen in love with you,' she told him as she moved towards him. She admitted it calmly, as if commenting on something trivial, outside herself.

'No,' he insisted, 'you've enjoyed my domination of you. It's an experience intelligent women are seldom offered because they attract weak men. And women always imagine themselves in love when they are merely enjoying sex. I think they have to make this connection; it makes them feel less animal.'

Why is he like this? Julia wondered. 'No, I don't think I *am* confusing my heart with my glands, as you are apt to put it. I've actually fallen in love with you in spite of myself! I don't really like you very much,' she admitted, half-smiling.

Massimo threw back his head, but his laugh was somewhat unconvincing. It was as if he might prefer to be liked rather than desired. He did not want her to desire him, he wanted her to admire him for his physical health, his intellectual prowess, for the respect he commanded, for his elegance.

'The trouble with you academic females is that you ignore your role as women. You think you want the upper hand in arguments, but actually it's only when a man comes along who won't give in to you that you find out what it is to feel. But I'm sorry you don't like me.'

'Really! I wouldn't have imagined that would matter to you.'

'Well, it doesn't much matter. It hasn't stood between us and pleasure, has it? The reason I've taken you sexually with some degree of delight is because I so despise your views. Co-operation, equality, pacifism – they're intellectual clap-trap. I sometimes wonder whether I'd want to fuck a woman of my own mind.' And as he insulted her, he leant over and fondled her breast.

Julia swatted his hand. She rose and went down to the water's edge. How could she, in the face of his contempt and condescension, feel the way she was feeling? A great divide had revealed itself between her thoughts and her feelings.

I'll not be seeing him again, she told herself. It doesn't matter. I'll go back home and within a week or two the whole thing will have blown over, will seem remote – like a bad dream. Or would it? She felt disorientated. It seemed that what was happening was happening to an aspect of herself she did not know. She had never before had an affair. She wondered why. What was it that had kept her faithful? Had it been lack of opportunity, or lack of need to be unfaithful?

She was content with James. She had never registered desire for anyone else.

She knew that among her friends and acquaintances adultery was a commonplace matter – at least sixty-five per cent of married women had affairs. Take Amanda Burgh. She had lovers the way other women had periods, regularly, and with some pain and inconvenience. Then there was Rachel, married to that pretentious pet-food producer Fred, a leading member of the 'Art for Architecture' set – when taking you on a tour of his Picassos, Nicolsons and Sutherlands he demonstrated a pride so inflated you could be forgiven for thinking they were his own handiwork.

Julia wondered if she herself was unattractive to men. She hadn't noticed anyone actually making a pass. Men had always been attentive to her, but no one had actually suggested bed after lunch. Low libido on her part? Perhaps she didn't give off the appropriate signals. Julia's thoughts strayed over her social contacts and her professional colleagues, and within the space of a few seconds it became clear to her that almost all the women she knew had either told her they had had lovers or told her of mutual acquaintances who had lovers. Julia was almost alone in not having sex outside her marriage. She wondered whether something within her had been positively seeking a threatening relationship rather than a consoling one. Why duplicate what she had? She had recently become aware of just how cosy her domestic life was. She had wondered whether cosiness might be an impediment to her ideals – letting them lie fallow without being challenged. She always assumed that she loved James; it was obvious, they were married. But did she? Really?

But surely, even if at some subconscious level Julia had been inviting a challenge, she could not be accused of inviting something as destructive as this affair? Massimo was going back to Italy and was not going to drag Julia, like some wooden leg, across Europe. He was unlikely to write to her or telephone her, or even include her in his thoughts. She might see him at the conference in Geneva in the spring . . .

'Will you definitely be going?'

'I'm not sure. I've been asked to speak on destabilisation but I'm not sure that I want to get into all that. It's a problem, being an Italian, and knowing what's going on from the inside. I can't be utterly frank.'

'D'you know who's behind the bombings?'

'No. Why d'you ask?'

'Well, I thought that might be the area in which you couldn't be utterly frank.'

'Come, it's our last day together, let's celebrate.'

Massimo packed the vestiges of the picnic into the basket and stowed it in the punt. Julia punted upstream towards the beech woods. Massimo had been quite specific; he wanted woods, with untrod paths. The air was hot and heavy, and clouds were gathering; there was going to be a storm. Massimo, however, looked cool in his aubergine linen shirt and white trousers.

'Can't you punt this thing a little faster? I've got a meeting at four.' At once Julia's pleasure diminished. He had limited time for her. And furthermore he wanted her to know it.

Massimo moored the punt at a clearing and spread the rug on the ground. Through the branches of the huge beech trees sunlight reached the clearing in a series of streamers, rendering the ground beneath dry and hard. Julia lay where Massimo told her to lie, she drew up her dress above her knees as he instructed. She felt intensely excited. She knew she was behaving like an automaton, programmed to please. She had submitted before and she would do so today.

Massimo threw himself on top of her. He was very heavy, her back was hurting and her ribs seemed strained to breaking point. She tried to protest but her struggle merely enhanced Massimo's pleasure and he put one hand over her mouth. He took her with vehemence and indifference. All her attempts to adjust her position on the ground failed. She tried to cry out, but all that emerged from her throat was a groan that could be interpreted as ecstasy – an interpretation she knew Massimo would be inclined to make. Then his hand slipped and his arm pressed against her neck. Julia was frantic: she was suffocating. Suddenly she heard a noise. Someone, or something was moving in the undergrowth. As Massimo achieved release inside her, a deer ran out of the woods, across the clearing where they lay, making towards the river. Its thudding feet – a sound that Massimo could not identify – disturbed him. He disengaged from Julia only seconds before she felt she would have passed out.

When she had regained her breath and her composure, Julia asked Massimo whether he realised that he had almost strangled her.

'You do so exaggerate, my dear!'

'No, you had your arm over my neck and I couldn't make you understand . . .'

'There's always something . . .' His tone was dismissive, appropriate, Julia felt, to her condition as an unequal partner. He could have killed her.

It was the storm that propitiously intervened. Suddenly, the clouds burst open, and within minutes narrow streams were flowing across the arid ground. Julia quickly arranged her dress, picked up the rug and threw it over her head, and ran for shelter. She had noticed a thunder-crack in an ancient tree.

'Will this last long?'

'I don't think so. It's just a summer shower.' Massimo looked at his watch. 'I don't want to be late. I'd quite like a drink right now.'

Julia knew that one of the paths in the wood led to a tributary of the river where customers of The Primrose Inn fished. If she could find the path, Massimo could have his drink in ten or fifteen minutes. It would be quicker to walk than punt – and they would be less exposed to the rain . . .

The bar was crowded with fishermen, in from the storm, discussing just how much weather drove them to drink. While Massimo consulted the man behind the bar as to what best to drink and how to get warm and dry, Julia sat on the window seat, stroking the cat and watching the rose petals tumble disconsolately to the grass.

The hot toddy was excellent. While Massimo drank, he watched the fishermen downing quantities of beer and measuring the air with their hands as they described their catches; pike and roach of gigantic proportions haunted the stream, it seemed. Julia wondered why it was that so few women enjoyed the quiet, contemplative sport of fishing. Perhaps it was the slaughter of the catch that put them off? When Massimo returned to the bar for more toddy, Julia stared at his back; it was large, well-proportioned and athletic. What sport did he play? she wondered. A man of his age must have to make efforts to keep his figure – and to keep fit. And then he turned and beckoned to her; he pointed to a door; he picked up a tray on which there was a jug of toddy and two glasses.

'What sport do you play?'

'Squash!' he replied. 'And Golf and women, of course!'

At the top of the stairs he ushered Julia into room number four.

'They only have four rooms, and as none's occupied, I had a choice. I chose the one with the biggest bed facing the stream.'

Massimo stood at the window with his arm round Julia's shoulders. The storm had gathered. The rain was pouring into the stream and swelling it, lashing the mimulus and flags. The tresses of the willows shook tremulously. Along the river, a row of unattended fishing rods, and umbrellas protecting baskets and nets, underlined the absence of any human being abroad. Massimo drew Julia into the room and helped her out of her dress and hung it to dry over the hot towel rail in the bathroom. He lifted her into bed. The couple lay entwined, watching the lightning tear the dark sky in shreds, as if the sky itself were no more than a sheet of cosmic paper.

Let this last! Let time just stop here and now!

For the first time Massimo talked to Julia about himself. He told her about his past . . .

Massimo had been born on the family estate in Apulia and had led a wild life with the children of the peasant workers in the ancient olive groves, the fruit of whose trees had sustained Vardis for tens of generations. He had been an only child, he told Julia; his father had combined his responsibilities as landowner with those of agent to a Fascist politician, and this

100

had taken him away from his estate for weeks at a time. Massimo's mother, the countess, resented her husband's absences and made up for his cavalier attitude to their marriage by drawing closer to clever young Massimo. Their relationship was consequently more intimate than is usual between mother and son. When war broke out Massimo's father was delighted at last to be *ordered* to enlist in Mussolini's cause. He had wanted to serve in Ethiopia, but his estate had been on the verge of bankruptcy at the time and he feared to absent himself until his new manager had familiarised himself with the particular problems of the Vardi domain. Throughout World War II the count was out of Italy – mostly in North Africa. He made no effort to get back home on leave.

Massimo told Julia how, since the Vardi estate was situated in the path of the advancing British, the huge old house at its core had become the target of incendiary bombs and shells. He described how, horrified by the fragility of human relationships and of bricks and mortar alike, he had steeled himself to become responsible not only for the safety of his mother but also for that of the village and the old peasants and young children who were all that remained on the land. From the age of ten he had become accustomed to giving orders and being obeyed.

When the demobilised count, his father, returned to his estate, he discovered his wife and son living like rats in the kitchen quarters of the old house – the only part of the building to have retained its structural walls. He could hardly believe the evidence of his eyes. He had married the daughter of a wealthy landowner from the Abruzzi; she had come to him under the weight of silks, satins, linens, silver and jewels. She had, in addition, brought the cash that eventually saved the Vardi estate from the long arm of the bailiffs, when he had been champing to fight in Ethiopia. This wife had now become no better than one of his peasants! Massimo remembered how his father had gazed, unbelieving, as his wife went about in torn old trousers, her hands gnarled, her hair matted, her posture bent and her skin the texture of orange peel. He remembered, too, how his father had reacted to him, Massimo

– fifteen years of age, but with a maturity that could be favourably compared with that of any man in the count's regiment. Massimo had had awesome confidence. But he was not a child. He needed no advice. He knew how best to tend the olive trees, how best to garner the crop, how best to officiate in matters relating to the old retainers. Above all, he knew what was best for his mother – and was determined to defend it. He had sensed that his father felt redundant, both on his land and in his family . . .

Massimo had resented the return of his father. He had no intention of sharing his mother with the stranger. He noticed with pleasure that his mother did not seem anxious to be shared; she did not appear even to like his father. Like a female automaton she saw to it that food was ready for him when he returned at night from his day-long, disconsolate wanderings over the estate; and when he complained that it was inedible and insufficient she removed the plate from before him and set it down in front of her son. No voices were raised, no discussions entered into. The countess was war-weary too. The count had lost the battle for a cause in which he believed, but the countess had seen her whole world shattered.

And then, while Julia listened, spellbound, Massimo told the next part of the story. One day he was sharpening knives by the well and the countess was making bread in the kitchen, when a jeep containing half-a-dozen uniformed men swung into the courtyard. Massimo stopped drawing the blades up and down the whetstone and the countess stopped kneading dough and wandered out into the yard, her hands and trousers covered in flour. The jeep drew up dramatically in front of her, scattering the loose dry earth. Six soldiers dropped to the ground as one. Both the countess and Massimo were impressed by their military precision and by their spotless uniforms and polished boots. It took no more than seconds for them to realise that these were not their men. The senior of the officers asked in Italian where the count could be located. Massimo gave precise instructions as to his whereabouts and the six soldiers set off in hot pursuit of their quarry.

'Neither I nor my mother was distressed when he was arrested and removed,' Massimo said reflectively. 'For my mother, the loss of a husband was irrelevant; hers had been an arranged marriage that had not the time or the circumstance to mature into a love-match. For me, the loss of a father was a relief. I had had sole possession of my mother from the age of nine and was not ready to relinquish it.' Nevertheless, Julia sensed that seeing his father taken away by the enemy, at his connivance, had left him feeling confused and guilty; it was a humiliation, but it was also treachery – even if it had been answer to prayer.

Within twelve months the count had been tried for crimes against humanity and found guilty. Before the sentence could be carried out he hanged himself in his cell . . .

Then Massimo told what happened after, and how he had come to Rome. When her future became husbandless, the countess had consulted Father Pagoni, a Jesuit from her natal Abruzzi, and it was his idea that she should lease out the lands in Apulia and build a future for her son in Rome. The money from the estate would be sufficient to support them both until Massimo was able to take over the role of provider . . . It was a sensible idea. The crumbling, burnt-out house and the ravaged land had become an albatross; and Massimo, excellent though he was in practical matters and at organising the peasants, also had an analytical mind, and wanted to train it for more cerebral work that might lead to academic honours. Mother and son had enthused together over a future they envisioned as being very different from the one the return of the count had seemed to presage.

If in her heart the countess yearned for her native province she had made no mention of the fact, but she saw to it that the apartment she took for herself and her son in Trastevere was in an old house, set in a spacious garden. Trastevere was not then a fashionable suburb; the countess had chosen the neighbourhood and situation for the view they afforded over the city, and for the abundance of trees. She feared to feel claustrophobic in the city. But of course, Massimo was delighted that, little by little, over the years, Trastevere became fashionable and he was not obliged to uproot his mother from a home she had come to love as he climbed ever higher up the academic and social ladder. By now, his place of residence truly reflected his standing in the world; aristocratic, intellectual and substantial . . .

Julia was stunned by Massimo's recital – so long and detailed, so totally unexpected, so entirely unsolicited. She did not know what to think. Did it explain him? Did it excuse him? Why had he told her? But one thing she was clear on. She felt herself so totally possessed by Massimo that his description of his early life acquired an erotic potency which reinforced her desire. It was she, now, who took him. She did so rapturously. Why was it that he swore at her and hurt her? What was it that sanctioned his brutality, his contempt? The absence of legal sanctions, she supposed. If he were to batter her body as he battered her being, he'd be given a life sentence.

But then it was that he made love to her with extraordinary delicacy and affection, his actions accompanied by a litany of endearments. It was a passionate pleasure to do as he bid her, to lick his body from head to toe, to swallow his sperm; and when he was replete, to obey his command for her to dress him, even to the extent of tying his shoes and combing his hair.

'Little mother,' he murmured. But she could not tell whether the comment expressed affection or contempt. Was it possible, she wondered, for a man to feel a combination of the two?

Julia went into the bathroom and washed in front of the mirror. Her neck was badly bruised. She had no scarf with which to conceal the spreading stain. She hoped that Massimo would not remark on the ugly colours.

'I shall miss my little adversary,' he told her, stroking her cheek.

'Will you? Don't you have others?'

He avoided the invitation to reassure her by suggesting they go down and get a drink.

'The bar will be closed but I suppose we rate as guests. I'd rather tea, myself.'

She would remember this room for his having been there. She feared that he would not remember it.

The television was on in the cosy sitting-room that smelt of a blend of cigar smoke, sherry and beeswax. The room had recently been vacated; the sun had come out again and the fishermen had returned to their rods. Tea and scones were provided and Julia was pouring the tea when suddenly the film that was showing on the television set in the corner was interrupted. A news announcer, seated at a desk with a map of Italy behind him, appeared, grim of face. Railway stations in a further five provincial Italian cities had been bombed, bringing the total number of stations affected to eight.

'A group calling itself "The Italian Band" has claimed responsibility.'

At Coldston, strikers, police and press had settled down to a regular timetable. From dusk to dawn groups of men stood round braziers outside the factory gates; from dawn to dusk they were joined by press and police and visited three times daily by their wives, bringing food and drink. Throughout the day the sounds of dispute rang out – reproaches against God, political leaders, factory bosses. Edmund and Margaret learnt that the causes of the men's discontent were more serious and had more justification than they had first thought – and were consequently more difficult to confront and put right. For example, the stench in which Coldston was enveloped was not just a result of the effluent from the factories. Years ago a tip had been dug in the field on the outskirts of the estate, to accommodate household waste from Oxford, not Coldston – Coldston's waste was shipped miles away. Eventually, after the factory bosses themselves intervened (for the noses of management are as sensitive as those on the shop-floor and in the school yard), the tip was filled in. However, three years later stench of a different sort was noticed; after a while it worsened, and small explosions occurred underground. Last month the Gas Board had been called in; the local authority engineers had been called in. Finally, it was admitted: methane gas had built up underground. But no one in authority had acknowledged that the inhabitants of Coldston were at risk and accepted responsibility.

Margaret was as much exercised over the social problems at Coldston as the industrial ones; in any case, she regarded the two as interrelated. She discussed with a group of women what the Council had so far done about the methane and, on hearing that nothing had been done, she canvassed some of the press and asked them whether they would be interested in making the methane gas under Coldston a subject of features for their papers – and for television. They were interested. Other cases of filled-in tips producing explosions were leaking out from closed files in Whitehall and locked committee rooms all over the country. The subject was ripe for exposure.

Margaret made her enquiries, and these rapidly led her to Mr Hardcastle, headmaster of the local comprehensive. Against the odds, perhaps, Mr Hardcastle turned out to be a dedicated educationalist who had come to the end of his tether. His pupils were all in poor or not very good health (they smoked, they drank whatever they could get hold of), they were fractious, and their attention was almost impossible to arrest – and once arrested, hard to keep. They had no ambition – which was hardly surprising since they fully understood that the sole purpose of school in their case was to keep them off the streets.

From a drawer in his desk – it was the school holidays, and Mr Hardcastle was at home – the headmaster took a faded page cut from an old *Guardian*, reporting the statement of a Tory MP that it had always been far too expensive to improve the educational standards of working-class children significantly . . . 'I've kept this near me all these years,' he told Margaret, 'so that I would never forget that my job in life was to prove him wrong.' He was delighted that Margaret had corralled the press, and was only too pleased to make the school hall available for their meeting that evening.

In the afternoon, however, Mr Hardcastle walked down to the factory gates and was quite astonished to see Margaret, standing on an up-turned orange crate, haranguing a large crowd of men.

'It's a fact,' she was saying, 'not an opinion, you know: bankers and industrialists are the most powerful agents in our society. So powerful that they influence every corner of our so-called democratic country. They control the media; they control the police. And you must know, surely, from your own experience, what industrialists are. Your position at Cold Products is little better than high-grade serfdom.'

The men nodded. The word 'serfdom' hit the spot.

'The reason for this state of affairs is the class system. It's the result of patronage. You're never going to get anywhere under this regime because you – not one of you – know no one in power. The only way you're going to get control over your own destinies is to own the means of production. Take over the factory! Make it into a co-operative!'

There was silence. Men tired of fighting for their rights could not muster enthusiasm for something that was going to take energy and time and organisation.

'I can't tell you what sort of a society you'll eventually create. But one thing I can assure you: even if what you create isn't one hundred per cent successful, it'll be one hundred per cent more fulfilling than anything done *for* you.

'In '68, in Paris, it was not only the capitalist but the industrial society that was called in question. And it was the students who pointed out that the relationship between men working for other men, as serfs, was a function of the class system. So the system had to be brought down. The revolution failed there but, eventually, it'll succeed. Take over Cold Products! Bring in young blood – old blood is congealed in old practices. Go to your union and demand that they finance you. Chuck out the management; they're only interested in profits: the less they pay you, the more profit they keep for themselves.'

Mr Hardcastle was alarmed by what he heard. Margaret had not struck him as having such extreme views when she came to his house. He would have to find someone much less revolutionary with whom to attend the press conference – someone like himself, who would address the problems of the community in less inflammatory tones. He would round up the Reverend Blaise, a man licensed to dissent, not only because of his dog-collar but because he couched his dissent in archaic language and drew on biblical parables to make his points. Blaise lived in Oxford on property that belonged to one of the colleges. He had had the opportunity of a living in Oxford which would have attracted a much more sizeable congregation than he had at Coldston, where he was lucky to get half-a-dozen pensioners to save. But he had felt a calling, he was anxious to do God's will. It was only when God's will appeared to coincide with that of Mr Marx that the Reverend Blaise found himself confused. 'Of course I deeply regret that gap between rich and poor,' he had once said to Mr Hardcastle. 'But I find myself facing the prospect of so-called equality with even less enthusiasm. And the means of acquiring equality would be so terribly destructive. What we want is surely a little more *kindness* on the part of everyone . . .'

By the time the two men entered the school assembly hall, Margaret was already seated behind a table, her eyes sparkling with fervour. On her right sat two trade union representatives and two flying pickets. On her left were some strikers and their wives, and Edmund.

'I thought it would be much more comfortable for us all to come in here and sit down and try to get the message about this strike clear. It's about much more than jobs at the refrigeration plant. So far neither television, radio nor press has given you a fair hearing. Will you bear with me? I'd like to dispose of one or two general points before you take questions.

'Here at Coldston we are no more than five miles away from prodigious wealth and privilege. But look about you. At Coldston there's nothing but craven poverty. The poverty is so deep-rooted that it's not a question of abolishing it with an injection of cash and then hoping that that will have cured the problem. The poverty's ingrained; it's a poverty of health, of culture – and of spirituality. The very fact that Oxford tips its garbage here . . . You can't have Oxford on the one hand and Coldston on the other without your people here feeling that somehow you're not worth much. You men are demoralised, not without cause. Your womenfolk are ill, understandably.

'We've all smelt the stench! D'you realise: Coldston's living on a time bomb? The Council says there's nothing to fear, but we all know what happened with a similar tip outside Newcastle, don't we? Four houses caved in and a baby was killed. Twenty-five per cent of the male population's unemployed at Coldston – and those in work risk being thrown on another tip, the unemployment tip. Now,' turning to the press, Margaret asked, 'are you members of the press going to publish these facts? Or are you going to persist in writing about men at Coldston not willing to make sacrifices for their country, and giving their Italian counterparts a boost? Have you asked any of the men what they were doing between 1939 and 1945? And if you *are* going to document every incident of violence on the picket line, will you be so kind as to mention the violence done to those men by the bosses and by society? You see, violence is not simply a matter of two men bashing their heads together, it's a question of one man or one society preventing other men from fulfilling themselves.

'There's real trouble in the country. Political ideals put the interests of the state, and the wealthy and powerful, above and before those of the working man. The working man – and woman – is never consulted about anything. In times of peace he's industrial fodder; in times of war he's cannon fodder.'

'So what d'you want for Coldston, Miss?' someone shouted. 'A socialist state? Have you asked the people here if they'd want to live in a Poland?'

'Because socialism has been repressive in some countries it

109

doesn't follow that it has to be repressive everywhere.' Margaret's tone was weary. 'You're falling into the logical fallacy.'

'Oh, a right little intellectual!'

'I don't regard it as a crime to have informed myself.' Margaret was furious. 'I regard it as a crime that not everyone has had my opportunity to do likewise. But for heaven's sake, this isn't a press conference about me. You see, you lot always have to personalise things. This strike is about ideas and ideals. I want to tell you about the alternatives that would keep the factory open and actually increase the numbers employed. I want to discuss how increased public expenditure combined with self-management could help Coldston out of the doldrums. At the same time I want to encourage the women of Coldston to gather their rubbish and tip it in the grounds of the Oxford colleges until such time as the tip here is made safe and the stench is gone.'

'And do you call that non-violent action?'

'Not precisely. But how much good does it do to a racoon if I wear a plastic coat?' She was incandescent with rage. 'Ultimately there is no point in strikes or boycotts because they are punitive of all sides. What is required is action that will help the people of Coldston – and we want support for that action *now*. We can't understand how it is or why it is that in the present serious circumstances that support is so slow in coming.' Margaret felt that she was spreading herself too liberally, like boiling milk from a saucepan. 'Now, some questions to Mick Aldery, foreman at Cold Products, please.'

'Mick! How much longer are your men going to continue this strike?'

'My men will continue the strike until such time as management revokes the plan to shut down the plant.'

'Don't you think your men would do better to take the money while it's on the table?'

'Would you take that money? I'm pretty sure you wouldn't. And I don't think you have any right to put that question unless you'd be prepared to accept the same redundancy money.'

One of the strikers interrupted. 'All we've got is our jobs.

You seen what Coldston's like and you know there's no work anywhere else in the country for the likes of us. We was told to buy our council 'ouses. 'Ose going to buy them from us if we was to get on our bikes and find work in Timbuctoo like Mr Tebbitt says. Tell me that!' There being no answer to that question, a short silence ensued. Then one of the managers in the crowd stood up:

'This is a free society. Factory bosses are at liberty to open and close factories as they see fit. They have the interests of the shareholders to consider. You'll all get social security!'

'Yes, you're bloody right there, mate! This is a bloody free society for shareholders. And if they're rich enough to have two or three 'ouses abroad, they can live in Florida, or wherever they like, and not even *pay* taxes. Social security, my foot! That's not what we want. We want work.'

'It's envy with you lot. Don't you see you benefit from a free society? Would you be happy in Russia? You'd get your arteries injected with turpentine if you criticised the system there.'

'Listen to me, mate! The only reason as we're allowed to express our views in this country is so that our fury don't build up and explode in *real* violence. They're wily men, our leaders; they know 'ow to stop revolutions. As for being accused of envy, funny how the rich always accuse the poor of that. But I've got another suggestion, think this one over: the rich need us. Without us their wealth wouldn't seem so great and good to them. They'd 'ave nothing to compare their fortunes with. And if they don't see us in our slums their own places might not seem so wonderful.'

Margaret skilfully engineered the debate so that those on the floor who wanted to speak were given the chance, and the press was forced to listen and note. She wondered how much they would report. The presence of a BBC tv camera man, and another with recording equipment, was consoling – even if the latter had not turned up until halfway through the proceedings. However, he was in time to record the bitterness the men voiced at having been encouraged to buy their council houses (rotten with unattended dry and wet rot) with mortgages they would not be able to keep up when the factory closed. Most of them would lose their jobs. Depending upon how long they had worked at Cold Plant, they would receive severance pay, a lump sum. Then they would be lumbered; there was almost no other work in the neighbourhood and they would not be able to sell up and move. Even if the university were to expand, no don, no student would consider lodgings at Coldston.

Walking back to Oxford with Edmund, Margaret was still consumed by impotent rage. 'I really don't understand the point of getting a degree if it doesn't make you feel. What's the point of a history degree, for example, if it doesn't move the graduate to reverence for the people of *today*? How many history graduates come out here to see what's going on? And you with your PPE. You actually know how the economy works. Are you proposing to see that in the future it works for the benefit of the poor?'

'Yes. At least, I'll try. I'm just as sickened by what I've seen as you are. I don't want to live in a country where there's such polarisation. I'll have to do something about it. I can't enjoy my privileges knowing that they're dependent on another's lack of privilege. When I was a boy I was quite religious until I discovered that the vicar didn't seem to care about improving the conditions of the poor – only about giving charity. Then I somehow lost religious feeling and got into travel and study and women. I think what I've seen out here is going to have a considerable effect on me.'

'Julia Bruton's invited me to dine at Marlowe this evening,' Margaret said. 'Will you be in Hall?'

'I haven't actually been invited, but I've no doubt dear old Jeremiah could sort something out for me. Let's dine together!'

Sir Augustus Eddington surveyed his guests from the top table. Between mouthfuls of venison he explained to Professor Lunquist that at Marlowe College they did not eat their Fellows. He waited, knowing that the professor must be wondering whether she had heard him correctly.

112

'You don't eat your fellows, Sir Augustus. I am most reassured to hear it.'

Sir Augustus never tired of this particular jape, the ambiguity provided valuable conversational ballast when it came to keeping conversation with delegates afloat. First the challenge; then the query; next, confusion; finally, exposition. It had the structure of philosophical discourse. He watched the beautiful professor add redcurrant jelly to a slice of venison, and as she raised her fork to her mouth he started on his explanation. He knew exactly how much time he would need – a full mouth of meat and sauce, followed by three or four French beans and a draught of claret.

'We have deer in our park – you must have seen them. Delightful they are. As an integral part of our college, they are Fellows. Naturally, to eat them would be an act of cannibalism – and so we eat others. That is to say, we eat the Fellows of Magdalen College.' The Master of Marlowe had never failed to raise a smile of appreciation with this explanation, and he waited for Professor Lunquist's lip to curl. He waited in vain, however. The professor was a solemn woman, and although not entirely uninterested in what the Master had been telling her, it was as an example of Oxford folklore that she treasured his explanation, noting that it was all the more valuable for being casuistic.

The buzz of conversation was continuous and approving; Marlowe had done its guests proud. As Sir Augustus surveyed the scene he felt well satisfied; another financial disaster had been postponed, the Dean had told him so. And he had been pleased to congratulate the Dean on both his foresight and his organisational skills – at the same time allowing the Dean to understand that the Master's own lack of organisational skills fitted him more perfectly for academe.

Margaret and Edmund had been seated at a side table through the good offices of Jeremiah Jenkins. Before leaving her room, Julia had rung for Mr Jenkins and handed the scout a note for Margaret, care of Edmund Marshall. She told Jeremiah that she had invited her friend to dinner that night in Hall, and hoped that even though she herself would not be present, Jeremiah would find a place for her. 'She may like to come along with Edmund Marshall.' Jeremiah, observing that Dr Bruton was somewhat distressed, hoped it was nothing serious. Julia reassured him. 'Will you be *driving* back to London?' he had asked, and on being told that she would, recommended her to take great care.

It was by chance that he had been walking through the cloisters to the porter's lodge with Julia's note in his pocket when Margaret and Edmund were entering the lodge on their return from Coldston. They had bumped into each other and Jeremiah had handed Margaret the note.

'Oh dear! Whatever's the matter?' Edmund had asked, surprised by the look of shock on Margaret's face.

'Julia's left.'

'Left? I thought she was delivering her paper tomorrow.'

'Perhaps that's why she left,' Margaret said caustically, adding quickly, 'But it's not like her. Utterly out of character. I think she must be ill. I do wish I'd known, I'd have travelled back with her.'

Now, oblivious of the lavishness of the feast they were consuming, Edmund and Margaret were talking hard. 'When Diderot was in Russia he remarked on the uncleanliness of the peasants, and on reflection said, "*Pourquoi auraient-ils soin d'un corps qui ne leur appartient pas?*" ' They found one another stimulating company, and parried quotes. Margaret was impressed by Edmund's firm gentleness and the fact that he seemed able to accommodate new ideas without seeming to be threatened by them. Edmund was impressed by the extent of Margaret's involvement in her work and the fact that she was prepared to be labelled 'unreasonable' in her determination to change society. In the late evening they were still talking in the garden, inhaling tobacco plant and listening to a nightingale. Edmund turned the conversation from work to ask Margaret about Julia.

'She's a wonderful supervisor,' Margaret said at once. 'Unlike most, she gives me all the time I need. She's generous and committed. She's one of only two lecturers in our department that one could term educated. When Julia's interested in a subject, she's informed about it; she doesn't wear her interests as badges, she gets really involved. She's astonishingly well-read. She can relate things to other things. She doesn't live in a political vacuum.'

'D'you see her socially?'

'From time to time I visit. Her husband's a decent man but he's a banker, of all things. He certainly doesn't have her depths. I often wonder how she can live with someone whose whole direction must be so different from her own.'

Had anyone known what had happened to Julia and had anyone asked her how she felt about it, she would undoubtedly have said, surprised. She would have laughed a short, bitter laugh and changed the subject. But it was much more than surprise that she felt; she felt dirty and degraded. She was unused to thinking about her feelings in so far as they related to her personal life. Since she had been married, she had taken it for granted that feelings look after themselves. After all, she didn't think about water, it runs from the tap . . . Whatever it was that had happened to her over Massimo was both unexpected and disturbing, but she couldn't identify all her responses to him. She knew that she had to get away from him, but she also knew that she was in love with him. She felt the desire both to be with him and to escape him. An internal war raged.

She remembered how in the past she had occasionally woken with similar feelings of disturbance. She put those feelings down to having had a dream, the details of which would not surface but remained obstinately in her unconscious mind; she must have found herself in some threatening situation and been disorientated . . . As with the dreams, so now with Massimo. She had no control over the anxiety aroused; she had to cope with feelings with which she was entirely unfamiliar. She felt unequal to this.

She had so wanted to please Massimo, but the only way he left open to her was to gratify him sexually. He wasn't interested in her personally, he despised her academically. And the worst of it was, it was precisely *because* he wasn't interested in

115

her as an individual, *because* he despised her mind, that he desired her – and desired to have her submit to practices that disgusted her.

If only he'd gathered her naked to him, kissed and caressed her and penetrated her lovingly! If only he'd capitulated to her, allowed her to risk expressing the feelings of tenderness, mutuality – even joy – that encroached upon her, despite his brutality.

She worried that the thought of Massimo would never leave her, that it would persist as a constant, continuous ache. The experience had opened up a chasm within her; she needed passion in her life. Did it only come accompanied by violence?

She had not noticed the journey. Not a single landmark on the darkening road between Oxford and Hampstead had impressed itself on her mind. She looked behind her, on the back seat. Thank goodness! She had not forgotten her suitcase and her papers.

It was well after midnight by the time James got home with Bates. He had noticed some way from the house that all the lights were blazing.

'Julia! You back?' he called from the front door and, walking into the drawing-room, he added, 'I didn't think it was burglars, more like *son et lumière* – without the *son*.' And he went over to Julia to kiss her, scratching her shoulder on the thorns of the roses he was carrying.

'Anything the matter?' he enquired when she did not speak, but without waiting for an answer he went on, 'Roger Perot cut these for us. Aren't they glorious?' And he walked over to the cupboard in search of a vase. Julia remained stock-still on the sofa where she had installed herself some two hours earlier.

'It's good to have you back, but why did you cut short your conference? Where shall I put these?' He did not seem aware of the fact that Julia did not reply. He set the vase on the Queen Anne table that stood behind the sofa – having decided against putting the flowers on the chest under the window – and then made his way to Julia's side. He sat down at an angle to her so that he could look into her face.

'Darling, you don't look at all well. And what's this?' pointing to her neck and gently tracing the bruise with his finger. 'My God! It looks as if someone's tried to strangle you. Do "conflict" and "peace" resort to those lengths these days to shut one another up?'

Julia did not smile with him. She picked up her scarf and wound it back round her neck. 'It's nothing,' she managed, 'I just don't feel . . .' And she got up and walked towards the kitchen.

James followed close on her heels. 'Would you like some coffee?' he asked. 'Are you feeling ill?'

'I'm not ill but I don't feel well.'

'PMT?' he asked concernedly. Julia raged inside, but she quickly calculated that this explanation offered her an alibi and she grasped at it.

'Yes. It was so severe that I just couldn't stay on and put myself through more political and conceptual hoops. It was obvious that my paper wasn't going to go down well, anyhow.' She sensed that what she had said was unconvincing, but she could rely on James not to probe. He always shied away from situations that looked emotional.

'Oh, well, I'm sure it doesn't really matter. It's not going to ruin your career. But it's a shame, after all the preparation . . .' And he got on with brewing coffee and pouring two glasses of brandy. All the while he moved around the kitchen, Bates sat by Julia's side, his head on her knee.

Julia was overwhelmed by the feeling of safety that James, Bates and the house bestowed. She looked around at the familiar kitchen and the objects she had lovingly collected. She watched James at the sink, clearing away some of the leaves he had removed from the stalks of the roses. She looked down at Bates. Everything was as it had always been, everything, that was, except herself.

'You can tell me all about the conference tomorrow. I can see you're exhausted. While you drink that down I'll run you a bath and get you a couple of Asprin.'

When James left the kitchen Julia tried turning her neck this way and that. It was horribly painful. She wandered into the hall. The briefcase and holdall that she had dropped on the floor when she entered the house had been neatly stacked by the side of the umbrella stand. James would, she thought. Tomorrow she would unpack . . . Not now.

When she had bathed and chosen a nightdress with a high neck, she slipped between the sheets of her twin bed and swallowed the two tablets James had left beside a glass of water.

'Do ring the Perots tomorrow,' James said. 'They want to know whether next week's picnic's still on.'

Is anything still on? wondered Julia. James blew her a kiss and turned out the light. She did not hear him ease himself quietly into bed.

Saturday

James had got up and gone out. He had taken Bates for a run on the Heath. Julia felt drugged. A veil had descended over her being and everything outside herself seemed remote. Only after some time had elapsed did she manage to pull herself out of bed and into some clothes and down into the kitchen. She heard the front door open and Bates stampede across the hall. James was calling to the dog; he would be wiping the animal clean of mud . . . shortly he would come into the kitchen. She would tell him . . .

'I've been having an affair!' She stood by the garden door, looking out on to the terrace with her back to James. James was standing at the other end of the kitchen, taking a bottle of milk from the fridge. He made no comment; she repeated her confession.

'Are you going on with it?'

'No!'

'Well then, there doesn't seem to be any point in discussing it.'

'Christ! Don't be so bloody reasonable!'

'What d'you expect me to be? I'm certainly not going to create a scene.' And then, after a pause during which he poured coffee for himself and added cold milk, he said that he was sorry *she* appeared to be so upset.

'Look! I want to talk about it!'

'No, Julia, that would be an unwarranted indulgence,' and he ostentatiously turned the pages of the *Financial Times*.

'*He was a fascist!*' she shouted. But James did not look up from the paper.

Julia felt frantic. She remembered that James prided himself on being able to spot the signs of indulgence at a hundred yards. His quiet, passive response angered her. She knew that he was feeling utterly confident in the rightness of it; she knew that he was incapable of confronting passion with passion – only with reason. But if he had hit her it might at least have relieved her of some of her feelings of guilt. Did she have guilt about sex? Was that why she had collaborated with Massimo's brutality?

She and James had agreed, in the past, that it was only sexual licence that the English ever condemned with real force – none of the other human misdemeanours aroused their ire to the same extent. Was James now bearing in mind his general objection to this tunnel vision? Or was he indifferent to her betrayal? But was it betrayal? She had not regarded it as such, why should he? Her thoughts were running ahead of her, she was unable to sort the chaff from the grain.

Had she betrayed James? His expectations of her no doubt included fidelity, but was this something that he could rightly assume? She had been rather more true to him than she had sometimes wished, having to remain quiet when his city friends expressed social and political views with which she did not agree. She had actually felt herself compromised on more than one occasion. James had never felt obliged to show the same restraint with some of her academic colleagues.

By letting another man see her naked, arouse her to an abandon that James had never succeeded in achieving for her, was she betraying him – or his rather immature and unimaginative love-making? Surely, she was entitled to her own gratification . . . And she probably wouldn't have embarked on this affair if her life with James had satisfied her erotically. An affair is not the cause of the breakdown in a relationship, it is a symptom. They had often agreed as much, in respect of other people.

James was a courteous lover. He had always been considerate. He had a small appetite for sex, himself, but when aroused, he always asked whether she was in the mood, whether it was a propitious time in the month and so on. He would tell her – rather mechanically, on reflection – that he found her attractive, and on occasions would admit to lascivious thoughts in the pub at lunch, when the prospect of rushing home and slipping between the sheets with her appeared rosier than downing another bottle of claret with old so-and-so and getting a headache. But being courtly was no substitute for being passionate. James had never bowled her over in a field or undressed her in the car. Indeed, he had always said that he was strictly a bed man.

She had not spoken ill of James to Massimo. She had not spoken of him at all. No, she had not betrayed James. It might very well be that in the years of her marriage she had betrayed herself, however. Had she ever, in fact, been true to herself?

She would never see Massimo again. He was the sort of individual who took pains not to let his sexual activities interfere with either his professional or his social life. He would simply pick up another 'lay' at the next conference. She would not go to Geneva; she was not going to stand by and watch Massimo seduce another female delegate. Smooth as asphalt; impervious as a giant bull sea-lion; a scrupulous planner; a man who would turn his mind quickly from anything vexing it. He would have forgotten her by now. It was terrible! He had just used her, and she had not only allowed it but welcomed it. How could she have gone on making love to a man who did violence not only to her body but also to her mind?

He was a fascist. He had clearly been involved in some capacity or other with the station bombings in Italy. Should she have informed someone? The bombings were, after all, the bloodiest terrorist outrage since World War II. Massimo believed in blind obedience to an aristocratic leader because he knew that once a man takes orders he no longer thinks for himself. He wanted that obedience from the mass of people; he wanted that from her. He had not quite succeeded with her but, in a way, he had done worse; he had influenced her to act immorally. She had known his views, and for that reason alone she should not have yielded to him. How was it that she had actually fallen in love with him? Or was it true, was he right, and she had merely confused being sexually attracted with falling in love?

He had not liked anything that she liked. The English countryside for example. While she took him round an English country garden, all he had done was to describe to her olive groves and vineyards. He had not admired the architecture of Oxford colleges, and instead of looking carefully at medieval Marlowe, had gone on about the virtues of Siena. He despised English style in all its manifestations.

He was unusually rich for an academic . . . How much of the neo-fascists' funds, she wondered, made their way into his pockets? Was he perhaps a member of the Masonic lodge, P2?

When she turned from the garden door and faced into the kitchen, she found herself alone. It made her anxious; she ran to look for James. He was not in his study, he must have gone out. She turned on the radio. A politician was answering questions on a phone-in.

'And what's yer salary?' asked the caller.

'Just over eighteen thousand a year,' the MP answered agreeably. And to the caller's suggestion that the *average* wage would be more appropriate for those who 'unlike yer nurses, yer doctors and yer teachers get subsidised meals and other perks', the politician earnestly explained that only by offering more than the average wage could the public hope to attract men (always men) of quality to represent them.

Julia was too dispirited to take up her pen and unload her derision. Matters that did not immediately affect her would have to wait. But her irritation threshold was peculiarly low. Her stomach knotted as she listened to the politician pronounce secretary 'secetary', and recognise 'recernise'. And when he spoke of 'mature behaviour' – meaning the espousal of his government's thinking – she thought her head would burst; and when he intoned 'responsibility' – meaning that owed by the poor to the rich – she wondered how it was that the mass of people didn't rise up, if only in indignation, and jam the radio waves. Was Massimo right? Does the mass encourage its own subjection? (He made me a prisoner and I didn't try to escape . . .) One thing is sure, she thought, politicians have an especially well-tuned sense of what and how much they can get away with . . .

'The majority of British workmen deplore the violence on the picket line,' the MP was saying. Julia wondered whether he had ever had a cup of tea or a mug of beer with a single British workman. Actually, she thought, what the British workman deplores is the violence of poverty and injustice.

The so-called Enterprise Society was not one to which Jesus would have subscribed. And this a Christian country . . . Founded by bigots, prejudiced moralists, on vulgarised Darwinism. Jesus would have chucked the Whitehouse School of Moralisation and all who belonged to it on the moneylenders' pile . . .

One of their number was being asked, 'And what does it mean to love your neighbour as yourself?'

'God knows!' he replied, and laughed. It seemed that the School of Moralisation positively welcomed the advent of AIDS, triumphant in the belief that God sees to it that vice carries its own punishment . . . Similarly with unemployment: 'The debris of society deserves its misery.' Some wit had said that the Minister for Trade and Industry had the franchise for boredom. Certainly no one could rabbit on more tediously about Britain's wonderful products, which were being exported in ever greater numbers due to the wonderful Enterprise Society, than he. But was he telling the truth? Was the whole world suddenly buying British? Julia thought of her French car, her Italian fridge, her German cooker and dish-washer. She had a Japanese typewriter and there, on the bookcase, was a box of Belgian chocolates. Her English tumble dryer, she had been advised, was not worth repairing after five years' use . . .

The sky outside the kitchen windows had turned black and it had started to rain. Tears came to Julia's eyes as she remembered Massimo in bed at The Primrose Inn. He had been tender, there. Oval crystals fell out of the sky; she watched from the window as they broke on the York paving-stones, turning the terrace from light to dark grey. She pushed open the window and remembered the river. The scent from the earth in the tubs on the terrace was delicious. Would she ever be able to think of Oxford, of Marlowe College, of Stanton Place, of corn shocks, without thinking of Massimo? Would this veil ever lift? Would the searing pain ever subside? She was not in control, not even of her own grief.

She picked up James's *Financial Times*. There was an article by Henry Neswel that she would read. She liked the critic's elliptical style. 'Bad fiction is like advertising,' he started, 'it uses ordinary materials and relationships and through a web of fantasy associates them with our imaginative longings for a world transformed according to our wishes.' He's right. He's spot on, she thought. Bad fiction is infantile; it reproduces the way of the infant who creates the breast that feeds him. All any of us wants is gratification. She felt a mounting bitterness. The admen and the cheap fiction writers know our weaknesses and feed off them royally. There are no values more ingrained than those controlled by our pockets and our sexual desires. Most of what is written and makes 'compulsive' reading has its eyes on the reader who needs to be distracted. It is as dangerous to the living as alcohol is to the liver. And the mornings-after are equally dispiriting.

Before her stretched the eternity of desolation that lies beyond the failed love affair. Irremediable grief bore down on her. The events of the past week were diffuse and would not form themselves into a coherent picture; they belonged to the world of nightmare.

All through the last week, the predominant mood, the enveloping atmosphere, had been one of violence – at Coldston, at Lord Stanton's, between the delegates and, above all, with Massimo. It had left her feeling threatened on all sides. And now James wouldn't listen to her, just as Massimo had had no wish to listen to her or understand her. Their refusals negated her. She had lost control over her destiny; all certainty had dissolved. Massimo had said that certainty was the most basic desire men had. Even when a man was to be hanged he still wanted to know the date of his execution.

On reflection, Julia realised that Massimo was not the first man about whom she had been deceived and with whom she had experienced an awesome loss of identity. There had been her father. And just before she and James had decided to get together, there had been André Fournier. She was eighteen at the time, André was thirty-five.

André Fournier was not the man's real name. He was not, as he claimed, related to Alain-Fournier at all – although he was extraordinarily well-informed on all the details of the writer's life, and had a passion for his work. Julia first became suspicious of André's claim to a French father when she caught him carefully pronouncing *fleur de lys* without the final 's'. The position became altogether clear when she was visiting André for tea one day and he slipped out for cigarettes. She picked up a biography of Alain-Fournier that was lying on the desk and discovered that not only had it been heavily annotated in André's hand, but that a list of dates and places relating to the most important events in the writer's life had been pasted on to the inside cover, presumably as an *aide-mémoire*.

André used to take her to the cinema, where he indulged his taste for exploring Julia's body in such a way as to arouse her to transports of delight that were not equalled until she met Massimo.

Julia would have thought little of André's illegitimacy had she known of it then. As it was, André imposed upon her – with vigour – the fantasy he had concocted, together with a range of religious ideas and practices which included long walks at night in unlit places when the moon was full, and a great deal of talk about sacrifices and blood. The difference in their ages led Julia to follow André's instructions unquestioningly, and it was only when he told her that they would have to sacrifice a cat to the moon later in the month that her eighteen-year-old self took fright and fled. But her mind had been less fleet than her limbs, and for many years Julia was subject to panic attacks at the full moon. It was only when, years later, she discovered that André's biography was as questionable as his religious practices, and she had been taken for a ride, that his influence evaporated.

Julia wondered whether having had so little experience of men had predisposed her to being taken in by them. She had always regarded James as the archetype of the understanding man, but perhaps James had only acquired this reputation because he had never been called upon to understand anything that might have threatened his assumptions, or questioned his ideals. He paid lip-service to some of her political views – he was a unilateralist – but tended to avoid discussions relating to social issues. What did it mean to be understanding? Some people who were indifferent – who had efficient shock-absorbers – were termed understanding. Very often all it implied was that X was not bowled over by a piece of information received from Y, whose revelation had annoyed or shocked the rest of the alphabet.

If she couldn't get understanding from anyone else, Julia decided, she would have to get it from herself. If only she could understand why she had done it. She wouldn't be able to discover the reason by using her normal thinking processes . . . She recalled the story of the man on his knees in the street being asked by a neighbour what he was doing. He replied that he was looking for a small coin he had dropped in the kitchen. 'Why, if you lost it in the kitchen,' his neighbour enquired, 'are you looking for it in the *street*!?' 'The light is better outside,' the man had replied.

She could not pretend that it had never happened – even if that was what James would prefer. In some way it seemed to her that her affair had been a seminal event in her life. Crucial. Momentous. And if it were not so, how much worse it would have been, for it was appalling to do anything that did not matter. Of course, James would prefer her to keep the mask intact. Appearances must be more important to him than she had imagined. Yet what is the point of experience unless it changes a person? She had heard Iris Murdoch say that the worst thing that could happen to *her* would be to discover that it did not matter how she behaved.

PART II

Autumn

The days crawled by. Time decomposed. Julia could not remember when she had last faced herself in the looking-glass. Such glimpses as she had caught, terrified her. She had given up brushing her hair and putting on make-up, and she had turned the full-length cheval-glass in the bathroom to the wall. She knew that she had lost weight; she was all skin and bones. What food she was able to swallow seemed to pass through and out of her within a couple of hours. Memories of Massimo faded, taking on a dreamlike quality. But he was still more real to her than anyone else. James, for instance.

She had no energy. She was listless. It was an effort to pull a cardigan over her nightshirt, and put on socks and get down the stairs. She was breathless and her heart thumped. Every morning after James left for work, she waited impatiently for the front door to slam and for Bates to return to James's study. When she heard these sounds she went downstairs to the kitchen and drank some milk; then she dragged herself upstairs to the bedroom and sat in bed or in the armchair with a blanket round her. She kept the curtains drawn tightly across the windows. She couldn't bear the light. She listened to Brahms's *German Requiem* over and over. Sometimes she had it on all day. Bates and the cat would moan behind her door or scratch until she mustered enough energy to get up and let them in. Her only response was to the animals; she stroked them. The only words she spoke were to the animals. She did not envisage doing anything. In the past, she recalled, she used to lecture, read, write, go to the theatre and out to dine. It all seemed a long time ago, in a remote past belonging to someone else. And she remembered going out into the country for long walks with James and Bates. She had been abroad . . . But the memories lacked impact, for they were not accompanied by any feelings – either of pain or pleasure. She was in a state of limbo.

By the side of her bed was a pile of books. She felt no urge even to open them. She had lost all curiosity. Inside her cupboard were neatly stacked piles of silk underwear, cashmere sweaters, stockings in every colour and design. In the wardrobe hung suits, dresses, trousers, skirts, smocks, shirts and jackets, by Jean Muir, Issey Miyake and Jasper Conran. She had no desire to look at them, let alone put them on. Instead, day in and day out she wore an old nightshirt and cardigan that James had cast off. She was conscious that her condition was an unfamiliar one, but she felt no alarm; she noted that she did not have the energy or imagination to feel alarm. All she desired – and this with her whole being – was to be left alone. As soon as she thought someone or something might impinge on her isolation, she felt panic. She would not, she could not see anyone. She peeped out between the curtains on to the garden. She might, one day, go into the garden. She might. She wondered whether this state in which she found herself was the living death of the Ancient Mariner. Would she need, in the end, to tell her tale until she was understood?

But that time, if it ever came, was far off. Now, she could not talk. She had told James that she did not want to talk to him. She had nothing to say. She had shut the door quietly in his face the morning after her return from Oxford, and had not seen him since. He had moved into his study, where he slept on the couch.

For the first time since they had been married, James felt irritated by his wife. She had had an affair! So what! Hadn't everyone in their circle, bar him, had an affair? Why on earth was Julia making such a production of it? He was excellent at looking after himself – and they had always shared the chores – but he wasn't going to take on the whole thing unaided, for ever . . . It was all very well for Julia, lying in bed all day, playing the same bloody piece of music and looking like Miss Haversham. But what was he going to tell everyone? Julia's had an affair with a neo-fascist and it's gone sour? She's ashamed, she can't face anyone? He wondered whether he was hurt. Did he feel cuckolded?

He had contacted their GP, Dr Grimshaw, and asked the elderly doctor to write out a certificate so that Julia could claim sickness benefit. Gladyse was lecturing in Ireland at the beginning of Michaelmas term and did not telephone. James agreed with her colleague at Paine that Margaret and another post-graduate student share out the tutorials, and that visiting lecturers should be contacted to do the rest. Grimshaw informed James, after examining Julia, that her blood pressure was on the high side but that otherwise he could find nothing physically wrong with her. He wrote out a prescription for tablets for the blood pressure, and for anti-depressants. Julia took neither; every morning she threw her daily dose down the lavatory. 'I think she could do with a good holiday,' Grimshaw tried. But he was no diagnostician. A hundred years ago he would have attributed Julia's depression to ancestor interference, or witchcraft. 'Time of life, perhaps,' he suggested to James.

Friends had accepted James's explanation of 'Julia's a bit under the weather . . . No, nothing serious . . . Grimshaw's prescribed some medication . . . says Julia needs rest . . .' But they translated the explanations into something more specific. 'Julia's overdone things, she's always overdoing it. She's approaching *un certain âge*.' (Wink, wink.) 'Her hormones are probably playing up. She's very ambitious; she's been thoroughly disappointed with the reception of "The Autistic Society". What a title! What could she expect? I imagine the marriage's gone a bit stale . . . She probably regrets not having had children, found it's a bit late now . . .' And the same friends were unanimous in deciding that their contribution to Julia's convalescence would be to take James off her hands. They invited him, every night, to accompany them to the theatre, to the cinema and out to dinner.

Margaret accepted neither James's explanation nor the

conclusions that his friends had come to. She alone ignored James's ordinance not to visit. She turned up regularly with flowers, *Vogue* and *Elle* and fragrant soap and bath oil. She tactfully never insisted on seeing Julia, but left long, newsy letters about how and what she was teaching, the students' reactions, and what was going on generally at Paine, and how the visiting lecturers were coping. Gladyse was offering them £23 an hour, and most of those the college had tried to get had declined to lecture for such an absurd fee. Margaret would have been hurt if she had known that Julia did not read her letters or look at the magazines or take any pleasure in the flowers. For weeks she did not bathe. Tirelessly, Margaret interrogated James about Julia's condition. Was she making any progress? Was she seeing a doctor regularly? She gathered from James's confused replies that Julia was very ill indeed – having a breakdown. She felt uneasy about James's ambiguous attitude. One the one hand he appeared concerned, on the other hand he seemed irritated, as if Julia were responsible for her condition, and making a meal of it.

'I have to say I was surprised that she left without giving her paper,' Margaret told him. 'It wasn't like her.'

'D'you know whether she had reason to be particularly apprehensive about its reception?'

'No! I don't know. But I do know that the Conflict group included some extremely right-wing delegates. There was an Italian who was obviously a neo-fascist, who seemed to be latching on to Julia. Knowing her politics, this did seem odd. I don't know whether he warned her off.'

The days became weeks. Julia continued to shut herself in her room with the receiver off the telephone, refusing to answer the front door bell. On Fridays, when Spick & Span's men came to clean the house, she locked herself in her room. James stocked the refrigerator and replaced the telephone receiver when he came into the house. He listened out for Julia's movements. He would hear the lavatory chain pulled and, occasionally, at night he heard her go down into the kitchen. Every Monday he rang Grimshaw and reported to him. (Julia had refused to see the old GP after the first visit.)

Grimshaw told James that Julia's method of regaining her strength by withdrawing was probably a sensible one. James accepted the reassurance gratefully. One day in early November, when he was belatedly removing the geraniums from the tubs on the terrace to over-winter them in the cold greenhouse, he noticed that Julia's window was slightly open and that the curtain had been drawn back. And then he remembered that not only had more fruit and salad than usual gone from the fridge, but a whole cooked chicken had disappeared.

Julia had not spoken to anyone for two months – only to the animals, monosyllabically. Now she tried out her voice in sentences to Bates and the tabby. It sounded odd, and she did not know what to say to them. 'Are you all right? Are you eating and sleeping well and taking exercise . . . ?' she asked the animals. And then she went to the linen cupboard and took out fresh sheets and a bath towel and a nightdress. She poured some of the oil Margaret had sent her into the tub, and when she had bathed and dried herself she rubbed herself all over with body oil. She savoured the heady scents. The exercise had pleased her, but it had exhausted her, and after it she slept. When she woke she did not play the Brahms but chose, instead, some Fauré piano pieces. She registered an unaccustomed feeling of hunger for things she liked. She went down into the kitchen and fetched a tray of food: lumpfish roe, bread rolls and salt-free butter, apple juice and fresh lychees. In the hall she found a parcel addressed to her in Margaret's hand. She opened it to find a copy of Costain's *English Postwar Painting*. While she ate, she flipped through the pages.

The naked truth – but not the whole truth! Before her sprawled a woman, naked on a couch, seen from some three feet from her gaping vagina. The model's face was frozen in an unblinking stare. Objective, scientific scrutiny, Julia realised, reveals only part of the truth. Perception is a representation of reality, not a reflection of it . . . This painter makes no effort to establish a relationship with his sitter; he makes do with a visual presence. Norman Stowe is a master of technique, and technique is vision. And if this is vision, it's horrific. Women feel, damn it! They love, they suffer. She put down the book. She was weeping. Women feel, damn it . . . Stowe was clearly not interested in any of that. He'd got this woman to collude with him in a denial of her humanity; in violation of it. Massimo had done that with her and she'd colluded with him – delivered to him the naked truth. He too had seen her as a slab of meat drained of all humanity. He too had failed to celebrate her, as he systematically pursued his own quest. Why do women collude?

She turned the page. Another Stowe! A young man sitting on a couch looking towards an older, clothed man who resonated money and power. The situation was unequivocal; the older man would buy the younger man's favours, and because the older man was rich and powerful he would take what he wanted and ignore the rest. He wouldn't notice the money the transaction cost him, and for many years the younger man wouldn't notice the cost to his humanity. She thought back to Coldston. She thought of James. Was this like James and her? Why hadn't Stowe shared the woman he painted with other women? He needed to violate them himself, no doubt. It's easy to sleep with a woman. It's more difficult to be intimate with her.

What is the purpose of a painting such as this? Julia asked herself. But she contradicted herself almost at once. That's a foolish question. Today art has no purpose but to be itself; it's decadent; it's become a commodity like other commodities. It's sold by merchants to people wanting to forge social personae.

The naked men and women painted by Stowe were a metaphor for contemporary society, a society in which scrutiny is objective, uninformed by imagination and compassion. All optics; no perceptions. To analyse is not to reveal – merely to organise. The paintings are well organised. They're not only scientific, they're managerial . . .

Stowe was dyed in the vat of his time, a Thatcherite painter moved not by spirit but by determination. A narcissist, who imposed his vision to the extent of denying others their identity, their autonomy. He can't love! Suddenly Julia realised that all this had its roots in an inability to love – the sort of love born of care, respect, knowledge and understanding. Stowe, too, was a product of the autistic society . . .

She had eaten without noticing what she ate. She had sat poring over Costain for an hour, in sustained contemplation. She closed the book. Her face was taut with dried tears. She felt that something within her had shifted, her mind had been galvanised. The clues to her dilemma resided in that inexpressible region that lies between thought and feeling. If she could work her way between the certainties to what lay flickering at the margin of her feelings, her thoughts, she might savour those mercurial flashes in which, she was starting to believe, lay the explanations. How can I bear witness to my experience when it eludes me whenever I try to pin it down? she wondered. She would need to explore the unknown aspects of her being that rose like sparks in a fire but, tantalisingly, exploded before she could take their measure. In the past she had always avoided prying into her own private affairs.

For some time, perhaps a couple of years, she had sensed, vaguely, that her life was dangerously bland – too much having, too little being. She had been on a production line, working her way from one small success to another. Yet she had known, at some intangible level, that she needed to be shaken out of her complacency, made to take risks. What had she been waiting for? She thought back to her early student days, before she committed herself to James. In those days she would never have colluded in a crime against her own humanity. Of course, when she was young she had thought more about herself. Since those days she had been thinking about other people; nations. But now that she had had the experience of being put in a compromising position that had disorientated her, she must think about who she really was. She must take thought for her conscience, for unless her conscience was available to reproach her, all would be lost. The cloak of dubiety in which Massimo had shrouded her was lifting. Perhaps Norman Stowe's sitters, unrevealed by him but certainly laid bare, discovered themselves in this way.

She was conscious that she suffered. She was conscious of the sufferings of the world. It was nonsense for James to insist that the world only looked bleak when the individual was feeling bleak himself. On the contrary, most people when they feel low are incapable of looking outside themselves. In her case it was more than possible that the years of studying the suffering and injustice in the world had taken their toll, exacerbated her feelings of impotence. And impotence created despair. She knew what there was to be done, but she did nothing; she was not only ineffectual but immoral. To feel adequate in the face of universal suffering she needed to forge a special relationship with herself – and then *do* something. Only then would she be potent. She would have to accept not only material discomfort but spiritual discomfort. She had become far too dependent on her job; it fascinated her, it gave her influence and status. Looked at squarely, she was just as much a prisoner of it as anyone else on any other production line. As for her liberal-with-a-small-'l' attitudes, at heart she had always known that they could never withstand fascism. Liberals accept the need for change in society, in the certain knowledge that they will not be called upon to make any personal sacrifices. All the liberal-minded folk Julia knew lived comfortably in pleasant surroundings on above-average incomes. She knew of none festering in tower-blocks twenty-seven storeys up in Tower Hamlets. She was not the first to observe, either, the way in which her acquaintances so easily reconciled high living with high principles.

If she were to stop colluding in what she judged immoral, she would have to make wholesale changes in her way of life. To start with, what was she doing living in this huge house while so many walked the streets by day, and slept rough by night? Enid and Arnold had *given* them this house! But even if she and James had earned the money to pay for it, was it legitimate to occupy more space than was strictly necessary? Only that morning she had switched on the radio while she bathed and heard a celebrated centre-Left interviewer challenge a guest, 'Is it true what the popular press says, that you binge on houses?'

'I'm afraid it is!' the far-to-the-Left actress giggled, part-prideful, part-embarrassed. 'I do. I've often wondered whether there's a medical name for it.'

'Probably only if the bingeing makes you sick. D'you know why you do it?'

'Well, you see, I was born in Wales but my father's Turkish, so it's quite natural that I should have a cottage in the Brecon Beacons to remind me of my childhood, and a sort of mud hut in Cappadocia to remind me of his.'

'But a little bird told me that you have also got a farm in Tuscany, not a thousand miles from one belonging to a very celebrated author. Was your mother Italian?'

'She was not,' the actress replied crossly, 'but if it's Crystal Farqueson you're referring to, yes we do share some land. We grow peaches together.' The interviewer made some odd noises with his tongue against the roof of his mouth. They could have been involuntary, an indication of 'Really now?' or intended to express incredulity.

'And what about the place in New Zealand!'

The far-to-the-Left actress seemed to be squirming audibly. Julia imagined that she was sweating and turning away from the interviewer, blushing. She had a picture in her mind of a rather plump, preening woman with sweaty armpits vanishing into her double chins.

'Let me see, now. Four houses in all?'

'No, actually. I've a dear little *mas* in . . .'

'A dear little *what*?'

'*Mas*. It's Provençal for farmhouse. Mine's near Arles.'

'Isn't it terribly expensive, maintaining all these properties? And you can't live in them all at once.'

'Well, you could say the same of suits. You can't wear them all at once, but I bet you've got more than one!' The actress had scored. The interviewer was renowned for his natty dressing – but he was good at ignoring points against himself and quickly came back on the attack. 'How did you come by the money for this profligate spending?'

'First,' and Julia could hear that she was settling to be frank, in the way that people are when they propose to say the unsayable, 'first, I'm hugely successful.' Game and set; the interviewer clearly was not. 'Secondly, I'm hugely rich!' Match. There being no answer to that, the interviewer tried another tack. He asked the 'hugely successful', 'hugely rich' actress whether she had ever thought of keeping just one house for herself and giving the others to people without a roof over their head. She answered that such a thought had never crossed her mind.

James had had enough. He had his job to do, and now he had the house to run single-handedly. He was impatient; Julia had been indisposed long enough. People just shouldn't carry on in this way over an affair. And it wasn't as if he was playing the heavy husband . . . He had noticed, however, that Julia had somewhat changed her regime; she had taken clean sheets and towels out of the linen cupboard, and she had not only bathed but cleaned the bath after she had used it. He had heard her moving about her room – she was not spending the whole day in bed. He cornered her one evening in the kitchen.

'I think we'd better start talking,' he said. 'But we're not going to talk about what happened, we're going to talk about how best to get you on your feet again. I thought I might have a word with Jerry Bach and ask him to see you professionally.'

'James, whatever you do, don't on any account speak to Jerry about me!'

'He might be able to help,' James muttered into the shoes he was cleaning.

'I just couldn't bear friends being drawn into this. I will *not* discuss my life with anyone in our circle. Especially not Jerry.'

'But Jerry's a psychiatrist.'

'Jerry's a psychiatrist married to Sally!' This was irrefutable, and James did not argue. Sally was one of those women who, in an attempt to revenge herself on her mother for appropriating the affections of her father, slept with elderly married men and sought – and received – continuous understanding from Jerry, who, as he said himself, had a low libido. How could Julia discuss what she had been through with a man who should be looking at his own life, and helping his wife grow up instead of condoning her baby-doll demonstrations? Anyhow, Jerry was a Freudian, and she wasn't going to expose herself to anyone of that school of thought. James might think she had problems to solve, *she* thought she had complexities to understand. Jerry would not understand her any better than James. In addition to which, he would be deaf to her political and moral dilemmas. He would go on – and on – about her sexuality. And instead of sympathising with her desire to find a more creative way of living that would accord with her moral outlook, he would regard her struggle for a spiritual dimension to life as a substitute for dealing with repression. His was a value-diminishing, even value-denying, philosophy. Together with capitalism, it had created the conditions for the world in which she felt uncomfortable. 'Psychoanalysis is that mental illness for which it regards itself as therapy,' someone had said. Nor would she allow her life to be reduced to dust.

'I'm worried about you, Julia. It's something like ten weeks since you returned so precipitously from Oxford. You've hardly washed since then. You've not dressed yourself properly. You've been listening to the same bloody piece of music all day and all night. You've seen no one and spoken to no one. You've lost pounds of weight. This just can't go on!'

He's too stainless, Julia thought. Too blameless. James has probably never had to face making the wrong decision. His immediate reactions have always been reliable. Insincerity's unknown to him; his good, sincere reactions translate themselves into reasoned action. But he is inclined to regard life as a box of goodies to which he has the key, and that all that's expected of him is to feast. Pity he can't be imaginative with me, now . . .

Julia did not notice that James was waiting for her to say something. She meditated on her husband. He was a gradualist; he could envisage change – but only slow change. He saw that change would have to advance on many fronts, but seeing her advance on one front, quickly, must have thrown him. In the past she had suggested to him that this reasonable, tolerant attitude of his was all very well, but what if *urgent* change were imperative? She had cited the case of the poor – they couldn't wait for the GNP to increase, or the pound sterling to advance against the dollar, if what they badly needed was a square meal in the present. Now it was her own case at stake. In the past James had resorted to saying that Rome wasn't built in a day; that had not satisfied her then, and it did nothing to console her today. No one could deny that he was a kind man, and intelligent in an unflashy sort of way, but was he truly understanding? He had never been depressed. He might sympathise with her but, try as he might, he could not empathise.

'I'm sure what you're feeling, what you're going through, is real. Don't get me wrong. I don't for one minute imagine that you're making it all up or dramatising. It's just, well, you know; we Brutons are rather straightforward folk.'

She should have known not to get involved with someone who was going to go into merchant banking . . . Banking was not simply a job, it was a way of life. What was embarrassing to face was that she had wallowed in the material benefits; life in the Fowler household had been aesthetically bleak, and James had not only provided her with a magnificent house but had given her the means to fill it with lovely objects. Her own salary was enough to dress her stylishly . . . She supposed that they were a statistic in the five per cent at the apex of British society . . .

She had married too young. Her progress, far beyond the aspirations her parents had had for her, to her present job and her book, had led her to think quite differently. It was mostly 'think'; she seemed to have jettisoned feeling along the way – not the sort of feeling that went in to knowing what was just and fair for others, but the sort of feeling that would have encouraged her to satisfy some of the desires she suppressed.

James had said before she was ill that he would prefer her

to give up her job and stay at home, and be available to entertain business contacts. That was something she would never do. She had noticed in him a mounting inclination to mix with those people – politicians and industrialists – who were likely to bring in business. She was not going to be an arm of that purpose. But if, all the same, she was willing to spend the money James made from deals she regarded as destructive, what did that make her? Certainly not 'straightforward'.

Knowing that the Brutons were 'straightforward folk', it was perhaps surprising that the first thing Julia did when she felt able to face the outside world was to accept an invitation to go down to Selborne, to Enid and Arnold. Had they been living in Hull or Coventry she would have declined their invitation, but she felt a deep longing for the English country-side, for her mother-in-law's hospitality and her father-in-law's passion for Gilbert White. Down there she hoped that she might find not only the Bruton decency, but wisdom.

Julia parked the car in Wasps Lane, at the far end of Selborne village from the Brutons' cottage, and walked towards the zig-zag path. The path had been cut by Gilbert White and his brother, and led from the village street up into the Hangers and on to the Common. A huge branch sprawled across the path. Julia looked up at the scarred tree from which it had been wrenched; it seemed to her that the open wound was being dried out and healed by the wind. Years ago in these parts, if the branch had fallen, and hit and killed a villager, the whole tree would have been sentenced to death – burned, and its ashes scattered. In less rational times it was believed that the spirit of the tree was responsible for such accidents, and unless the tree paid the full price, the blood of the victim was not avenged. Julia wondered, would the wound heal, as she hoped, or would the open sore become infected, and the whole tree be poisoned?

She was standing not on the public path but in a cottager's garden. The fallen branch had felled part of the boundary fence. She looked at the cottage. The row of old shoes by the back door looked diseased. The back door was ajar, held open by a crock filled with rotting vegetables. The coat on the hook might have done double service as the dog's blanket. A chain attached to a pole sunk deep into the ground was evidence of the existence of a dog, but there was no dog about. Overhead, clouds were sailing confidently along a pale blue sky. Suddenly, the cottage door was hit by the wind's fist and the crock smashed, spilling its contents of withered carrots and mouldy potatoes at Julia's feet.

Julia decided that she would climb into the Hangers alone. If she waited for Arnold to accompany her, he would overwhelm her with his enthusiasm for White. She would wait until they were seated comfortably in the cottage to hear about the pyrites and ammonites White used to find, and their exact location. She would discover the mole-holes for herself and the 'secret dormitories' of house-martins. She knew all the varieties of mushroom and toadstool peculiar to the area, and Arnold would tell her later where the young boys used to find the wasps' nests they sold to White. But on this walk she did not want to receive information; she wanted experience. 'Conversation enriches the understanding, but solitude is the school of genius.'

She was grateful for the steps Gilbert and his brother had cut into the hill. She was grateful for the wooden bench placed at the summit of the path, before the entrance to the Hangers. From it, she sat and looked down on the village through a thin screen of green and bronze foliage. The rustle of late autumn rang consolingly in her ears. But as she turned into the gloom of the woods she was filled by a sense of awe.

Underfoot, fallen leaves and beechnut husks from many years' harvests, crisp and dry, registered every footfall. No hair-thin robin's legs or slithering snail could pass in silence. She remembered a clearing where there was a three-hundred-year-old beech stump. She would sit there and wait for deer. But after an hour, none had approached. She could hear the animals in the thickets, but they were well camouflaged and she could not see them. Occasionally, she heard one dart away from the far side of the thicket, away from her scent.

Along the path that skirted the wood and led to the

Common, an abundance of mullein, foxgloves, dog roses, old man's beard and brambles, together with other plants to which she could not attach names, grew with unfettered enthusiasm – and for their own sake. Riders sometimes mashed the lane, and villagers walked their dogs, but the flowers remained unpicked and the blackberries and elder-berries never came to jam or wine but rotted on their bran-ches. Everything was dying down, preparing for the future. She peered over a hedge. In the pasture the grass was bedraggled, and above it crows were reconnoitring for carrion. The ancient church, squat and square, crouched behind its wrought-iron gates in a garden of graves and weeds. She remembered how the graveyard sloped and how in a dark corner, out of the sun, was concealed a pond with an under-world of water-logged plants. The memory made her shiver. The graveyard at Binsey:

At dusk
Under the skin of molten pewter,
A shoal of dead fish.
Memories.

Someone – she had forgotten who – had written that the passing of belief in the immanence of God within nature led men to see the world as mindless, and therefore unworthy of moral or aesthetic consideration. He had forecast that man's alienation from nature, together with advanced technology, would lead to the end of the world. Julia was not convinced that the most stony-hearted of men were unmoved by nature – notwithstanding their atheism. Of course, the property speculators and chemical manufacturers who built unsym-pathetically over the land and polluted the rivers and killed the fish were beyond salvation but, oddly, many of them were church-goers; worshippers. It was simply that from Monday to Saturday they worshipped Mammon . . . The desire for profit resides deepest in those who fear the most; they have an overwhelming need to keep all their options open.

No doubt such men seek out island paradises for their

vacations, Julia thought, places undiscovered by other property speculators and manufacturers of chemicals. If it lost them money to rip open the land for gas, to dig deep into its bowels for minerals and cover it with detritus, they might well be persuaded to turn their attentions to other things. The only situation a businessman cannot endure is the absence of profit. It's a glass eye to an eagle.

As she turned on to the Common she noticed within two feet a barn owl staring at her from his perch on a hawthorn. He had apparently never before encountered human kind; he stared transfixed. And then, hearing something stir in the wood, he swivelled his head ninety degrees so that his feet and the back of his head faced forward. There was something so comical about the sight that Julia laughed out loud. He took off – his feelings hurt, perhaps. His flight was graceless; it was as if a cat were swimming through the air.

She loved the common. It never failed her. She could not walk across the grass, whether long and pink or closely cropped and luscious green, without tapping some deep interior satisfaction. She was not bored, that was the best of it. She had never registered boredom before these past weeks of shock. And then, when she had felt well enough to imagine herself in some occupation, it had been terrible to discover that she was without all energy. Previously she had imagined that boredom was the distemper of the rich; now she knew that it was the inability to be absorbed in life, and that it was as much an illness as depression and shock. The fact that the rich were bored did not necessarily mean that it was money that created boredom; rather, that the bored pursued money as a distraction.

She'd been bored with herself; she'd been bored with the world. It was *la morne incuriosité*; apathy. Bruton would put it down to dry heat in the liver and spleen, but she knew otherwise. It was disillusion. And the trouble with boredom as it had affected her was that it was all-consuming – she had become utterly self-centred. 'The man who loves only himself cannot, it is true, be accused of promiscuity in his affections, but he is bound in the end to suffer intolerable boredom from the inevitable sameness of the object of his devotion.' To be absorbed means to forget self.

It was one o'clock when Julia pushed open the garden gate and walked up the lavender-lined path to the porch at the front door of Enid's and Arnold's cottage.

'Darling! How lovely to see you!' And holding Julia at arms' length, Enid said, 'Let me look at you. Yes, you *are* thin. James warned me. I'm so sorry you've not been well. Was it one of these bugs that've been doing the rounds?'

'Not really, Enid. I'll explain later.'

Enid had prepared things that she knew Julia most liked to eat. While Arnold gathered up the glasses from which they had all drunk sherry in the conservatory, Julia and Enid carried a platter of smoked salmon into the dining-room. The cottage looked lovely – chintzy, with oak furniture, flowers everywhere, and hand-woven rugs spread across the polished oak floors. A *clematis orientalis*, planted by the door of the conservatory, strayed against one of the dining-room windows and pressed clusters of mustard-coloured flowers against the panes.

'This must be precisely how the average American imagines an English paradise.'

'How nice of you to say so, darling. We love it, and I'm glad you do too.' Enid was serving guinea-fowl that she had braised with vegetables from the garden. Arnold poured a vintage claret. Julia took pains to deflect the conversation from herself to Arnold's research and Enid's gardening. She did, however, admit that the conference had been 'a bit much' and that she had left before delivering her paper. She said in self-defence that she had assessed the political climate and come to the conclusion that those who would not receive the paper well far outnumbered those who would be sympathetic to it. 'I didn't want to be faced with awkward questions that I didn't feel entirely competent to answer.'

'I thought you argued your case cogently in the book, Julia. Did you have trouble with it when you had to reduce it for the paper?' Arnold showed concern.

'It wasn't so much that. I just found that I couldn't stand

the hostility. There was a much stronger "conflict" presence than I'd expected. In a way, the fact that I didn't deliver the paper – which, of course, they'd all had sent to them weeks before – illustrated better than anything I could have said, what I feel are the problems of communication.'

'More charlotte, darling?'

'No thank you, Enid. I've done very well indeed.'

'I thought you and Arnold might like to have a chat while I get on with the dishes. I don't want you coming all this way to stand at the sink, Julia. I want you two to get together.'

Perhaps James had said something . . . ?

'So! You got up into the Hangers before lunch, my dear! Good for you! It's marvellous up there at this time of year. D'you know, I go up every other day, and sometimes as much as a week or ten days will go by before I bump into anyone else. Occasionally a forester's there, or someone on horseback . . . I get to see a lot of wild life. Did you see deer?'

'Sadly, no. I heard them, though.'

'What a pity you didn't see them. They're shy, of course. They don't eat from my hand, I have to admit, but they do come and look me over.'

Arnold told Julia about the progress of his book, and how the move to Selborne had not only changed his life but improved it incalculably. 'But I didn't make this move for any other reason save that of being on the spot for my work. I think it's probably impossible to actually change one's life for the better through planning. We all yearn for something we can't define, something perfect. It's as if we're born with a model of paradise within us. I think I've found something of it here. I'm very fortunate.'

'Can you explain? Can you describe what you've found?'

'Peace. I think that's the nub of it. I feel re-integrated, as if the parts of my shattered self had come together.'

'Has Enid found this peace, too?'

'I don't think she's found quite what I've found. But I'm easier to live with these days, and she's made happier by that. Enid's a tidy person – rather too tidy for her own good, I

146

think. She finds emotions a bit chaotic. Likes to see the pyjamas in the drawer marked pyjamas – you know what I mean. She tends to be intolerant of my wanderings. I've tried to explain to her my need for solitude, but I think it hurts her to be told that real discoveries are made alone.'

Julia felt a surge of love for the man. He had encountered the sublime. He would understand her.

'The great thing to remember, Julia, is not to strive for certainty!'

Oh, the sweetness of those words!

'If you bind yourself to any one thing, come a great force, and you and your support will be dashed to pieces together. You must always give yourself room for some uncertainty. You know what Keats prescribed. "Negative capability . . . when a man is capable of being in uncertainties." '

'I know what you mean. A delegate at the conference, whose political outlook really terrified me, said that because man couldn't stand uncertainty it was up to the powerful to provide him with certainty. He said that because the mass of people know they're not going to win power for themselves over the productive means, they welcome, positively welcome, being organised so that they feel not *part* of the country – the community – but the country itself. A mighty battalion: one man under vigorous leadership. I suppose all men do feel certainty in the same way; it's uncertainty we experience individually. This same, awful man said that the mass need to feel as man first felt when he was part of nature under the authority of God. I was so struck by this. Have you noticed how people who believe in totally different things will yet use the same examples to illustrate what they mean – and interpret the examples to meet their own ends? Anyhow, so far as I can see, it's as dangerous to provide certainty for others as it is to seek it for oneself. "Negative capability" is an excellent goal.'

Enid brought in coffee. She was on her way out into the garden to tidy the vegetable bed. Did they love one another, Julia wondered, or was theirs merely the familiarity of long association?

Arnold, anyway, was clearly not comfortable, being ordered about by an anal obsessive . . . He took up an American literary journal to read an article on White. Julia rested her head against the back of the sofa and looked up at the oak beams. The only sound was coming from the apple boughs spitting in the grate. She was going to have to change her life radically. And, once acknowledged, this was something she would not be able to ignore. She wanted to put herself within grasp of illumination. She would need to be sure that what she was doing, and where she was doing it, were not factors that would militate against her discovery of peace. Her sense of identity could no longer be dependent on her job, and the luxury and status bestowed by an above-average income – but only on her own self-knowledge. She would have to let go. She would need to detach herself from belongings, from job, house, marriage. She would have to cease seeing herself climbing a ladder to more and to better, and live fully on the rung on which she found herself. The only matter to confront was human suffering. That didn't necessarily mean packing up and joining Mother Theresa; it might mean Hackney . . .

'Since I've been living down here,' Arnold said quietly, 'I've been considering what it really means to be alive and human. I've come to understand that to be alive and human isn't simply to be a person – a person in the process of accumulating knowledge and experience, imitating what other men have done and do, acquiring values that don't stand up to any sort of scrutiny, earning money doing jobs that aren't fulfilling – and, above all, entering into relationships that positively inhibit one's growth. No, to be human is to be free and fulfilled. The real problem as I see it is this: until you've experienced a sense of fulfilment, you don't know that that's what you've been after.' Arnold spoke slowly and emphatically and Julia could see that he had more to say and that he was pausing to gather the unruly strands. She did not interrupt him.

'The other day, I read something I think might be of interest to an academic like yourself. Among certain primitive tribes, knowledge is owned, rather as a collector owns a work of art; it provides status and can be bought and sold. The anthropologist wrote about this as if it were singular. He was evidently quite unaware that in our own primitive society the same applies. We in the West still don't understand that knowledge, like art, is a ware that can only be appreciated by those who know the difference between good and evil.'

'I've been thinking seriously of giving up teaching.' Julia sought to express something of what she'd been going through over the past months. Arnold had paved the way by his own intimacies. 'Although I may not have realised it consciously, at the back of my mind it's partly for that reason – that knowledge is just a commodity, and that it's only available to a privileged few. My other reason is that students are selected on the basis of proficiency at examinations and, to my mind, being adept at passing examinations is invariably an alternative to thinking. Anyhow, the universities are no longer truly independent, and in my field, where it's obvious that morality must dictate all judgements, morality is presently regarded with suspicion. I don't know whether you caught it, but the Minister of Education actually announced on the air that he proposed to abolish Peace Studies in schools . . .'

'And what about science? It's certainly not backed by moral strictures!'

'Precisely. And unless it is, we could see a "purification" programme in this country.'

Arnold seemed about to object but Julia insisted, 'It's not such a far-fetched idea. After all, we all know who are the despised members of society. There's not a day goes by when some politician isn't dictating how we should lead our personal lives, who we should be keeping out of the country, who shouldn't share a bed with whom, who shouldn't be allowed to demonstrate . . . If I stop to consider how I ought to spend the rest of my life, I know it wouldn't be by contributing to those values, but by trying to heal the disfunction between the actual and the ideal. I'm not going to allow those who tell me that I'm an unrealistic idealist to have it all their own way. If I stay in the department at Paine I shall either be accused of overt political influence by Gladyse Baker, or I shall find myself colluding in a system I despise. Corrupt acquiescence is not something I want to find myself guilty of.'

'I went to hear our local MP speak,' Arnold said hurriedly. 'It was really only because I wanted to take an evening walk, and I thought going over to Alton provided a good excuse and the right amount of exercise. I arrived a bit late and the man was in full spate. As I came into the hall I heard him say, "What we want is the Enterprise Society. We all want to see much more get-up-and-go in this country!" I turned on my heels at once and made my way home. In my view, what we want is much more care, respect, knowledge and understanding, and that will come only with a lot more sit-down-and-think.'

Julia wondered whether Arnold still attended Quaker Meetings. She would not confide to him that she did not – nor did James. She believed in some sort of spiritual reality, a uniting force. But she did not like the club atmosphere of religious practice. Arnold had said that at the heart of things was a kind of blessedness, one he had experienced not only in the Hangers but in silence, in music and in the scent of tobacco plants at dusk. He said too, with some force, that he was sure insight was not born of theories. And his final words to her were a warning. 'There is no connection between the individual will and the world.'

On the journey back to London, Julia pondered over what she had said to Arnold. She *had* thought of giving up teaching, that was true, but she hadn't consciously weighed the reasons as thoroughly as it had seemed when she spoke to him. His company had acted as a catalyst. Much had become clear, she seemed to have found something of herself. Once known she could never un-know it . . .

Her thoughts settled on her students frantically trying to take down everything she said in an effort to acquire her 'wisdom'. They didn't understand that this was impossible, and no one explained why; they couldn't understand why it was that they choked on undigested gobbets of information. They had no idea that all that was available to them at the university was information, and that even knowledge – let alone wisdom – did not necessarily result from absorbing it. Poor things! They – some more than others – diligently memorised facts, considered data, even learnt to discriminate, and marvel at another's critical faculty. But there was no guarantee that any one of their number would emerge the wiser.

In her own defence, it occurred to Julia that the good teacher is often the man or woman who has encountered great difficulties and overcome them with patience and understanding. For to live creatively and acquire wisdom is to have turned error and hurt into a capacity to empathise. A good teacher can lay this perception at the disposal of students. On the other hand, there are students who are not susceptible. Nor are we all born to die for the rest of mankind, she reminded herself firmly.

The journey passed without Julia noticing the miles she was burning up. She was feeling more positive about herself, and about Arnold. In the past she had found her father-in-law a little remote, but now she had discovered otherwise and resolved to visit him more frequently. She wanted to retain his friendship - although she wondered whether he would be able to accept that her life as his daughter-in-law was coming to an end. It had been odd, the way he had spoken about change. Had he intuited something, she wondered, or had James hinted that their relationship was unstable? She was sure that, together with her teaching and her material comfort, her marriage would have to go. All she felt towards James was gratitude. Heaven knew why! He had lulled her into a sort of complacency. They had lulled one another. If a caricaturist had wanted the perfect NW3 couple, the Brutons would have done admirably. What had passed for her self-fulfilment had been a fraud; she only appeared self-fulfilled. In the judgment of other people she was unusually fortunate with her looks, her financial security, her education, her marriage and her academic status. She had rather accepted this assessment of herself. She had never looked closely at her situation. She had enjoyed the reflection she received from the glass held up to her by her husband and their friends.

In the West, in Christianity, we are taught the wickedness of selfishness, she thought. We must love *others*. But if we are to love others as ourselves, surely we must first love ourselves? Calvin and Luther be damned! How often she had submitted to her mother's exhortation, 'Don't be selfish, Julia!', meaning, 'Don't do as you feel, do as you're told; don't be yourself – the standards to be attained are standards set by authority.' Why had she gone along with her mother? She had always known that these standards were false. And look where they had taken her parents! But the fact was that if she had not respected her parents, she had feared them, and although she had stopped listening to their precepts as she grew older, she had been left with a disturbing inner conflict. On the one hand there was the leftover sense of duty, an echo of 'mother knows best', on the other the knowledge that only if she could fulfil herself, 'love' herself, would she achieve the genuine self-interest required to make herself properly human.

However, to deal with her existential position, she would need more than psychology and ethics – she would need some sort of revelation. She could not prepare for that – only prepare to wait for it.

'Just tell me this, Julia. What's having an affair with a neo-fascist over a period of five days got to do with deciding to chuck your job, your home – and, presumably, your husband? Are you planning to live with the fascist? Have you gone all romantic or feminist or some other "ist" of which I'm unaware?'

It was bizarre listening to James talk this way. He had absolutely no idea of her essential nature. True, she had had very little idea of it herself. But he also seemed to have no idea of the way she was feeling.

'Neither!' she spat. Damn the feminists! In Hampstead they tended to be like the liberals – tolerant of change for themselves so long as the inconvenience was felt only by their husbands. She had watched the so-called feminists at parties; middle-class graduates bleating over their lack of freedom while their *au pairs* did their chores, brought up their children, serviced their husbands; women who spoke of the books they would write if they had the time, the explorations they would make when the children were at Bedales, Dartington or Millfield. And then she had watched the poor besotted husbands, men who rushed in overcrowded trains to the city at 8 a.m. limping back only when the Market was closed – and experiencing their first heart attack before they were fifty. Nor would she be joining the frivolous set that meandered in Knightsbridge until it was fruit-juice time at Harrods – women who, their desire unfulfilled by their husbands' caresses, sought fulfilment in their husband's bank accounts. Such women died of boredom, disappointment, frustration, laziness and greed because they never discovered their rights as human beings. No, she would not be joining that sisterhood either.

'Look, James, I know it must seem to you like terrible selfishness, but I need some time. Can you be patient for a while?'

'I thought I was being extremely patient.'

'You are. But I'm asking you to go on being extremely patient for a while longer, while I try to sort myself out. I know all this is grim for you and must've come as a shock, but I think I'm emerging from the worst of the depression. There's Christmas coming; I thought we might re-make the arrangement we had with the clan – you know, the dinner you had to cancel when I was ill . . .'

'Oh! Really!' James was astonished. He clearly had no idea that Julia might be contemplating such a thing. 'When?'

'Well . . . I thought either on Boxing Day evening, or the day after that. They'll all be finished with family "dos" by then.'

'Probably not even on speaks by then.'

For the first time since she was back from Oxford James had made a remark to her that did not reflect upon her. She took a breath and said, 'D'you think you could hear me out calmly over what happened in Oxford?'

'Only if you insist, and only if you think it'll help.'

'Well, it might help us both – especially if you feel that I somehow betrayed you.'

'What possible other interpretation could be put on your adultery?'

'Well, oddly, it had nothing whatever to do with you – or us. It was one of those peculiar things in which the environment probably played the largest part. It would have happened anyway, no matter who I'd been married to – if the circumstances of the marriage had been like ours.'

'So, it *did* have something to do with me! *I'm* somehow at fault.'

Julia saw that she might well be going to make things worse rather than better. She had various alternatives available to her, and one of them was to lie to James, to spare his feelings. But she was not inclined to adopt that alternative. She did not believe that, in the long run, it was the kindest thing to do, and anyhow, she was more inclined in the present to do what benefited her.

'I was, I admit, hypnotically attracted to the man. But I had no other positive feelings for him but sexual attraction.'

'You're disgusting! You lost your self-control. I'm really surprised at you Julia – you who pride yourself on being thoughtful, rational and integrated. What the hell do all those epithets signify if, at the drop of a hat, you fall into bed with a man you deem loathesome?'

'If you really want to know, the sheer unexpectedness of the situation is probably the clue. It showed up how in my life everything is over-programmed. I probably needed the experience of something unexpected arising to make me see that.'

She saw at once that she was in deep water. There was no point in going on. James was not interested in her examining her motivation. He had made up his mind that what she had done was unpardonable and that it had done him harm – although he did not specify *how* it had harmed him, and Julia imagined that the hurt was only to his pride. He wasn't going to be argued out of that – you couldn't argue James out of anything that seemed to him to affect him personally. But

Julia knew that what she had done *was* pardonable. It had disorientated her and made her an impossible companion for her husband; in the long run, however, it might be seen to have done her own life a great deal of good.

'Don't deprecate inconsistency, James. Sometimes it's a sign of the richness of possibilities rather than an impoverishment of judgment!'

Winter

Of course, it was tantamount to inviting a swarm of clothes-moths. They'd all pick holes in her if she confided anything of what she was thinking. But it would be interesting to discover whether, after four months of isolation, she would be able to pick up where she'd left off with them, or whether she'd find them intolerable. They were not really *her* friends, they were *their* friends. Quite different.

She was in the kitchen with James, idly roughing out a menu, and at the same time remembering yet again the pleasure of her visit to Selborne.

'By the way,' she said suddenly to James, 'did you say anything to your parents?'

'About what?'

'Me! Us!'

'Why?'

'Because Enid was *so* careful not to find herself alone with me. You know she can't stand any sort of heavy scene. She's like you.'

'When she rang I simply said you were feeling low. I had to, she wanted a word with you and if you remember, you weren't taking calls. She didn't ask any questions. She wouldn't ask a question if she didn't expect to like the answer. Was Arnold as tactful?'

'It wasn't tact I needed from him. He was wonderful. He's really found himself down there, with Gilbert White. And what he had to say about himself and his own experience was reassuring for me.' And as James cleared his throat, preparing to speak, Julia pre-empted his questions by begging him *not*

156

to ask her, then and there, the precise nature of the changes she envisaged in her own life. He would be asking the sort of questions the press asked the students in Paris in 1968, expecting to be told exactly how the revolution would look after it had come about . . . 'I just know that the job's got to go,' she said. 'I know that all this comfort's got to go.'

Julia paused. The expression on James's face was so blank as to be vacuous. She felt a twinge of sympathy for him, and it was in a less strident tone of voice that she reminded him of the man who visited Bonnard and found him living in a simplicity bordering on poverty. 'He noticed that there wasn't a single comfortable chair in the house and so he arranged for one to be sent round. When Bonnard took delivery of the chair he was so appalled that he made the delivery man take it back to the shop at once. He explained to his patron that he didn't ever want to consider comfort. A concern for comfort, he explained, could lead anywhere, but certainly not to anywhere worthwhile.'

'Am I to gather from that exemplar that you propose sleeping under the arches?' The conversation had entered a minefield. Julia did not reply.

James sighed audibly. 'Are we ever going to get back to normal?'

'I'm not at all sure that what you call "normal" is worth getting back to. Anyhow, I need to go forward, not back.'

'I thought we'd been happy. I thought you enjoyed your teaching, and the house and me and everything . . . You're simply running away . . .'

Poor James, thought Julia, but now he's whining. It's my fault, of course. I always appeared content. I gave every indication of being satisfied. Now comes the guilt.

The last dinner party she had attended had been at Stanton Place. She recalled the details of that evening. She had forced herself to remember everything – the drive to Stanton, the meal, the conversation at table and in Lady Stanton's dressing-room, and later in the drawing-room. And the awful, passionate sex on the way back to Marlowe College. As she kneaded dough, spun sugar and picked over vegetables, she found herself understanding for the first time how it was that Massimo had triggered the change in her which, at some unconscious level, she had actually been preparing for for years. It was that life with James had become a charade – that without thinking, they had been endlessly rehearsing a domestic comedy whose lines had been written by society, and neither had stopped to consider whether their long run was justified . . . It was a relief that James was now tactfully avoiding the bedroom, spending as much time as possible away from the house. It was astonishing how he had misunderstood her decision to invite twelve to dinner, believing it marked her return to normality.

'Who are you thinking of inviting?' he had asked.

'Amanda Burgh, for starters. She's always amusing.'

'The marrieds are terrified of her,' James muttered. Amanda was a highly attractive divorcée. But whenever she needed a man on her arm at local parties, she was usually accompanied by Justin, a free-floating gay. 'Who else?'

'Well, Justin, of course. The Howards, the Andersons, the Perots and the Lewises, I thought.'

'Must we have the Lewises?'

'James, you've been friendly with Fred for years. You've always said, "Beneath that rough exterior is a soft heart". After all, he helped you with the Boys' Club. Are you now going to admit you were only friendly with him for what you could get out of him?'

'Of course not!'

'Well then . . . And of course, Jerry and Sally Bach.'

'Are these all our friends?'

Julia wondered what he meant. Did he mean, were they their only friends, or was he questioning whether they were really friends? Had her suspicions transferred themselves to James?

'You always thought of them as friends in the past. We've known Helen and Justin since Oxford,' she said defensively. But as she made out her case, Julia realised that these 'friends' were not friends in the real sense but a group of people available to make up numbers at parties. They constituted a team that played musical chairs around the houses of Hampstead. If one of them died tomorrow, the funeral would assume the shape of one of their parties, and he or she would be forgotten – in any real sense – until the next party when, sentimentally, he or she would be recalled for no more than five minutes. In her mind's eye Julia saw a pond with a hole at its centre made by a dead weight. She watched as the circles from the centre widened and finally disappeared into the undergrowth at the bank.

She would wear her black wool Jean Muir with the scooped-out neck, and her amber beads. She was very thin and rather pale, and would have to make-up carefully. She would take pains to orchestrate the evening well. She hoped there would be no awkward questions asked. She wanted these people to remember her as hospitable, elegant and decent – qualities at a premium in their judgment. She knew that the food would taste delicious and that the table would look beautiful. She would use the Sarah Walton sand-grey stoneware plates. She had made napkins to go with the plates only a few days before she left for Oxford – grey ones with sand binding, sand with grey binding. She would use the Danish glass and the Robert Welch stainless steel cutlery . . .

'Will you do the wine, James?'

'Yes, just tell me what we're eating!'

Julia went through the courses, and James made a note on the back of an envelope before going down into the cellar. It was quite like old times, Julia thought.

Half an hour before the guests were to arrive, James brought a large glass of very dry sherry into the kitchen. 'To prepare you,' he said.

She took a sip, and then put down the glass; she needed both hands free for the mayonnaise. As she trickled olive oil slowly on to egg yolks, she sensed that James had something to say. He was standing at the opposite side of the kitchen table, watching her intently. She felt awkward; she hoped that he had nothing contentious to bring up.

'This is my real Christmas present to you,' he said.

It was true, she had felt rather surprised by the umbrella he had handed her on Christmas morning, even though it was a handsome, colourful, Italian umbrella.

'You get on with that, and I'll open it for you,' James said, prising open a dark blue leather jeweller's box and taking from it an antique cameo brooch.

'It's lovely! It's beautiful!'

'You've always wanted one.'

'Did you get it in Italy?'

'No, Bond Street, and I had to arrange for the safety-catch to be fixed, so that's why it wasn't here on Christmas morning. The jeweller delivered it half an hour ago.' James approached her, intending to pin the cameo on her dress, but she would not let him.

'It won't go on this dress.'

'I thought it was the sort of thing that would go with anything,' he objected.

'No, it would spoil the effect to put it on this!'

Julia knew that had she been kind and considerate – had she loved James – she would have worn the brooch through her nose to please him. She loved the brooch, and she was aware that James observed her pleasure. But they both knew that it had not bought her; nothing was changed . . . he was presuming . . .

'You look wonderful, Julia!' Justin said, a mite over-enthusiastically, as he gave her a bear-like hug. He was the last to arrive, and now the familiar group were all present, conversation flowing fast and strenuously over the weirs of general interest as they drank their pre-dinner drinks.

Dazed, Julia had registered the compliments as everyone told her how wonderful she looked, as each pressed a Christmas present into her hands. But after a while she had stopped participating; whichever man she was with, an arm casually draped over her shoulders, would continue talking to others, not noticing that she was not speaking. Instead she watched, attentively. All these people: self-confident, attractive, more or less intelligent, utterly predictable . . . James appeared in his element . . . 'I'll just go and . . .' she murmured. But as she slipped from Jerry's arm, no one noticed her leave the drawing-room to put the finishing touches to the meal. She did hope they would not discuss her, have the details of her recent past picked over like bones. She didn't want the bones of her life turned into pipes and her skull into a drinking bowl.

'My mother-in-law speaks five languages and has nothing of interest to say in any one of them,' Barbara Perot was saying ten minutes later as she buttered a piece of Melba toast.

'It's like people who go abroad and traipse over archaeological sites and wander in and out of cathedrals and castles, yet never think to visit the Tower of London,' Amanda remarked.

'My mother-in-law eats grapes with a fork and has a way of pronouncing "Po-si-ta-no" ' – Cordelia pursed her lips and gave an imitation – 'which has ensured that I shall never go near the south-west coast of Italy. Every time I hear that word my stomach knots.'

'*My* mother-in-law . . .'

Whenever Barbara Perot and Cordelia Howard found themselves in the same room they competed for the title of most abused daughter-in-law as some women compete for the worst health. Now Cordelia said: 'You know mine did an OU general degree? Well naturally, after that she concluded she was an art expert, and now she's got herself on some list or other that has her racing through the Shires with a box of slides, dispensing culture to the natives. Last weekend Jo and I were up at the cottage so I hadn't a leg to stand on – I had to drive the ten miles to Bakewell to listen to her lecture – *lecture*, mark you – on van Gogh. It was toe-curling. I was so relieved that Jo had to stay at home with the children or we'd have disgraced ourselves.'

Cordelia now arranged her mouth so that her lips gathered in a sphincter and enunciated, ' "He was born in 1853 at *Groot-Zundert*" ' – magnificently mispronouncing the Dutch – ' "and he painted in London in 1867 and in *Ramsgate* in 1876, if you please." ' Here she made a pointed pause, as if waiting for signs of astonishment, before continuing in elderly, patronising tones, ' "And you may not have known but he was trained as a missionary in *Bruxelles*. Yes, he *was*," ' she insisted. ' "And he was so saddened by the poverty of the miners he lived among that he became a sort of social worker to them. He was sensitive, you see. And it was because he was so sensitive that he took to painting. Yes! That was it!" ' Cordelia mimicked the triumph of intellectual discovery as her own audience laughed. ' "Then he took some lessons in art at *Anvers*, but the professor found *van Gogh's*" ' – the Dutch again splendidly mispronounced – ' "drawing so poor that he discouraged him from taking further lessons. He told him that he'd never become an artist! Imagine! So poor Mr van Gogh, who never sold a single painting in his lifetime, decided to accept the invitation of his dear brother Theo and go and live in *Paree*, and then in 1888 he left for *Arles* where he painted the Sunflowers – you all know them, I'm sure. And then he went mad." ' Here she paused for effect, before resuming in an exaggeratedly solemn tone, ' "He was committed to an asylum in 1889, and I'm sorry to have to draw my lecture to a close on such a terrible note, but in 1890 he committed suicide. I know, it's a very sad tale, but we mustn't allow ourselves to be depressed by it. We have the lovely landscapes and portraits to look at. We don't have to linger on the old boots and potatoes and the ungainly peasants and miners, do we now?" '

There was a general roar of laughter as Cordelia finished. 'Now, Barbara, cap that!' she said.

Julia recalled: 'If the shaking of her breasts could be stopped, some of the fragments of the afternoon might be collected . . .'

Barbara launched into a recital of her mother's tea parties. 'The talk never goes further than a comparison of recalcitrant servants. My mother and her friends have a lexicon of terms for the women who come in daily to pick up what they drop on the floor, wash what they leave in the sink, and polish what they stain. "My treasure", "dear-Mrs-Daily", "my cleaner", "Mrs Mop", "Mrs-daily-do", "the lady who does for me", and the one I hate most of all, "my woman": it's somehow extraordinarily eloquent. They don't have to have sixty-five names for the fishmonger or the gardener.'

'Barbara, I must tell you about a peach of a letter I got last week from the editor of the woman's page of a left-of-centre newspaper we all know and love. I submitted eight hundred words on that very subject – the iniquity of middle-class women employing working-class women to do their dirty work for them. This woman wrote back saying that while she shared my views, she didn't think her readers were "quite ready for them".'

'Chicken! But Amanda, you're always ahead of the times. Didn't something similar happen to you with a piece you offered *Housewives* on racism?'

'It did. And it was a much more serious matter. I was comparing the treatment of Pakistanis and West Indians in this country, now, with the treatment of the Jews in Germany in the early 1930s, before the Nuremberg Laws. Some editorial jerk rang me and told me that they'd had a meeting about my piece and concluded that I must be Jewish, with some personal axe to grind. What sort of tits do they employ? I ask myself. Racist to a woman . . . So then I submitted a piece on homelessness, only to have that rejected on the grounds that "our readers would not find it possible to identify with the problems of women sleeping rough . . .".'

'I was asked to do a piece on Flora Thompson for *Up-Country* – only because the editor has a cottage in our village and we meet in the pub,' Cordelia said. 'Not only did it appear cut to shreds, with all the hardships of Flora's life either watered down or expunged altogether, but it was illustrated with drawings of elegant young ladies of the period in smocked, sprigged muslin. It's a mystery to me why well-heeled journalists and amateurs write for *Up-Country* – it isn't about the country at all. It's to farming and country matters what Barbara Cartland is to love.'

'That's why it's successful. *Urbes in rure.* Very safe,' Justin muttered.

'Lady Caroline Glanville was at Cambridge with me and she reviews for a periodical whose name I won't utter – not only for fear of being sued but also for fear of reminding you of its ghastly existence. Daddy's on the board: Caroline's given space. The editor know which side his toast is caviared.'

Conversation raged as Julia's guests worked their way through her first course. She had prepared a terrine of veal sweetbreads, a fish terrine involving sole and salmon, and a vegetable terrine; there was onion bread, herb bread and toast Melba – and the wholesome aroma that filled the dining-room told everyone that Julia had baked that afternoon. The oval platter with the *crudités* was over twenty inches in length; on it she had created a pattern worthy of Delaunay with French beans, carrots, cauliflower, baby turnips, spring onions, radishes and artichoke hearts, their colours made more vibrant by the careful positioning of shiny black Kalamata olives. At either end of the platter she placed bowls of mayonnaise. She was pleased to have provided an abundance. She could not bear the Andersons' habit of always serving uninteresting food with a surfeit to drink – clearly, both Helen and Charles hoped the food would go unremarked . . . No one had remarked on the appearance of her table. Had they noticed, she wondered?

Fred Lewis's voice was heard. 'Corton Levi? He didn't come to Britain for the sake of our way of life. Where on earth did you get that idea from? He came to get away from his mother. He couldn't stand the prospect of his mother attending his private views – if he'd stayed in the US there would have been no corner safe from her. Fortunately, she's allergic to water, can't sail on it or fly over it. That's why Corton's here. He can't stand this country.'

'Don't be absurd, Fred!'

'One's not being absurd. You don't know what it is to have a Jewish mother.'

Julia remembered that she had met Corton Levi at Fred and Rachel's, and had wondered at the time whether he had been invited to lend weight to Fred's expertise (Fred had spent thousands on Levi's work) or because Corton and Rachel had something going. Levi, she remembered, was a middle-American who had adopted Surrealist manners in his teens and still tended to open dinner party conversations with such remarks as 'What shit is this I'm eating?' or 'You queer or sommat?' It appeared that this 'exuberance' was not merely tolerated but actually rejoiced in by everyone, from royalty downwards. On the one hand, what could you expect from an American-Jewish artist, on the other, wasn't it perfectly ghastly! And weren't they broad-minded to a fault to put up with it?

Jerry Bach said, 'Marcus Harrington's writing a monograph on Kossoff and has asked me if I'd let him reproduce my "Family in the Bakery" for it.'

'I saw Marcus last week, myself. One lunched him,' Fred quickly interjected. Fred had unwisely failed to buy Kossoffs when they were within the budget he set aside for works of art, thinking that the subject-matter was too Jewish, and that therefore they would not be a good investment. Since then prices had rocketed, and he'd been obliged on more than one occasion to defend the absence of the painter's work on his walls. Not only did Fred hate to miss a bargain, he couldn't bear his judgments to be questioned.

'Marcus came to look at my Wesley Cromes. He says they're absolutely first-rate. He's writing a piece for *The Connoisseur* on them.' Everyone understood from this that Fred hoped this article would inflate their value. In fact, as everyone knew, the Cromes were one of Fred's biggest mistakes – he'd been taken in by Hart-Saunders of the Quadrangle Gallery in Cork Street, who was badly in the red at the time, and had recognised a sucker when he saw one.

The consumer society: adults suckling to feed the inner void.

Into the small silence that had developed, Justin said, 'I went to see the Black South African Mine Dancers at the Coliseum. What magnificent physiques they have. I felt particularly poorly endowed. And such a sense of rhythm! What is it, I wonder, that gives those men such rhythm?'

'Avoiding the hot coals of injustice?' Julia offered quietly, suddenly reminded of her parents. She rarely thought of them these days, and when they did swim unbidden into her consciousness, she was filled with feelings of shame, rage and fear, remembering how her father had once sneered at her when she was forcefully rejecting his values: 'You're only as good as your genes, my child!' She'd had the courage to break away from Jack and Jill; she must find more courage, and break away from all this if she was to mature . . .

'Did you read about that ex-barrow-boy who markets electronics and said that if he could make a profit out of long-range nuclear missiles, he wouldn't hesitate to do so?' Charles asked.

'Yes, he was on the box. Hasn't he been awarded an OBE? He's a perfect example of what the Enterprise Culture throws up.'

'He certainly made me throw up,' Helen said. 'Talking of which, Julia, your food is absolutely fabulous and very easy to keep down.'

'I'm so glad you're enjoying it.'

If Helen likes my food so much, Julia muttered wordlessly to herself, I wonder why it is she serves such stodgy muck. Eating *chez* Anderson, one passes from hunger to satiety without going through anything remotely resembling sensuous pleasure . . . It's not as if she couldn't afford the best ingredients, and even if she does prefer to read about cooking rather than cook, couldn't she get the *au pair* to do it? It was never a *funfest* dining with the Andersons . . .

No one noticed Julia leave the table with the used plates and dishes. And when she returned with the pheasants, the bread sauce, the raspings and the vegetables, it was only James and Justin who stopped talking and cleared spaces on the table for her to set down the main course. Everyone fell to; Julia watched as her guests passed the dishes and poured the gravy. James and Justin filled the glasses with claret. Warm appreciation murmured its way to her and to James. Somehow she didn't feel entirely present. Since Massimo, a gulf had opened up between the outside world and what went on inside her head. She fought to keep out thoughts of the Italian, and looked towards Fred – he could be relied upon to irritate her sufficiently to distract her. For one thing, he always referred to himself as 'one'; not 'I', not 'Fred', but 'one'. Who was it who had identified the habit as an attempt to make egotism respectable? Years ago, at Oxford, she had contributed a piece to *Isis* entitled 'Third Person Nebulous', based on her experience of a weekly tutorial with a Fellow of Magdalen . . .

Jerry and Fred were jousting over their respective art collections again. Julia wished she could wave a wand and make the collecting of painting and sculpture the most unfashionable occupation in the whole gamut of occupations. If only she could gather a posse of distinguished critics to argue that real aesthetic experience is only to be had from *objets trouvés*, gathered by the collector himself . . . Then we'd discover the meaning of taste, then we'd be able to separate the men from the boys and identify those for whom works of art are as necessary for the nourishment of their souls as food is for their bodies. Much of what is collected is just rich men's graffiti. The fashionableness of art is inimical to its function . . . What had all Fred's art-collecting ever done to modify his values? Long before it was encouraged and made legal by Tina's government, Fred had been the proud possessor of a Swiss bank account. And he was on first-name terms with a man in the Inland Revenue, with whom he always managed an 'arrangement'. As long as there was the chance that the Tate or the Hayward would ask Fred to lend something from his collection for a retrospective, so that he would see his name in the catalogue, he would not only risk being burgled but continue to spend his money on art that he neither particularly liked nor remotely understood. Just like a number of other wealthy citizens whose enjoyment of art was confined respectively to a knowledge of its market value, and an appreciation of which of the family portraits could be relied upon best to offset death duties . . .

Julia's glance slipped from Fred's pseudo-intellectual beard down the table to lovely Rachel. No wonder, perhaps, that Rachel went her own way, hit back at 'one' by sleeping with the artists who gave him the chic he otherwise lacked. Rachel had Fred in a vice; being cuckolded was not flattering to him precisely, but the attentions of the artists – even those with the flattened vowels and glottal stops of the 1960s – was. It was no mean thing to mosey into the galleries on Cork Street with the beautiful Rachel on one arm and the latest fashionable artist on the other. Poor Fred! What a mess!

To Julia's right, Jerry Bach and Roger Perot were discussing hormones. Across the table, Cordelia was criticising a recent television series on World War II. 'Jo says it was quite right for us to have burnt Dresden to a crisp,' she said defiantly.

Odd, Julia thought, how some women seem to have to believe in the omnipotency of their husbands. She herself wouldn't trust Jo to tell a fresh lettuce from a slug-eaten one, or Monday from Tuesday for that matter.

'We had a thoroughly unpleasant job to do and couldn't risk defeat,' Jo elaborated. 'The bombing of civilians hastened victory. It's no good being wise after the event. Anyhow, in those days moral judgments were regarded as purely personal matters. We allowed the experts to take all decisions relating to political and military matters.'

'Don't you think anyone knew that bombing cities wasn't actually necessary from a military point of view?' James asked.

Jo was clearly feeling uncomfortable, and like an animal he sniffed out the most vulnerable member of the pack and asked Julia whether she wouldn't be willing to back the bombing of Johannesburg if she knew that the result would be the overthrow of the present regime, and the establishment of majority rule.

'I think I might,' Julia agreed, softly. Suddenly, beneath the level even of her conscious thought, she heard another voice speaking.

I'm too tired. Perhaps the pockets of all those who once believed in the possibility of moral influence have been stuffed with the stones of self-interest and we are all sinking to the bottom of our jacuzzis . . . No one is going to put himself out for the homeless, the unfed, the unclothed, the Black . . . Divide and Rule! It's a strategy that's never failed the self-interested.

'But I thought you were a pacifist, Julia!'

'I thought so too. I was, I think. I'm not sure what I'd call myself today. I used to believe in the efficacy of non-violence.'

'Used to?' James was raising his eyebrows in a maddening way. She was going to have to explain herself. If only she could sit this one out . . .

'I'm not sure what it is I believe now. I used to think that non-violence gave the oppressor a chance to stop in his tracks for long enough to perceive the humanity in those he was whipping and beating and starving and warring against.' The image of Massimo floated into her mind and her blood ran cold. 'But when I consider what's going on in South Africa, for instance, I see that the continuous oppression of the Black majority by the White minority has so brutalised the *Whites* that they no longer have it in them to respond to another's humanity. You can't respond to something in another if you don't have it in yourself. Suffering hasn't resulted in a compassionate world. Look at the behaviour of the Israelis towards the Arabs in their midst! You'd have thought that the Jews of all people would understand what it feels like to be a subject people. Submitting to violence in an effort to bring your aggressor to a loving relationship with you simply hasn't worked and won't work. I don't see how it ever can. Christian idealism is beautiful in itself, but I have no confidence in its application.' She should not have given in to his violence. At the time it had not occurred to her, but had she struck back, perhaps he would have entered into a more equal relationship with her . . .

'Jo told me . . .'

But Julia was not listening. Instead she found herself wondering whether she had ever totally believed in her husband. She had taken it for granted that he was a decent man – but being affable is not the same as being decent. She thought about his choice of friends, and the boring evenings she had shared with them, listening to folk music that she loathed, drinking unblended malt whiskeys and exotic liqueurs brought home from very foreign places that upset her digestion, and not taking issue when someone expressed a view she profoundly disagreed with – James would have felt uncomfortable if she had spoken her mind and unwittingly upset someone. And James had never needed the original or

169

the brilliant. He argued that that type of individual always took the stage and performed, and that upset the balance of a social gathering. Perhaps what he had really meant, however, was that such people made him feel inadequate. He'd always stuck up for the bore and the fool. He said that he felt for them, believing that beneath the conversation of the man who says too much about too little, an anxious soul is yearning to be liked. As for the fool, James said, he was only a fool on a given number of topics. He might have nothing to say about art and other matters on the set list issued by the universities – and James always expressed some doubt as to the wisdom of placing too high a regard on universities – but he might well have a vast knowledge of and passion for something he'd never been encouraged to reveal. 'I'm a fool about children, about fashion, about contemporary music,' James would boast, adding that he hoped no one would cast him out socially because of it. 'Who am I to label a man a fool and thereafter ignore him?'

It sounded decent enough, but Julia remembered that when, one evening at the Perots', a man in the lawn-mower business had button-holed James and bombarded him with talk about hovers and blades, he had been none too amused . . . Perhaps James made more allowances for fools than bores. Julia wondered about consistency.

> Do I contradict myself?
> Very well then, I contradict myself
> (I am large, I contain multitudes).

If she was going to leave all this, the meaningless chatter that took the place of action, where was she going to go? She had her savings; she would be able to set herself up modestly somewhere. But where? Something in her sank; she would need so much energy to leave James and the house, and reconstruct her life. But once she had acknowledged that this sort of life was incompatible with her real needs, there was no way back – only forward.

She tried to imagine, as the dinner party continued merrily

around her, what it would be like without James. Rather bleak, at first, she imagined. Rather like giving up running water or electric light. Come to think of it, it might be a good thing to go and live somewhere really primitive and fetch water from a well and live by the light of an oil lamp . . .

What would she do? How would she spend her time if she had no lectures to prepare, no one to cook and clean for? True, she had had to give in to James and allow Spick & Span to clean the house for her every Friday, but with a house as large as this one there was always plenty to do without having to scrub and polish and so on every day. She would be without occupation. That was not conducive to well-being . . .

This party she was giving, was it so different from the one at Stanton? The Stanton lot were racist snobs who belonged to a sort of right-wing fraternity with a particular vision of how Britain should be. These people, her guests, were liberals-with-a-small-'l' who belonged to a sort of complacent middle-of-the-road fraternity that rather liked things as they were. The Stanton lot played soldiers; the Hampstead lot played the market, and to the gallery . . . Surely these, her guests, were infinitely preferable to Stanton and his dreadful cronies? Surely? And yet . . . In the end, perhaps neither group would be able to create the sort of world that she, Julia, would choose to live in . . .

'Tell me then, what's robbing a bank compared with founding one and working in it?' Roger challenged Charles Anderson, who was known to have been offered a very lucrative post with a city bank. 'Illegally accumulated capital from drugs, for example, has become the very foundation of legally founded banks.'

Julia silently agreed.

'O, for God's sake, don't you start. I've quite enough with Helen. Julia, help me!' Charles called down the table. 'I've told Helen, if she wants to go on teaching part-time, and simultaneously run a fistful of charge accounts at Harrods and the like, I'm simply obliged to quit the Civil Service for better renumeration. Incidentally, d'you know what they've offered me?'

It was a staggering sum. Julia wondered whether Justin and Jo would feel a twinge of envy. She knew that James would be none too pleased to hear a sum approximating his own annual salary disclosed for everyone to savour.

Bankers don't produce goods, miners do that. It would be cleaner to live with a man who made things, not deals . . .

'Why d'you suppose that, having been silent since he handed the tablets to Moses, God has suddenly found his voice and spoken to the chief constable of Manchester?'

'In the US he speaks to politicians.'

'She wants to show the British that She makes no distinction over here between public servants!'

'Amanda!'

'A society that pays its police more generously than its educators is saying something, and we should be listening to its message.'

'A God who only addresses the powerful needs to be kept an eye on . . .'

'The reason why plastic is unsympathetic is that it's indestructible,' Justin was saying. 'The apogee of unnaturalness is plastic flowers. Man has no inner model to enable him to respond to plastic flowers: all his prototypes are organic – they come into being, they grow and then they wither and die. That's why we're willing to fork out lavishly for cut flowers at the peak of their perfection; we know that shortly they're going to decline into death on our dinner tables. Their decline from consummate beauty provides us with a sort of solace. It's something like the release we get from tragedy.'

Man that is born of woman, hath but a short time to live, and is full of misery: he cometh up and is cut down like a flower.

'One really ought to visit the National Gallery more frequently,' Fred was confiding to Sally. Rachel butted in to say that she always went once a year, in December. 'One should venture further than the shop for Christmas cards, my love,' Fred advised her affectionately.

. . . 'I'd say it was as unlikely as the sight of Bernard Levin milking a goat.'

'Or an insurance agent leaning over backwards to meet a claim!'

What was? Julia was confused. She was finding it increasingly difficult to pick up the threads of the conversations weaving themselves all around her, or follow any one of them to its conclusion. She would catch short blasts, she would register one-liners – but nothing cohered. She was grateful to be left out of the conversation and hoped that her infrequent contributions had been sensible. Was she being treated respectfully? Or was she being ignored? She could not be sure. Perhaps she could find an excuse to leave the table?

'One always stays at the Cipriani . . .'

Where had she heard that before? Julia wondered. Quite recently . . .

'The reason why Brenda does so well with men . . .' Oh dear! Jerry was going to tell Helen the whole sorry history of his sister . . . 'is that, being demonstrably unattractive and in danger of being neglected, men feel protective of her, and that lessens the feelings of guilt their lust might otherwise provoke. Even super-achievers feel guilt,' Jerry added, to the satisfaction of all the men present and the disgust of Julia.

'I'm afraid I have to admit that so far as I'm concerned, Brenda's a wingless bird, a scentless flower.' Fred was getting his own back.

How can they talk about Brenda like that? Julia raged silently. She's uncharm, everyone knows that: it's the most terrible thing to be. Worse than BO.

'She's got something of the waxed waterproof of Virginia Water about her,' Charles continued. 'And a too keen desire to be liked.'

'I know. Precisely! Army officers seem susceptible to that.' Jerry was gratified to feel he understood Brenda so well but regretful about the details.

We explore ourselves, we explore one another. We expose our views, our problems, our complexities . . . by exposing those we can face, we imagine that we're being honest. We're not honest, not any one of us, we don't face moral questions. And if we do address them, we find we can't do much about them because we live in an immoral world. That gives us the excuse . . . I shouldn't pay my taxes. If I'd the least moral fibre I'd say no and stand firm. I'd refuse just so long as there's homelessness, and harassment of the poor, and humiliation of the disabled and discrimination against minorities. 'NO!' while the nation buys coal from countries where it's mined by children. 'NO!' while there are no sanctions against South Africa. 'NO!' until we withdraw from Northern Ireland and get the UN in.

I was right not to deliver my lecture. I would have been morally quite wrong, knowing myself as I do, to have stood before all those delegates and mouthed reason, non-aggression and pacifism a few hours after being involved in a sado-masochistic affair with a neo-fascist.

'Julia! Julia!' Someone was speaking to her. It was Charles. 'What was the subject of the paper you were giving?'

'Oh, it's a bit complicated . . .' Julia was emerging from her reverie like a deep-sea diver emerging at the surface. 'I was trying to work out whether a refusal to defend oneself shows disrespect for the gift of life.'

'You were referring to the arms race, were you?'

'Well, yes, but I was pointing to a more fundamental question about the way in which victim and vanquished are part of a single, rather appalling symbiotic relationship.'

'She's too deep for one!' Fred chipped in, laughing. 'The trouble with you, Julia, is that you take yourself and everything else in life far too seriously.'

I've heard that before.

'Do I, Fred?'

'You should be more like Rachel and have hobbies.'

I'd like to tell Fred how very much like Rachel I've recently been with my 'hobby' . . .

'You're right, Fred. I'm always telling Julia that she's far too cerebral. It's not attractive in a woman, is it?' James was laughing.

'Well, there's nothing wrong with Julia on that score,' Justin parried, rushing to the defence of his hostess. But

174

none of the others took his assessment seriously. He was a homosexual, after all.

Massimo loathes women as they are. He desires them only as he imagines that they should be. Perhaps all heterosexual men do. If only all these people would dissolve and Massimo appear. But how would I conduct myself?

The great humped wave of conscience was breaking over Julia, it threatened to engulf her. The suds of the waves' undertow appeared grey, and as the waters withdrew they left a vacancy tenanted by nothingness.

She looked up from her plate. She looked around her. *Were these people, this dinner party, so different from the people and the party at Stanton? Both groups are dedicated to either creating or maintaining circumstances in which they – and they alone – feel comfortable and prosper. Of course, liberal humanism is decent and moral, and fascism is foul and immoral, but if liberalism were truly to justify itself it would be by becoming the route to socialism, and this was not its intention. Liberalism had not withstood fascism, and it never could; all it did was to provide a safe haven for people by diverting their minds from the real issues. Liberals risked nothing; they did not so much as risk their liberty to free others from serfdom.*

The conversation, so far as she had succeeded in following it, had been bitchy, bitty and shallow, a theatrical performance played for its participants. Everything that had happened to her recently had struck her as some sort of performance, with a script that she had not written and not even agreed. When she lay naked in the fields with Massimo she had hardly been able to believe that it was she playing that role . . . She felt shocked. She was ice-cold. She had not known what were the full dangers of the affair with Massimo, and now that she had suffered the wounds so grievously, she knew she could never again embark upon anything like it. Was it this realisation that had, for a while, taken from her the urge to survive? Had she felt that desire could only be satisfied sexually? For she did know that to be devoid of desire was death. She would survive, she knew that now, for desire was strong within her but its object was quite different . . .

'Would you turn up the heating?' she whispered across the table to James.

She did not want Massimo; she had had him. Waiting for such experiences yields the greatest pleasure – the years of subdued contentment, the occasional ripple on the placid waters, and then the encounter. Finally: desire satisfied is desire obliterated. Something at a close. But her past was shattered; shards of a violent, passionate struggle lay on her memory and scratched her mind.

. . . 'He said he was going to the Indies this year, with an older man.'

'Per anum ad Antiga!'

Oh! NOT in front of Justin.

'Actually, he's a Liberal advocate.'

'You mean that when one of the half-dozen Black Africans who have made it comes to him for advice, he doesn't actually refuse to take his money.'

'I suppose that's what I mean,' James said regretfully. He did not like having to admit that Jo's evaluation of a mutual acquaintance was a fair one.

'Did Adam get into Harchester?' Jerry asked Fred.

'He passed the entrance examination. But, no, he didn't get in.'

'How come?'

'The Jewish quota was full.'

'The what!'

There was silence. Everyone felt uncomfortable. Just because Fred was in many ways impossible, just because he wore an I'm-rich watch and drove an I'm-rich car and referred to himself as 'one', was no reason for his son to be discriminated against.

'What are you going to do? What action are you taking?'

'What can one do? Everyone knows these quotas exist, everyone pretends they don't. One should never have entered Adam; one shouldn't have played into their hands. One shouldn't have given the bastards the satisfaction of reminding one that one's here on their sufferance. Anyhow, Adam knows it would be worse to be a Pakistani – we don't get lighted excreta through our letterbox.' Fred turned towards Roger who was asking him where he supposed Britain's reputation for tolerance came from.

'It's all PR. Of course, they let the Jews in when they needed their financial skills way back in the seventeenth century, and of course they let the West Indians in when they needed menial workers. The British don't put themselves out when it doesn't suit them. Look what's happened with the Boat People.'

'Have you come in for anti-semitism, Fred?' James asked him.

'Of course. As a Jew one's always in a quandary. Does one accept intolerance, or pretend it doesn't exist? If one pretends it doesn't exist and works for those people and institutions who maintain it doesn't exist, one can do very nicely, thank you. Once I've done the necessary and got myself a knighthood, I can't see the schools and clubs of this country turning down my applications and my son's. One did the thing too hastily, the wrong way round. One should have got the title first and *then* entered Adam. Now he'll go to St Paul's where he'll win all the prizes and be called "a clever little Jew-boy", and he'll either turn out like me, heaven forbid, or he'll become a Marxist. On the plus side, he's much less likely to be buggered at St Paul's.'

Julia was speechless. She was outraged, embarrassed and felt a surge of sympathy for Fred. He overestimated his own charm but he was saved by his vulnerability. She did not know what to say without the risk of sounding patronising. She rose quickly, and took dishes from the table to the kitchen.

'Well, Julia, still living your life in D minor?' James was at the fridge, taking out the Danish cream circle filled with seeded muscats and putting it on the kitchen table. It was clear, it had been clear throughout dinner, that he was utterly fed up that she had chosen not to wear the brooch. 'You've been rather unsociable this evening.'

'D'you think anyone's minded?'

'I've not the remotest idea,' he said coldly. 'I think they've all had plenty to say to each other, one way or the other.'

At least she hadn't been thinking out loud. It had been worrying her that the conversation that went on in her head these days could be overheard.

'I'm going to serve the hot chocolate soufflé first, so would you leave the Danish circle and the marron cake on the side table, and bring in that jug of pouring cream and put it on the dining-table?'

Back in the dining-room the conversation continued over familiar ground. Why was it assumed that the highest salaries attract the best teachers and doctors? Perhaps they only attract the most acquisitive. Why are the lowest wages paid to those who do the most dangerous and unpleasant jobs? Julia could answer these questions, but she did not have the inclination or the energy. She passed Fred the chocolate soufflé, and while he spooned the mixture onto his plate she heard him say that he and Rachel were moving into a Queen Anne house on Kew Green so that Adam wouldn't have too far to get to school.

'On the one hand they berate us for our materialism, on the other they encourage us to buy honours,' he was saying.

'I think it's a mistake to look for consistency in human behaviour,' Jerry advised Fred.

'Surely, consistency is a sign of maturity,' James butted in.

'Well, it may be a sign of an individual's own maturity, but it's certainly not a sign of his maturity if he goes about insisting on its existence in everyone else.'

'I'm in favour of the status quo,' Fred continued, ignoring James's interruption. 'The gap between rich and poor gives the poor something to aim at; either they try getting rich themselves, or they show a proper contempt for the system. I'm in favour of stockbrokers, bankers, fast-food franchises, private medicine and private education. One likes to live in a prosperous country that's cutting a figure abroad. One shouldn't simply give everything to the needy – it makes them reliant.'

'Really, Fred, you're absolutely appalling.'

'Amanda dear, all one's saying is that the system suits me. One's not suggesting that it's the way it should be. No doubt Paradise will be run on very different lines. And, I have to say, I regard Norman Tebbitt as the angel of death . . .'

Good on you, Fred! And yet what a confusing man he was. Julia could understand why it was that he was invariably invited by the small circle she and James belonged to; he was a good listener, he was generous, he entertained lavishly and, above all, he provided a focus for the circle's unanimous scorn. Such an individual was essential at a gathering. And now that they knew how humiliated Fred and Rachel and Adam had been, they had become his creditors.

'It used to be said that the saddest sight of all was that of a solitary horse standing in a field under a tree in the pouring rain. Today, I think, poets would turn to the image of foreign tourists examining a bill of fare in the rain, on a Sunday in Leicester Square.'

'I think it's the sight of a family – mother and father pulling a couple of unwilling children under ten into the British Museum on a Sunday afternoon.' Barbara spoke from dire personal experience.

Heaven and hell are within us. Every evening we organise distractions for ourselves so as to avoid contact with the great disappointment of being stuck with a stranger until 'death', please God, 'do us part'. (Or do we, perhaps, meet up again?) The distraction is more often than not the theatre, where couples are either more heroic than the spectators so that there is vicarious release, or so unfortunate as to make us, the audience, preen with emotional pride.

'I'm certainly not giving up our second home,' Cordelia was telling Justin, who was arguing that while so many were homeless no one had the right to two houses.

' "*Over a whisky watered down with ice, Justin specialises in being very nice.*" '

Julia said suddenly, 'The public laughed at medieval executions when the brigands were poor. Today they step over the poor sleeping in the streets. It makes me sick.'

The laughter directed against Justin faded into uneasy silence. Julia wished she hadn't spoken. She had read (where had she read it?) of a homeless, destitute mother, suffering from depression, her stomach speaking of neglect, who had boarded an Inter-City train and, as it rushed through the open Northamptonshire countryside, had thrown her baby out of the window. Only then had she qualified for a permanent roof over her head, albeit in a mental institution.

'Are you feeling a little restored?' Jerry had come to the back of Julia's chair and was putting his arm round her. She shuddered.

'Oh, yes.' She was so pleased when he moved away. He must be making for the loo.

'How's the book doing?' Helen had a book out too. She should have asked her about it.

'Moneywise? As I expected.'

'And critically?'

How could she ask such a question? 'Hm, well, the critical response has been mixed. I expected that. Is it not inevitable that a book about the problems of communication should meet those problems itself?'

A wave of cold discouragement formed and broke over her. As Jerry returned he had to pass her chair, and whispered, 'Can I be of any help? Would you like to talk?'

'It's kind of you, Jerry, but there's really nothing to talk about.'

There was nothing anyone could do. She wished that dinner was over. Perhaps James would deal, alone, with the coffee . . . She wanted out. She felt exhausted. She wondered how she had found the energy to prepare the gargantuan meal. She had enjoyed making the dishes but had only managed to eat tiny portions. Someone – more than one person – was laughing horribly loudly . . .

'She may very well be the tit of the iceberg but I will say this for her – she dresses divinely.' Sally was evidently green with envy of someone. Julia looked her way; like an owl catching a mouse, Sally closed her eyes each time she raised her fork to her mouth.

'So she bloody well should, with Morton's bank account to draw on. It's not that money can buy style,' Cordelia conceded, 'but it can buy advice. Gloria's spent her youth at the hairdresser's and with make-up artists – as a prelude, no doubt, to spending her middle years with plastic surgeons . . .'

. . . 'How would you define humour, Jerry?'

'A release from tension? Standing common sense on its head? I don't think I can define it accurately; it has something to do with objectivity . . .'

'Incongruity?'

It will soon be over . . .

'The whole history of the world would be different if decent men hadn't remained silent,' James was saying to Fred. He had been galvanised into showing Fred that the latter was among friends. He engaged him in conversation about the Boys' Club, in time for Fred not to hear Rachel boast, 'If I'm to spend two hours in the dark it certainly won't be in the theatre!'

Julia looked towards James. He was nodding vigorously at the general laughter, but she knew he despised Rachel and the clan's response to the innuendo. Jo was obviously uncomfortable, too, but the glazed expression on his face bore witness to another cause – his tongue was investigating a piece of pheasant lodged in a molar.

'The reason *I* don't go to the theatre is that I refuse to consider myself as "bum on a seat". The only sort of seat provided for someone of my income is one from which I can neither see nor hear,' Amanda was telling Cordelia.

'Anyhow, all the playwrights are writing about us these days!' Sally butted in.

'All?'

'Well, you know what I mean.' And Sally looked down at her plate, coyly embarrassed. Her face was perpetually poised for admiration. She wore a light but continuous smile as if she had some private joy that she did not wish to share. Julia considered this smile. It crossed her mind that it might owe its origin to one of those gadgets oriental women are said to lodge in their vaginas to provide them with multiple orgasms throughout their idle days . . . Sally could look quite pretty, actually, but in fact regarded herself as outstandingly beautiful. Her elderly lovers, anxious to keep her strictly for themselves, repeated phrases from an earlier, more elegant age, and made her feel distinguished. She was a child still, with the exaggerated sweet tooth for adulation of a Shirley Temple.

'Everyone thought we were crazy at the time,' Sally was saying, 'but we got it for a song. In the corner of the Ardèche where we are, there are lots of little men who simply love to be asked to do things for us – turn a chair leg, put in a missing beam, lay tiles – that sort of thing. Then we go down to the village café and drink *un coup* with them. It's all they expect.' Sally went on to talk about the idyllic cottage, its situation, and how Jerry and she had such special times together there. 'Such interesting people have places near us, writers and painters, and the Duke . . . But I shouldn't really tell.'

'It's her dolls' house,' murmured Jerry.

. . . 'It's a sobering thought: by my age Schubert had been dead ten years . . .'

. . . 'Did you read of the very rich forgerer, given six months for some minor offence, who drove to Wormwood Scrubs in a taxi and told the driver to wait . . . ?'

'Well, now that we've demolished the theatre, the cinema, the novel and the reputations of all our acquaintances, let's restore ourselves with coffee and brandy.' James pushed back his chair, but no one rose to follow, and he sank down in it again.

Had they done all that? She hadn't noticed. She hadn't been anywhere since Massimo. She hadn't read anything, either. The biggest trouble had been not being able to concentrate. It had been fine, cooking; she had managed some mending; her mind seemed to have dissolved . . .

'The point is, Fred, works of art are registered in experience – not in the retina.' Charles was employing the tone of patronising reasonableness he used on his children.

'I bumped into that funny old chum of yours, Michael Parson, Fred,' Roger interrupted. 'We played squash. He tells me he's become chairman of some quango or other. What did he do? And to whom?'

'Gave a very substantial sum to the Party, dear man.'

'Is that the only way to get anything out of this government?'

'Oh, one imagines so,' Fred said in a tone that was meant to make James feel a perfect idiot for imagining otherwise.

'Well, it certainly accounts for the fact that my old friend Arthur, who's been looking after drunken Irish destitutes, living rough with them and sharing their lives for fifty years, goes unremarked, unpaid and unaided. It's not that Arthur wants any personal recognition – he'd hate that – but if what he was doing was only acknowledged by the powers that be, it might mean that someone in the Home Office would really help him solve the problem of homelessness. Something fundamental might get done.'

'Has the Prince of Wales acknowledged Arthur?'

'No. The Prince may have his heart in the right place but most of his advisers don't. Anyhow, his hands are tied behind his back.'

'Oh! That's why he walks like that!'

'Shut up, Fred. That's why the POW sticks to buildings and plants. He's prepared to face ridicule in the gutter press but not the monarch's ire. Anyhow, I can't see Di approving of his sleeping rough in cardboard city, even for one night. My dream is that he'd get himself kitted out as a beggar and for twenty-four hours cohabit with the others in Waterloo. He'd get pushed off the pavement and served last, if at all, in the shops. And he'd be ignored by women. It'd come as a terrific shock to a man in his position. I think it could change everything.' Amanda fell silent, savouring her dream.

'Life weighs half a pound,' Sally was saying. Julia imagined that Sally's might not weigh as much . . . 'If you weigh a body just before and just after death, you can prove it.'

'How astonishing! Did you hear that, Roger, Sally says . . .'

. . . 'She's reached the age when a promise *not* to sleep with the producer can win her a part,' Fred was telling Jo.

'Nothing more rigid than a sanitary towel has been between those legs in years!'

'Fred! You're sheer poison,' Amanda laughed.

'Cocteau, writing about a chameleon, said that its master put it down on a tartan rug and it died of over-exertion.'

Did Fred really read Cocteau? Julia looked towards him. He was still eating – but didn't seem so much to be eating his chocolate soufflé as engulfing it. Like an amoeba, he closed round all his nourishment, be it artistic, sexual or alimentary. He appropriated it. A portrait painter of imagination would have drawn Fred spherically, wound about prey.

What happens to conversation when the guests have gone home? Does it dissolve, or does it leave its imprint on the walls of dining- and drawing-rooms? What happens to words and phrases once fashionable, now discarded? Is there a shelf in an Oxfam shop to which they repair? Are 'charisma', 'symbiosis', 'wizard' and 'top hole' stacked with others against future use by those without verbal means?

'His first girlfriend was Lady Somebody, his second was an actress, the one he eventually found consolation with was a British Caledonian air hostess he met on a bus. I asked him what they had in common and after a very long pause he said, 'Well, she drinks and I drink.'

'Who are you talking about?'

'Piers-the-putrid!' Julia and Helen had known Piers at Oxford.

'Oh, him! "Too lazy to work and too nervous to steal." Who was it said that?'

. . . 'If you've not worked out when it's best to put your conscience before the law by the time you're seven, you probably won't ever. Civilised standards of behaviour are best understood by those for whom uncivilised ones don't achieve personal betterment . . .'

. . . 'My view is that if Scargill had looked like Gregory Peck, he'd've had all the women of the nation eating out of his hand. He's actually a man who tells the truth. The mines he said the Board would close, the Board closed. The miners whose lives and livings he made every effort to defend have lost out. The trouble is – or one of the troubles is – he's physically repulsive . . .'

. . . 'He said we simply didn't understand one another. We couldn't. He said it was understandable, seeing that we were different sexes.'

Oh my God! Silly-Sally. Does she ever listen to herself?

'He had a talent to abuse!'

'Clever old Fred! By the way, Fred, you used to know Maria Coleman, didn't you? She's doing TV ads for outsize bras these days.'

'One always knew she was keen to act, but one is surprised she's willing to expose herself to the wanking public . . .'

. . . 'What else drives you mad, Helen?'

'Bishops who love being bishop more than doing God's work. Politicians who say "to be perfectly frank" and "I want to make this absolutely clear", when what they really mean is "I'm certainly not going to provide you with the facts, you oaf, I'm going to obfuscate!" '

Even people in unique circumstances – of wealth, social position, on a hot-line to God – are utterly ordinary . . .

'I allot two first prizes to Dr Edward Norman, Dean of Peterhouse, with that awful fluting voice of his, who broadcast that "people are on the whole rubbish" in the course of one of his Reith Lectures. What d'you imagine Lord Reith would have thought? And one-and-a-half first prizes to Lord Gowrie – Minister of the Arts, no less – who told the nation that it was impossible to live in central London on thirty thousand a year. How do these people get away with it? Why aren't they lynched?' Amanda was apoplectic.

'We're a phlegmatic people, Amanda.' James was applying his well-tried emollient.

'What I hate is musak in Sainsbury's at eight-thirty in the morning. I hate pop music in shoe shops, the M25, skimmed milk – and so much else.' But Julia couldn't be bothered to think what. Had this dinner reduced itself to a parlour game? She hated games, whether they were played on grass, concrete or interior sprung mattresses. She watched as Fred, too well fed and too well wined, attempted to rise from his chair. He reminded her now of an octopus trying to decide which part of itself to prise off the rock before tumbling in its entirety into the sea.

Fern seed in the shoes makes people invisible . . . Had they noticed that she hadn't initiated much? Had they minded? Or had they found her intolerable, believing, perhaps, that she was plotting? Or if not plotting, criticising? What she must do was absent herself, withdraw, go into the wilderness . . . She looked down at her hands lying in her lap. One of her fingers was bleeding, and the button on the cuff of her dress was missing. Unconsciously she had torn at both, she supposed.

'I wonder whether you'd excuse me.' Julia got up from the table. 'I've not been very well lately and I'm exhausted. I think I'd better retire. It's been lovely seeing you all.' She seemed to hear herself stuttering.

Of course, James would be furious. It wasn't the way to behave. It would embarrass their guests. They wouldn't know what to say to her, to James . . .

As she left the dining-room she heard Charles telling Jo about a scandal involving some Lord or other who was discovered to be keeping twenty Philippinos in slavery on his estate in Oxfordshire. 'They're illegal immigrants and he gave them Hobson's choice – work for him for food and lodgings in the stables or he'd turn them in to the police. If they got repatriated they'd face starvation.'

'The name of the Lord was Stanton,' Helen remembered. *Oh my God! That as well!*

Did she have a right to leave James? That was to say, in her own moral judgment, without thought of what the world would say or think, did she have a right? He had done her no harm; indeed, it could be said that he had done her great good in that he had provided royally for her materially, been faithful to her sexually, encouraged her in her studies and rejoiced openly and sincerely in her professional successes. The fact that he had not touched her at the deepest level, and had ignored both the stirrings of her doubts and the emergence of her true nature, was as much her fault as his; she had suppressed the first, and only discovered something of the second when she had withdrawn from him.

Might she destroy him if she betrayed their years together? It was a disturbing thought. It had taken her long enough to appreciate the obligations she had to herself, but did she not also have obligations to James? Between individuals, as between nations, the present is dominated by memories of the past, and change either goes unremarked or else arouses suspicion and disbelief. 'Power is the ability to make another suffer the burden of change,' Dr Light had so rightly observed during a seminar at the Oxford conference.

If she were to open up the whole can of worms – tell James precisely what she felt – he would find it virtually impossible to accept that their marriage was the impediment to her fulfilment when it was clearly the very fount of his own. If she were to suggest that the premises upon which their marriage was founded were false, he would react with incredulity. Yet that was the case. Robert Louis Stevenson wrote that marriage was 'a friendship recognised by the police'. She had savoured the thought when she came upon it, but it struck her later that Stevenson's statement was as wrong as it was right. Friendship is an astonishing gift, calling upon the most subtle of human qualities; but marriage has a different goal, and to reach it the qualities of friendship must be touched by something more – some mysterious splendour. It was this that had been lacking.

James had always been prepared to spend the whole of his life making a castle of his house. Since coming down from Oxford he had devoted his waking hours to the provision of wealth for people and institutions already stacked with it. She might have preferred to live with a man committed to creating good housing for those condemned to live in squalor, or to travelling the world and bringing clean water to people who lived off sewerage. But it had never so much as crossed James's mind to devote himself to something socially relevant. He gave one evening a month to the boys' club that was the special responsibility of The Society of Friends, and he gave financial support to the Society's prisoners' appeal. But that was his lot. He knew that he was privileged but, as he put it, 'What am I supposed to do about that? I can't give back my education – anyhow, who would I give it to?'

He was a practical man; his approach to injustice was dispassionate. He looked at the prevailing circumstances in Britain, he weighed them, he found them wanting. But in a few years time a different government would be elected, a more compassionate one. Until then he would just wait and see.

Did this sort of attitude mark him as a patient man or as an unimaginative one? For James, change was a slow process that took place on many fronts and within the existing order. 'Evolution not revolution,' Julia had heard him recommend more than once too often. And working within the existing order had led James to behave as if hierarchies were natural phenomena. 'Some lead; others are led!' Hadn't she heard that somewhere else?

Were Julia to tell James that their relationship lacked the essential ingredient that transforms friendship into marriage, after his initial reaction – silence and disbelief – would come conciliation. He would seem to agree with her, for he could not bear to find himself engaged in hostility. He would suggest that together they identify the qualities Julia found lacking, and inject them into the relationship. As if that were an option open to them! He himself would never have dreamed that anything was lacking. He loved stability and did not distinguish it from ossification. He liked to be seen as reasonable and co-operative. 'Whatever you want, Julia. Whatever you say!' She remembered how often he uttered these phrases and how they always seemed so kindly and generous – but they led nowhere and had cost him nothing.

If from time to time James found himself bored, he did not sit around feeling sorry for himself, or making Julia's life a misery – he sought distraction. He turned on the television, and if that failed him, the radio, and if that failed he walked to the Everyman . . . His solution was to be fed – not to feed himself. He was exploitative. And because the largest part of his life was spent exploiting the have-nots on behalf of the haves, he did not question this tendency. It was only while Julia was thinking this out that it occurred to her that James might well have gone into politics. He had the constitution; he was personable and could be impulsively generous but, *au fond*, he was conceited and egocentric.

But what was the point of fault-finding? She was only indulging herself in an effort to justify her own behaviour, and giving in to the universally held view that if A was wrong, B was right. If she were to look into herself she would find as much to condemn as she found in James. Had he exploited her? Had he got what he wanted from her at the expense of what she wanted for herself? It was legitimate to consider those of James's traits that had influenced her own life to its detriment. He had been attracted to her at Oxford because she had been at the centre of a group he had wished to infiltrate. He had told her so. He had known about her involvement with André and how she had been held in thrall by the older man. Taking her away emotionally from André and from her peer group had probably given James a sense of his own potency.

He had never wanted to do research; he said that in his field quite enough had been garnered without his adding to the weight of paper . . . He appeared not to value personal discovery. In the past this had looked to Julia like evidence of his modesty and his practical bent, but in the light of her present thinking it seemed closer to inertia. She started to wonder to what extent he had manipulated Arnold and Enid into giving them the Hampstead house. Did James need to be given to, constantly?

Did he *really* care for her? she wondered. Did he feel responsible for her? On the surface it had always appeared that he cared; he had encouraged her to develop and had sustained her. But he had only encouraged her academic interests; it had been fine for her to expand intellectually, but as soon as she showed change at an emotional level he had felt threatened and had withdrawn.

He had never really got to know her. He had found her

desirable because she was physically attractive and mentally agile, and thus a credit to him on two fronts. But, she recalled, her individuality had always irked him. When she expressed ideas and feelings – even desires – that James found aberrant, his response was irritation, and immediate departure from the room. Later, when he regained control, he would beg Julia on no account to humiliate him with her eccentricities in public. He had never found a way of dealing with the unexpected in her. So long as she gave him no trouble he seemed to assume that she was not only in full accord with him, but utterly content – and this must mean that he could never have been deeply interested in her. James was not someone who could live, personally, with difference; instead of being attracted to it – excited by it and by the idea of negotiating with it and ultimately accommodating it – he preferred to make Julia in his own image. He rejoiced only in the uncontentiousness of their marriage. He had never acquired objectivity; what passed for it in his case was detachment. It was becoming obvious to her why he made no intimate contact with those with whom he worked: by practising a sort of withdrawal, he could avoid all threat.

She must come to terms with the unpalatable fact that because James had never truly recognised her individuality, she had been partner to evading it herself. She had submitted to his domination of her, confusing it with loyalty. He had made her a prisoner of his comfort and, until now, she had not felt like escaping. Clearly, she had masochistic leanings. It had never occurred to her that this was so until Massimo, and when faced with the revelation she had felt sick. Dependency was not something that she had wanted to discover in herself. She had become dependent upon James, the benevolent sadist, who wanted her success – just so long as it reflected well on him.

In recent years she had done no reading outside her fields of research. Anything that did not have direct application to her academic work was ignored, so that while she was examining the build-up of weaponry, restating the case for pacifism, relating personal behaviour to the behaviour of nations, it had not occurred to her to fortify her arguments with examples from fiction or images from poetry. Yet she owned a huge collection of books, her study was lined with them from floor to ceiling. In addition to the books she needed for her teaching and research, there were all the volumes she had acquired since she was a child – books on natural history, architecture and painting, poetry, travel, religion . . . And there were her father's books. Jack had passed on to Julia over one thousand volumes that he had decided against shipping out to South Africa. Jack Fowler had been a traditionalist, he collected 'the classics', but if his collection had no surprises in it, it had few gaps. Perhaps it was Jack's relentless thoroughness that Julia had found off-putting. At the back of her mind she had had the intention of re-reading systematically from Jane Austen to Emile Zola, but faced with Jack's neatly ranged essential reading she had felt overwhelmed, and had never so much as opened *Emma*.

It was a chance remark made by Fred Traisom – not to her but to another delegate in Hall at Marlowe – that had dislodged something of Julia's resistance to the classics in her study. She overheard Traisom remark that he recommended the reluctant fiction-reader to start with contemporary authors and work back, slowly, into the past. When, at her own table, she heard Justin discuss with Jerry the way in which Sartre describes the odd sensation of not recognising the familiar, she had made a mental note to read *Nausea*. Reinforcement from the existentialist might well throw light on her present condition.

'Existence *is* prior to essence!' Justin had insisted, and the metaphysical proposition clearly had its attractions for Jerry. 'It's got the great advantage of being verifiable,' he continued; 'look at the case of wolf children, adopted by animal mothers, and brought up in animal surroundings! They have the *form* of human beings but you can't call them human; they don't grow into the human condition. Like all animals they have the urge and ability to imitate – but not to discriminate. And they lack conscience and can't empathise with people.'

It was the very lassitude that made the task of reading

Nausea from start to finish so daunting, which prompted Julia to turn first to its final page:

A book . . . A book. A novel . . . Naturally, at first it would only be a tedious, tiring job, it wouldn't prevent me from existing or feeling that I exist. But a time would have to come when the book would be written, would be behind me, and I think that a little of its light would fall over my past. Then, through it I might be able to recall my life without repugnance. Perhaps, one day, thinking about this very moment, about this dismal moment at which I am waiting, round-shouldered, for it to be time to get on the train, perhaps I might feel my heart beat faster and say to myself: 'It was on that day, at that moment that it all started.' And I might succeed – in the past, simply in the past – in accepting myself.

The prospect of being able to recall her own life without repugnance would be enough, even if acceptance did not follow automatically. The thought filled Julia with pleasurable expectation. Academic work has a different purpose . . . So many academics lack imagination . . . they fail at a personal level because their intellectual development has been at the expense of their emotional development. She took down a copy of 'The Autistic Society' and read her chapter headings. She studied her flow charts. She recalled how she had planned the book, and how her argument had been wholly tendentious. All the research that she had laboriously undertaken had been in pursuit of evidence for a judgment at which she had already arrived. She had been single-minded; she had argued with clarity; but because the book had nothing organic about it, it had failed. She had raised brick upon brick in an orderly succession to arrive at a reasonable conclusion. But a reasonable conclusion is not enough – to describe society is not to change it. Until such time as all men agreed to relinquish power, nothing would change.

It had been agreed by a number of reviewers that her most suggestive idea was that war was the uncaring society's autistic object. Being uncaring, society could only pass on to its citizens the sense of its own destructive body – not the freedom that points to good, transitional objects and ultimately to self-fulfilment. An autistic object *is* the person; it produces the sensation he desires, the sensation of the object being of preeminent importance to one whose intellectual and emotional development is arrested. He clasps pain, recognising in the hurt in and of his own hand that he belongs to it, can identify with it: the hurtful, uncaring state. The autistic individual's agonising sensation of 'not-self' is mirrored in the lack of identity experienced by citizens of the uncaring state; they are made slaves (in that they are not free), able only to identify with the evil from which they themselves have emerged. Their anger, rage and violence is what they are – and what the state requires of them, giving the state both a reason for looking after only those it favours, and for using the rest for matters (war, industrial slavery, etc.) which protect its favourites.

She had examined the armature of contemporary British society: political authority created structural violence. Society was not run on rational lines. The governing élite did not, could not, justify its position on the grounds of having superior morality or greater powers of perception than the governed. The difference between the two was in their relative strengths. The 'not-me' only maintained a semblance of balance by locking into the hostility of the uncaring mother-state. Political authority was maintained at the expense of the wishes of over half the population. The terror of the 'not-me' that the autistic individual experiences is the xenophobia of the dispossessed. There was, she found, a telling resemblance between the symptoms displayed by a citizen at the mercy of a system whose concern he is not, and an infant that has experienced maternal deprivation. Autistic reactions divert attention away from the uncaring state and the unloving parent in favour of self-generated sensations.

The infant of the 'refrigerated mother' fails to construct himself. If he does not know himself, he cannot know another and cannot come to a commonly agreed picture of reality. Lack of communication begets lack of communication and increases the self-orientated quality of what is perceived. The distorted view of one leads to the distorted view of the other, and a closed circuit in which there is no exchange is impossible to interrupt. The dispossessed citizen can only distract himself from his condition by being sensation-dominated. His emotional and cognitive developments are halted, either because he refuses to learn from a society that ignores his interests, or because the means to develop his talents are not available to one of lowly financial and social status. He is accused of being disruptive (in trades unions, for example), but whilst appearing self-centred he has in fact very little sense of self. In his poverty of ideas, imagination and material wealth, the image held up to him by society is of his worthlessness. He is obliged to remain *out* of touch with reality, in order to retain the germ of self – even the idea of 'not-them' – for to be *in* touch would involve accepting society's assessment of him. His own apprehension of injustice is returned to him as envy; his claim that he has a right to some sort of life – as opposed to mere existence – is returned to him as his assumption that the world owes him a living. The process of integration being unknown to him, he cannot build a complete identity. However, his hostility can be harnessed. Like the autistic individual for whom existence is sensation-dominated, the dispossessed citizen can be made to feel good by being sent to war; he feels justified in returning *to* the state – if not against it – the sensations of hostility that developed when the state made him worthless, for that way lies his own survival. Her thoughts strayed to Stanton and the sort of uneducated youngsters that Lord Stanton would seek out and recruit.

In her book Julia had shown how violence is always present when people are forced physically or mentally below their potential realisation. 'You don't need to be hit to experience violence,' she told her students. 'Unequal life-chances are violent; the individual is pumped into subordination by them.' She felt that the worst aspect of acquired autism was that of impotence; for even non-violent action – the very thing that might alter the subject citizen's condition – requires a sense of identity to activate it. While some weak members of society – pensioners, the disabled, the underprivileged – demonstrate spurts of non-violent action, the autism that affects them undermines their action. They do not even have the power to make the system unworkable, for their use to the system is negligible.

Two things had struck Julia. First, we cannot understand the nature of the state; second – she had spent far too little time reflecting upon man's real nature and how he should best live in order to fulfil himself. She had observed the results of ignoring man's essential nature; she now realised that she herself was in danger of falling into the same trap.

Why had she become a university teacher? It was all too obvious: to impress Jack and Jill, whom she despised. She had inherited pedantry from Jack, and had ignored the importance of the imagination in line with Jill. Why had she laboured so hard to gain the respect of people she neither liked nor admired? She needed to turn her psychological insight inwards, towards herself. How was it that she had spent her professional life arguing cogently for the understanding and freedom of others, and yet submitted herself to arbitrary authority and never demanded understanding from herself? She had, in the past, regarded herself as a liberal pluralist, claiming that to some extent all authorities were equally valid – and invalid. Later, she had drifted towards anarchism, and recognised no single authority. Had she arrived, at last, at nihilism, rejecting all authority?

Spring

Julia drove to Doughty Street, where Margaret rented a small flat. 'Where arc we going?' she asked, as Margaret stowed two baskets in the boot of Julia's car.

'If you take the Guildford road, I'll direct you from there.'

The sky was overcast. The countryside that lay self-consciously at either side of the motorway – as if its function were to provide more embellishment for the functional man-made artery than it could manage – looked weary.

Julia's depression had lifted somewhat. James had left for a provincial town in northern Brazil where he was going to discuss financing a factory run by Catholic priests, together with their Indian converts. He had been given about three months to travel round Brazil, drumming up business. There were people from his own firm working in a subsidiary outfit who would put him up in the major cities. He had not specified to Julia the precise date of his return. From the moment of their uneasy leave-taking, Julia had felt less tense, freer, and somewhat more optimistic.

She had made a thorough tour of the house when James left. So much of the decoration, including the pictures and the pottery and the embroideries, she took for granted and hardly saw any longer; they had become plastic musak. Had she cleaned the picture glass herself instead of allowing Spick & Span to do it for her, had she washed the lovely old pottery and the Tibetan bhudda, she might have kept on more familiar terms with them. But did she really need all these *things*? She thought back to the woman at Coldston and her pyrex bowl with its festering bananas. Would she, Julia,

have opened up her house for that woman, had the circumstances been reversed? She shied away from the question,
feeling fraudulent. She was a fraud. She knew it and could
not now un-know it.

The twelfth-century church of St Laurence at Wychwood
was one of the smallest in the south of England. Margaret
was pleased to note that Julia's spirits were raised as she
absorbed its features. She had realised that if she were to
succeed in prising Julia from home, she would need to offer
her a tempting goal for an outing. She knew that both Julia
and James were interested in medieval wall-paintings, and
those at Wychwood were in a particularly good state of preser-
vation. What she could not have known, however, was that
the last occasion on which wall-painting had been on Julia's
mind had been at Stanton.

It was fortunate, then, that the decoration at Wychwood
was abstract, and being empty of Stanton's images it did
not immediately arouse disturbing memories in Julia. The
decoration consisted of an all-over pattern of lozenge-shapes,
linked on all sides, rather resembling the patterning of ancient
flooring. The lozenges were painted in burnt-sienna and
covered the wall space above the three pairs of white columns
in the nave. St Laurence was properly Norman, with a miniature gallery, clerestory, and open roof held aloft by stout
oak timbers. Being so small, the church reminded Julia of a
craftsman's model, or one of those buildings tucked under the
arm of St Paul or St Jerome in fourteenth-century paintings. A
block of stone roughly hewn into chimney-pot shape stood
just inside the west door. At first Julia did not indentify it,
but eventually she made out a shallow saucer-shape scooped
from the top of the boulder and realised that it was an early
font. The twelve oak pews were plain, and polished so thoroughly that the pale sun, cautiously drifting in through clear
glass windows, made them glow like treacle. The only orna-
mentation was on the capitals of the six rounded arches –
irregular lozenge-shapes, almost certainly the inspiration for
the later wall-decoration.

Here was a monument made by anonymous craftsmen to

the greater glory of God. The men who raised St Laurence took for granted their shared symbolic order. Unlike the artists of today, the artist-craftsmen of the twelfth century had been no mere ornaments of society – 'with nothing to say and no technique with which to say it,' as James so often repeated.

'The whole life of feeling seems present,' Julia said quietly to Margaret.

'When I was in Cuba I was struck by the way everyone seemed to share in the political and social aspirations of the country. I realised that although theirs was a secular society, the inspiration for it was their religious tradition. I was enormously moved. The Cubans aren't working for the greater glory of God these days, but for the greater glory of man. They say "we" all the time – not "I" – and not in the manner of "we are a grandmother", I hasten to add. I found something reassuring in the fact that although the church had failed the people, religion hadn't; it's the basis of their community spirit, whether they acknowledge it or not.'

There would be no more 'quiet thinks' with Enid, Arnold and James at Meetings on a Sunday morning, reflected Julia. She doubted that she would ever pray again.

'I don't think it's important to believe in all the tricky bits of religion,' she said to Margaret as they sat down on one of the pews and contemplated their surroundings. 'But I would find it comforting to be part of a tradition. I feel isolated in my scepticism.'

'If belief in God stops children pulling the wings off flies, it's a good thing, but because it doesn't stop grown men going to war, it's a failed thing.'

They should have backed out of the tea-shop just as soon as they pushed open the door and caught sight of the interior. But the proprietress, hearing the tinkle of the bell, turned from squeezing a blackhead from her chin in the mirror over the fireplace, and faced them boldly. It would have been difficult to turn tail. Joan – of Joan's Tea-Break – was standing surveying the cake trolley; half-consumed cakes and chocolate *gâteaux*, icing cracked and crumb dusty-dry, were disintegrating on plates that had not been washed since the confections had first been placed on them. A bluebottle was darting back and forth from the icing to the windows.

'What a nasty day!' Joan said triumphantly, adding, 'We don't normally open till eleven!' As she spoke, she waved her arm this way and that in an effort to confuse the fly. However, she added quickly, seeing as how she'd brewed coffee for herself, she would make an exception this morning and open a little earlier. Neither Julia nor Margaret pointed to the Open sign on the door. Defeated, they pulled out chairs and sat down at a table covered with an off-white tablecloth.

'What is it that prompts people who can't, to paint?' Margaret murmured to Julia as her eyes scanned the works of the Wychwood Amateur Painting Society displayed on the walls. 'It's a good thing that people who can't don't career round the skies in by-planes . . .' And then her eyes alighted on the china dogs on the windowsill, the Spanish dolls and the olive-wood boxes with views of Jerusalem . . . The shop felt damp. Mould would be growing behind the pictures.

Joan carried cups of coffee to their table and, with her finger mid-centre of a chocolate digestive, put down a plate of assorted biscuits they had not ordered. She was obviously unhappy. She was in her late forties, her hair wispy and thin and bleached of colour. So too was her face; and her eyes were ringed with shadows and the corners of her mouth encrusted with cold-sores. She appeared not to be wearing anything much under her flowered blouse and too-tight skirt; her body quaked like jelly as she walked.

'I looked like that when I was ill,' Julia whispered to Margaret.

'I very much doubt it,' Margaret answered emphatically.

'You didn't see me! It's an odd thing, not bothering. We're accustomed to bothering – about everything, particularly appearances. Giving up's a real watershed.'

'A positive move?'

'Not at the time. But like everything else in life, it's a gesture that can be turned to good account and become positive. I suppose that's one of the signs of recovery.'

They drove along secondary roads through Surrey and into

Hampshire. Along their route they passed sumptuous Edwardian houses in over-neat gardens, their topiary too perfectly clipped into too-fanciful forms. Behind twelve-foot walls of weathered red brick lay expensive boarding-schools and exclusive golf clubs. All the buildings had been erected in clearings cut in a vast forest. The setting was idyllic, but the effect was lifeless. There was not a soul about.

'It's all been manured with bank notes.'

'They've left far too many hollies and pines.'

'Is that what makes it so remarkably depressing? Or is it the schools? It's as if the air itself has become so impregnated with the sobbing of homesick children that it's solidified.'

'Why d'you suppose people have children if all they do is banish them to institutions?'

'Habit, I suppose. They've been doing it forever. I sometimes wonder if I shouldn't feel compassion towards women who can only achieve some sense of identity by breeding.'

'And I sometimes think that if I were truly compassionate I'd be able to feel for the unhappy rich as well as for the poor,' Margaret added ruefully.

They drove on slowly until Margaret directed Julia down a twisting, unmarked lane that had been cut through the forest by the side of a fast-flowing stream.

'Are you sure you know where you're taking us?' Julia asked anxiously, as she steered the car round the hairpin bends.

'Of course I do! My grandparents lived near here. When I was little we came here often.'

Margaret was the only person with whom Julia felt absolutely comfortable these days. The two women had no need to explain themselves to one another, they shared political and social attitudes, and enjoyed arguing over details. They had a silent understanding that personal matters were personal. If Margaret wished to confide in Julia or Julia in Margaret, that was each one's individual choice, but no unsolicited questions would prompt a confidence or seek to elicit more information than the other proffered.

Julia sometimes thought that she saw herself – her better

self, when young – in Margaret. Or perhaps she found in Margaret the daughter she had never had. Margaret, less complicatedly, had found in Julia an excellent teacher and a good friend; the age difference hardly struck her at all.

The lane soon gave out, and there seemed nothing but a sheer cliff above a quiet, still gorge. To reach the place Margaret had chosen for their picnic, they had to leave the car well above the ravine. It looked as if the steep incline would be impossible to negotiate even on foot, particularly with two large baskets, but Margaret went on ahead, and Julia saw that the exposed roots of the vast old trees provided steps – the descent was feasible.

The stream that ran in the hollow by the side of the lane here rushed full tilt over the hillside to its destination – three huge ponds in the valley below that disgorged, eventually, into a subterranean pool. The two women could hardly hear themselves speak above the roar of falling water. But as soon as they finished their descent, and took the path that circled the first pond and led on to the second and the third, the fall of water became a distant murmur in a hollow of silence.

The trees were in bud but not yet in leaf, and the pale sun shone through the branches.

Margaret walked purposefully. She knew exactly where she intended to put down the ground-sheet and lay out the food. A felled beech would serve as back-rest, and thick moss would cushion them against the unyielding ground. She had brought along French bread, English cheese, fruit and a flask of coffee. Julia registered that Margaret had catered adequately but simply. It was in keeping with her personality. She, Julia, would have gone to unnecessary lengths.

They sat overlooking the water. There was no sound of human life. The sun was now warm and bright. The burgeoning trees seemed to be gazing at their own images reflected in the pond. Where the water was shallow, clumps of kingcups blazed. A duck was circling the pond, pursued by two drakes who pushed after her in the reeds, then followed her on to the bank where she snapped at insects. Finally, they pursued her into the air, quacking noisily, to the head of the ponds –

up, round, and back to the point at which the waters sank underground. It was some time before super-drake emerged triumphant, and the valley resumed its peace. Julia and Margaret watched the couple linger harmoniously among the kingcups.

'It's paradise!'

'I knew you'd like it.'

But Julia was having to struggle to banish thoughts of her last picnic. It would help, she felt, to drown her thoughts in non-stop chatter – but it would be criminal to interrupt this present peace for which they had driven so far out of London. Anyhow, she didn't want to impose on Margaret, nor did she wish to appear neurotic and self-obsessed.

'Have you noticed how everything that's bright at this time of year is yellow?' she said. It was a neutral subject. It showed that she appreciated Margaret's choice of place. 'There are the kingcups' – and she pointed – 'the gorse behind us, the celandine . . . and I just spotted a yellow wagtail, and now there's that brimstone butterfly . . .' Both watched the tiny brimstone – no more than an inch in length – flitting in the sunlight. But Margaret did not respond to Julia's observations, and in a short while Julia, uncontrollably, spoke again.

'I suppose I'd better tell you, now, that I've decided not to go back to Paine.'

'Ever?'

'Ever!'

'D'you want to tell me why?'

'I'm not sure. I'm not sure that I'm ready to commit myself to a definitive statement yet.' She paused. She was feeling upset and uneasy. She wished that she had kept quiet. Like Margaret. Margaret had the control she lacked. She realised that it would be difficult to spell out to Margaret that she was giving up teaching because as an academic she had found her ignorance positively heightened by knowledge . . .

It was not that she had stopped asking questions – as happened to so many who teach – but that, having found many of the answers, she had spent too great a proportion of

202

her time shoring them up. 'The Autistic Society' was a case in point. Looking back, she could see that she had risked very little of herself in revealing how the state created the psychotics it deserved. Now, as an agent of the state – as educators had increasingly become – she must make the difficult move. If, in trying to change society, all she did was to throw sauce over stinking fish, it was less than enough. She must change herself; she must become the sort of individual who is impervious to the destructive intentions of society.

'I'm leaving James, too,' she told her student. There! It was out. She felt better for having given form to her decision. Both women continued to face on to the water and watch the brimstone.

James was decent, thought Julia, but he had always failed to recognise that what he did to ameliorate the privilege of a few ensured that the many would go on suffering for all time. 'Isn't it better,' he would argue, 'to create jobs – however little they pay – than to condemn men to unemployment?' She had seen his point, and in disagreeing often felt that she was being unfair to him. But James seemed unable – or was it unwilling? – to grasp *her* point of view: that by 'helping' in a piecemeal fashion, he was letting the state off the hook and storing up more callousness for the future. His behaviour was like that of well-meaning amateurs who work for nothing, or very little, and by so doing prevent the less wealthy but professionally qualified from finding employment. She had seen something similar at Paine. Gladyse had asked postgraduate students rather than visiting lecturers to fill in for Julia. The post-grad students, living on exiguous grants, could be bought cheap, and since they were themselves victims of the educational system, it would have been unreasonable to expect them to refuse the work – or to insist on getting the rate for the job.

'So far as your thesis is concerned, Margaret, I think it would be best if you transferred at once to Gerald Smith as your supervisor.'

'Really?' Margaret sounded incredulous. 'I think Gerald

203

would be more suitably employed modelling knitting patterns than dabbling in international industrial relations!'

'He's not altogether stupid, Margaret. I know he tends to try a bit too hard, but better that than Godfrey Essenden who doesn't try at all. No, the thing I particularly object to with Gerald is his habit of calling me by my first name more times in a short conversation than a close friend would do in a year. He wants to make it appear that we have an intimate understanding – and we don't!'

'It's patronising, isn't it?'

'That too. My only other suggestion would be for you to approach Gladyse herself.'

'I'd rather take up pot-holing. You know her political stance.'

'Indeed I do! And that's why I think you'd be much better off with Gerald. The problem with Gerald will be that instead of ignoring you, in the time-honoured way supervisors do ignore their students, Gerald will want to see you every five minutes and will wax offended if you don't constantly consult him and defer to his ideas. Nevertheless, I think he's your best bet. And you can always discuss things with me.'

'So! You're going to be around?'

'I think so, at any rate for the time being. I mean, I'll be in London. I'm going to look for somewhere congenial to live.'

'In town?'

'Yes. I need to find a temporary stop-gap while I sort out what it is I really want to do and where I want to do it. I'm looking for something cheap and cheerful.'

'Would you like to have my place for a while? Would it do? I'm going to be abroad for the whole of the summer. I'm going with Edmund – you remember, the chap I met at Oxford. He's got the use of a house somewhere remote in the Jura. We thought it would be a lovely place to work.'

'Margaret! That would be a perfect solution for me. Thank you. What a help!' And Julia felt all the gratitude she expressed.

'By the way, I've got a cat.'

'That's OK. There's a small garden . . .'

A sudden sense of relief filled her; a huge problem had been felled at a single blow. A shaft of optimism as beautiful as a ray of sunshine fell on her immediate future, and at once, all else forgotten, she turned to Margaret to discuss rent, when Margaret would want the flat back, whether the shops in Lamb's Conduit Street were any good for provisions, and what the neighbours were like.

'A guaranteed income for one and all – whether they work or not, so no one would ever again fear starvation!'

'No woman obliged to stay with a brutal husband!'

'Only free education!'

'Only free health care!'

'Free housing!'

'Free basic foodstuffs!'

'That's a new one!'

'It's quite feasible; no one can eat more than a loaf of bread a day and drink a pint of milk. If they took more it would only go bad. It could be limited to war-time rations.'

They were driving back to London, remembering that in the past Margaret had half-seriously conceived the idea for a board game to be called 'Ideal Society'. It would proceed along the lines of Monopoly – Capitalist Society. The goals, of course, would be non-acquisitive, and the skill of the game would be in the diplomacy the individual players employed to establish the Ideal Society.

'Come on! It's your turn. Let's get all our goals together first. We'll work out how to pass "go" and "collect" later,' Julia said.

'Clothes! Free basic clothing!'

'Why not!'

'Eradication of patronage . . . Absolutely free press, tv, etc.'

'Right of access to all public documents; public ownership of knowledge!'

'Eradication of competition – in school, university, industry, everywhere!'

'It could work. I'm sure it could. The crass will always maintain that given half the chance no one would be productive, but then, the crass are so often the non-productive paper-pushers. . . I believe that people would *want* to be employed. If they weren't *competing* with one another all the time they'd feel an obligation towards one another. And they'd need the satisfaction that comes with doing something stimulating. We'd have a situation in which people would want to do what their consciences indicated they should be doing.'

'And they'd only produce what was needed by everybody – not luxuries for individuals but necessities for the community. The trouble, or one of the troubles, with the present situation is that private, individual appetites are satisfied while public ones go hungry.'

'What would we do about the forces and the police?'

'Put them under democratic control. *And* see to it that dissenters are protected.'

'Eight per cent of the population still own about eighty-five per cent of the wealth of this country. Private ownership of land would have to go, along with private ownership of everything else.'

'We'd keep our own toothbrushes . . . !'

'Somehow we have to create a society in which self-discipline replaces the values of the market place, the prime minister, and lackeys such as Sir James Stirling, David Willetts and Rupert Murdoch – my current *bêtes noires*.'

'I certainly wouldn't share this dream with anyone but you!' laughed Julia. 'If I talked to colleagues and gave them so much as an inkling that I hoped for solutions like these, I'd be accused of living in cloud-cuckoo-land and made to feel I was an idiot – or worse. I'd be seen as a threat to society. But if you make it all into a game, it could have the effect of making less cynical folk have a good think.'

Julia had seriously considered the benefits of simple living only when faced with the immediate problem of sorting herself out. She saw that privilege and luxury had meant self-mutilation for her. In her quest for a more meaningful way of life

– dare she hope, 'creative life' – she would need to find the circumstances that would ensure that her work (whatever it was to be) could emerge directly from her psychic life. She recalled what Kris had written about Michelangelo's unfinished work – that it was actually better than his finished work for being nearer the state of conception; a projection of an inner image. Nothing academic about that! It is not nearness to reality that makes the great work of art but the nearness to the artist's creative source. And if she couldn't aspire to 'art', precisely, she knew that the great divide that had always existed between her feeling and her thinking selves was going to have to be bridged if she was to succeed with anything she now wanted to pursue. And this bridging, like any creative process, might be painful.

A year ago she had been invited to take a seminar at a provincial university and, en route, had stopped in a small village to admire a mill. She had wandered along the path by the side of the river until she came to the bridge, which she had crossed to mid-point to watch the river course downstream. Absorbed in the force of the flow of water, some minutes elapsed before she sensed that she had company. A small boy wearing a black-and-orange-striped T-shirt was standing by her side, his head thrust between two of the stone pillars that formed the balustrade of the bridge. He too was watching the water pull strands of water-weed downstream. When Julia looked up, intending to continue over the bridge, the child quickly drew his head back through the pillars, and faced her.

'What's your name?' he asked.

'Julia! What's yours?'

'Daniel Football Jones.'

She wondered whether she had heard correctly, but looking at his grazed knees and bruised, muddy legs, she concluded that she probably had. Pointing across the river, the small boy told Julia that the house standing alone on the river's bank was his house, that he wasn't at school because he'd had measles, and that his baby brother wasn't very interesting.

'He can't even walk!' he said scornfully. And then he reached out and took Julia's hand.

'Come with me!' he said, and tugged at her arm. He drew her across the bridge and down a narrow path cut by the footsteps of small children.

'Mind the muck!' he ordered unselfconsciously, letting go of her hand the better to negotiate cow-pats left by a thirsty herd. Once at the river's edge he settled on his haunches in a clump of mimulus.

'Isn't it beautiful!' he gasped.

Standing a little behind the child, Julia looked out in the same direction. At this point the river was leaping over large black boulders.

'D'you see?' he asked, pointing to a family of ducks sheltering in the waterlogged plants at his feet. 'They like me. They let me scratch their backs.' And he gently stroked the back of the drake with a hazel switch.

Julia looked across the river into the child's garden. Brilliant white tea-towels were flapping dry on a washing line slung between ancient, gnarled apple trees.

Daniel Football Jones got to his feet. 'Follow me!' he ordered. The path he trod was overgrown with stinging-nettles and brambles, but this did not seem to worry him.

Suddenly, he stopped. 'Look!' he said, and in the single word Julia registered his awe. Fouling the river's edge a few yards ahead lay the rotting carcass of an upturned car; it was wheel-less, window-less and door-less. The decomposing form was sprouting rosebay willowherb, and in the hot sun it gave off a peculiar smell of rust and damp.

Daniel wandered round the carcass in ecstasy, drawing his hand carefully over such smooth areas as remained, picking with his tiny fingers at loose nuts and bolts. Julia tried to draw him away from his speechless rapture towards a daisy-spattered green, but she had no success; the child was transfixed by his treasure. And when she said she was going, taking the path through the village, Daniel Football Jones declined to come along; some imaginary line, beyond which lay forbidden territory, was a signal for him to turn back towards the bridge, to return home, back to base. 'I mustn't. I'm not allowed!' he told her.

In his striped black and orange T-shirt he reminded Julia of a honey-bee. And like a bee he was keenly aware of the frontiers drawn round his territory, which must not be traversed.

The little boy clearly had loving parents to establish his boundaries, and he felt secure within them. Julia knew a pang of envy. But it was no use wanting to be a child, and anyhow, hers were not loving parents. The adult, to dignify the term, must establish his own boundaries. Where am I going? I've crossed the marriage boundary and the career boundary. I'm free, and it's terrifying.

It had been raining. The ground was sodden, so too was the air. London was not yet fully roused, but the distant hum of traffic in Farringdon Road to the east and Southampton Row to the west reminded Julia of the thousands of commuters who would be making their dutiful way to polished desks and occupations that merely paid the rent. Those emerging from the underground would find streets fly-blown with rotting fruit peel, wet newsprint, plastic bottles and dog dirt. Those who drove in by car would be arriving bad-tempered and sweating, with 'stupid cow', 'idiot' – and worse - drying on their lips.

The window on to the steps that led down to the garden was open, and the Tubby-Tabby was seated beside it, looking trussed like a capon, staring out in deep contentment. The cat shared with Julia a pleasure in the scents of earth and shrubs and the security of bricks and mortar. Margaret's garden was no bigger than her sitting-room, but because it was sheltered on all sides it boasted a cordon peach tree. Margaret had left instruction: as each fruit swelled it should be wrapped loosely in brown paper (provided) to protect it from the sparrows and the wasps. 'That is,' she wrote, 'if you want to have peaches to eat as well as to watch.'

The peach tree was Margaret's only luxury, otherwise she seemed to have exercised an austerity that Julia found peculiarly congenial. The sitting-room was furnished with a paper-hanger's table, two upright old school chairs, two capacious armchairs, a tv and a record player. The floorboards were the original eighteenth-century ones and in very poor condition. Margaret had sanded and polished eighteen inches of border, and in the middle of this square had thrown durries. The walls were painted a matt salt-white, and the venetian blinds and chairs damson-blue. Planted in a wide, shallow bowl, placed between the two long windows, was a forest of miniature oak trees, twenty or more acorns that had sprouted to a uniform height of ten inches. Julia was to tend this planting too. The bedroom led off the sitting-room. Its walls were painted damson, the furniture white and the curtains and bedspread – made from heavy Victorian tablecloths – were salt-white, too. Margaret explained the advantage of such a simple colour scheme – it was an easy matter, thereafter, to find suitable contrasting colours for accessories. The scheme struck Julia as obsessional – another anal obsessive like Enid? she wondered – but not oppressive. Unlike her own house, which had developed organically, the decor of Margaret's flat had been planned and executed in the space of one month.

'I don't see myself as a home-maker,' Margaret explained. 'I need a machine for working in.'

Indeed the flat ran like a well-oiled machine. All its surfaces were stain-proof, there was nothing in it to collect dust. The environment reminded Julia of her Filofax. Jerry had given her a Filofax for Christmas; it had deeply depressed her, but at the time she had not been able to work out quite why. On reflection she had realised that it was wholly inappropriate to her needs – the complexities of her life could not be filed between covers. Could this order, this austerity of Margaret's, she wondered, provide the necessary environment to generate invention? Or does invention emerge from less ordered surroundings – from less ordered personalities? Creative people have strong egos. They may appear chaotic, but being able to tolerate chaos suggests that they can tolerate dissonance within themselves – even make use of it. Less creative people deal with their inner chaos by planning an outer order.

The truths she had been confronting were increasingly ones more evident to a theologian or an analyst than to an academic. And now the images had become peculiarly geographic, what with bridges to be slung and frontiers broached. As she brooded on these topics Julia observed that only theories formed in her mind, and she remembered that Arnold disdained theories. Was nothing more immediate available to her? Had these two-and-a-half decades of theorising put her beyond the pale? Her dissatisfaction was interrupted by the telephone.

'Arnold! How lovely to hear your voice. I was just thinking about you. Nice thoughts . . . I'm fine. How are you?' And she listened while Arnold confided that he had been waiting for Enid to go into Alton to do some shopping before ringing her. He wanted a good long chat. They were all fine. Bates was thoroughly enjoying his country vacation. The garden was looking better than ever. Enid had bought a vegetarian cookery book and Arnold feared that he would shortly turn into a green shade. They had had a long, newsy letter from James. Had she heard from him?

'Of course I'm lonely!' she admitted to his enquiry. 'And of course I miss him – in a way. But I know I have to be on my own for a while. Sort myself out.' And she gently refused his invitation to Selborne for the weekend. Would she at least come down for the day? She would love to – eventually.

Arnold knew her well enough not to insist, but Julia sensed that by talking at length about other things, he hoped she would get caught up in his world and want to see it again for herself. He had discovered a hitherto unknown correspondent of White's. 'It's a considerable coup, my dear. A lady . . .' Enid had driven to Beth Chatto's and invested in some rare plants for the shady part of the garden. And both of them were up to their ears in committees and demonstrations over the proposed motorway. Arnold had clearly been in need of extended conversation and he was leaving no stone unturned . . . They had found a pub four miles away and sometimes walked over for lunch. They had adopted a stray kitten. Arnold's waterworks were giving him some trouble and he thought a prostate operation was inevitable. Julia murmured concern and interest, enthusiasm and outrage. But her heart was not in the conversation and she took up a felt pen and started to doodle.

'I do hope you don't have to have an op . . . Yes, Enid would be very anxious . . . Please don't worry about me, Arnold . . . I know you care and I'm grateful but everything's going to be fine. I'm starting to see my way ahead . . .'

Immediately she had replaced the receiver, she went over to the record player and put on her record of Gerard Souzay singing Heine's *Dichteliebe*. She couldn't remember when last she'd played it. She couldn't remember when last she'd thrown open the windows and belted out the 'numbers' with Souzay:

> *Im wunderschönen Monat Mai,*
> *Als alle Knospen sprangen,*
> *Da ist in meinem Herzen*
> *Die Liebe aufgegangen.*
> In the lovely month of May,
> when all the buds opened,
> love unfolded in my heart.

At the end of the cycle she listened carefully to the words. *She* knew why the coffin had been so large and so heavy.

> *Ich senkt auch meine Liebe*
> *Und meinen Schmerz hinein.*
> Do you know why the coffin
> should be so large and so heavy?
> I laid all my love and my grief
> in it.

But now it was well and truly buried. No exhumation was necessary. A feeling of deep contentment crept in, slowly and quietly. She was confident it was going to envelop her.

James

Massimo

'my country is the world'
PAINE COLLEGE
self-glorification

LOVE

Conference

Conformity   Insecurity

Awareness of
fraudulence

Illusion of
Omnipotence

Inhibition   Shame

Disillusion

Resignation

BREAKDOWN

FLIGHT

Independence

Insight

New life style
'My religion is to
do good'

Ambivalence

Conscious/Unconscious
Thought/Feeling

Creativity